# WINGS

## THE BBC TELEVISION SERIES

Barry Thomas has been writing for television for twenty years and was Script Editor for the very successful series, *The Onedin Line.* He once adapted Gogol's *The Government Inspector* for comedian Tony Hancock, collaborated with Francis Durbridge on the marathon eighteen-part thriller, *The World of Tim Frazer,* adapted *How Green Was My Valley* for live transmission from the Cardiff studio, and has been Script Editor and writer for *Dr Finlay's Casebook* and *Z Cars.* In spite of a fair bit of experience he is still naïve enough to marvel at the work of directors and actors who do the real job of getting the shows on the screen.

He is the creator of the television series, *Wings.* He was a navigator in the RAF, and for a short time – not short enough! – he was a parachute jumping instructor. This gave him a taste for insecurity and so he became a writer. Born in Barry, Glamorganshire, he now lives in Walton-on-Thames with his wife, Connie, and their five children, and has no time for hobbies.

# WINGS

## OVER ENEMY LINES

Barry Thomas

*To Diane
With memories
of a very happy time
spent in Baldwinsville
Fond Love*

*Peter R. Hudson
Churchill Fellow
1980*

British Broadcasting Corporation

First published 1978 by the
British Broadcasting Corporation
35 Marylebone High Street
London W1M 4AA

ISBN 0 563 17427 7

Printed in England by
Love & Malcomson Ltd
Brighton Road, Redhill, Surrey

FOR CONNIE

The BBC1 television series *Wings* was created by Barry Thomas and is produced by Peter Cregeen. It is written by Barry Thomas, Arden Winch and Julian Bond, and directed by Donald McWhinnie, Jim Goddard, Gareth Davies and Desmond Davis. The cast includes: Tim Woodward as Alan Farmer, Anne Kristen as Molly, John Hallam as Harry, Sarah Porter as Lorna, Reg Lye as Tom, Michael Cochrane as Charles Gaylion, Celia Bannerman as Kate, and Nicholas Jones as Triggers.

# 1

In August 1914, the British Expeditionary Force, under the command of Field Marshal Sir John French, embarked for France to take up positions between Maubeuge and Le Cateau. Among them, viewed with curiosity and amused disdain, was a small group of officers of the Royal Flying Corps: their purpose was to look for suitable landing grounds for the four squadrons enthusiastically preparing their stick-and-string aeroplanes for war. Though what their actual role would be no one quite knew. 'They could frighten the enemy horses, I suppose,' one Staff Officer grumbled. 'Beyond that, I can't for the life of me see what possible use they'll be. God knows why the unsightly monsters were ever invented.' Oh yes, he knew that Britain trailed behind Germany and France in the field of aviation, and quite right, too. Britain had more sense. She knew damned well that aeroplanes were an expensive waste of time. Noisy, smelly creatures, advocated by a few eccentric individuals whose ideas were unworthy of attention.

One such individual was Captain Owen Triggers, RFC, who had caught the flying bug in France in 1911 while watching 'an aerial performance to defy all natural laws'. Cutting short his stay—he was on leave from the Royal Engineers at the time—he took the next boat back to England to enrol for flying lessons, at a cost of seventy-five pounds, with the 'Aero Club of the United Kingdom'. Gaining his pilot's certificate, Triggers secured an attachment to the Air Battalion, joined the Flying Corps when it was formed in 1912, and went off to France on the outbreak of war with that gallant, puny and despised force of one hundred and five officers and sixty-three machines, mostly of foreign make and of varying degrees of un-reliability. 'And in many cases, totally bloody unair-worthy,' Triggers raged at his nervous new observer, who had been warned about Triggers' sudden outbreaks of blazing ferocity. 'I sometimes wonder why I ever left the Engineers. I mean, here we are, living like gipsies in uni-form, sleeping at best in bivouacs and barns, at worst be-neath the rain-soaked wings of these damned death-traps, moving hither and thither with the military whim and the press of the Hun advance, making reconnaissance reports that the General Staff seriously mistrust and don't bother to act upon, despised by the rest of the Army who imagine we're having a nice easy comfortable war compared with their muddy, bloody lot, and for what? We don't do any-thing positive. We don't actually fight. We just report on the fighting. We're just spectators! Flying journalists! I'm beginning to believe the Generals are right. The aeroplane is not yet ready for war.'

Triggers' new observer had been strongly advised to remain silent when Triggers was in one of these moods, but he couldn't resist making the comment that wars were noted for speeding up progress and development, so might not the aeroplane prove its worth before the great conflict came to an end?

Three months later, Triggers and his observer were shot down four miles east of Arras. The machine caught fire but Triggers managed to put her down. He escaped with minor burns on both forearms, but his observer, who had been wounded by Archie fire, was trapped in the blazing machine. Triggers, unable to reach the screaming man, took out his Webley revolver and shot him through the head. Soon afterwards, when he heard he was to be 'rested', posted back to Blighty as an instructor, Triggers made no pretence of disappointment. 'Perhaps the aero-plane will prove its worth in this war,' he told his CO, 'but it won't worry me one little bit if I'm not here to see it happen. I can't wait to get to Beechwood Reserve Squadron. A sleepy little airfield two miles from the south coast, amid lush green fields and quiet lanes, with a friendly pub or two close at hand. God, after life here in France, it sounds like heaven on earth.'

But although the war seemed a million miles away in the peace of Sussex, death was just as close. Indeed, perhaps closer, for the innocent, fresh-faced young trainee pilots were far more deadly than the Hun. Triggers' first pupil was a rash young cavalry officer who turned through two hundred degrees on his third attempt at getting airborne. 'You're not in the cavalry now,' Triggers barked, inspecting the badly damaged lower wingtip and giving a word of apology to the poor rigger who'd been sent running for his life. 'It's an aeroplane, not an "aerial mount". We don't go charging it as if the propeller were a power-driven sabre.'

Triggers' next would-be murderer was a feverishly keen young man straight from school who was 'doing his bit' in the most exciting way on offer, confusing patriotism with cricket and scoring it in crashes. 'Dickie Parvitt's crashed three times,' he chirped, 'but I've only managed it twice.'

'Manage it once more,' Triggers snapped back, 'and you'll find yourself on the next train back to wherever you came from. There are plenty more young idiots like you. But aeroplanes are in short supply.' That evening in the Mess, he told a fellow instructor: 'I don't mind dying for my King and Country – but it irks me to do it for some stupid schoolboy Hun.'

Referring to pupils as 'Huns' soon caught on and in the next few weeks there was a significant reduction in the number of crashes, an all-out effort to banish the stigma. Or was it the result of the formidable list of 'Do's and Don'ts for Fliers' that appeared on the walls of every hut? The life-saving reminders were to be drummed into the heads of the high-spirited young daredevils and might have been the topic for endless jokes had not Triggers added a personal note: 'You will all laugh at this list, of course. Some of you may die laughing.'

The machine on which pupils were introduced to their precarious new trade was the Maurice Farman 'Longhorn', a docile creature, and reasonably safe, even in the hands of the most ham-fisted. Called the Longhorn on account of the pair of long skids that curved up before the main planes, the Farman was an immense arrangement of booms, struts and piano wire, seemingly designed to occupy the greatest amount of space whilst filling as little of it as possible – a skeleton for some fearful monster that had never been fleshed out and so remained a lovable freak. The whole conglomeration sat on two pairs of bicycle wheels, the pupil and his instructor perched one behind the other in a canoe-shaped 'nacelle'. Here the controls were duplicated, a lever for the elevators and swivelling handlebars for the ailerons. Pushed along by a seventy-horse Renault engine, the Longhorn climbed at forty-five, attained a top speed of about sixty straight and level, and landed (engine off) at the velocity of a determined cyclist. These low speeds and the comforting ocean of wood and fabric between occupants and ground ensured that crashes were rarely fatal. 'That's what makes you all so damned brave and careless,' Triggers snarled at his pupils as they watched a grumbling mechanic dislodge the undercart from the roof of the Sergeants' Mess. 'Wait until you go on to the Avro and the BE2.' These were more conventional, faster machines, requiring far more skill and delicate handling. 'Mistakes you make on the Farman will kill you on those machines.'

During the following months Triggers stretched himself in mind, body and nerves, teaching his pupils to fly as safely as possible in the ludicrously small number of hours allotted for training. The RFC in France was in desperate need of pilots. Triggers understood the urgency, but still felt the guilt of a job only half done whenever he watched his latest 'fully-fledged' pupil take off and turn east to wing his way above the railway line to Folkestone and the two large crosses cut into the chalky coastal fields. The crosses were one mile apart and, if seen quite clearly, then visibility was good enough for the Channel flight, and the pilot would now turn south, midway between the crosses, and fly on until the French coast was reached. 'You'll know when you're there. You'll smell the garlic.' There was always that uncharacteristic flippancy whenever Triggers wished them goodbye. His advice took them as far as the French coast; his responsibility for them ended there, thank God, and after that he didn't need to care two hoots what happened to them. He did care, of course. Too much, perhaps. 'Note your compass reading and keep to it, no matter what it indicates. A compass in an aeroplane is about as accurate as my grandmother's bedside clock. It's the vibration of the machine that does it. Especially after making a turn. If they intend a compass to be useful they should fill it with brandy.' Always the same jokes, always the same farewell 'gift' – a motor-car inner tube! 'If you do come down in the Channel, it'll keep you alive long enough.' For what? 'To regret not having joined the infantry. Good luck! And if you do what so many have done before you, fly in a semi-circle and land in Kent – I'll have your ears for elevators.'

As the weeks went by, each more slowly than the last, Triggers became increasingly restless. His enthusiasm waned, his temper grew even shorter. And whenever a new instructor arrived, a chap just back from France for a 'rest', with all the latest news of what was happening on the squadrons there, Triggers would be strangely silent.

'So you want to get back there, eh?' The Squadron Commander looked glum. Triggers was the best instructor he'd ever had. On top of that, he liked the man enormously (aside from that ferocious temper, of course; no coping with that, you just walked away from it). Yes, he'd be sorry indeed to lose Captain Triggers, but there it was, if that's what he wanted, he'd put in the request for a posting back to France. 'May be a little time before it comes through, mind you.'

Yes, Triggers understood that. But his request was to be granted much sooner than he expected.

A pall of brown dust rose behind the British Army staff car as it jolted down the rutted track towards Ste Marie airfield. The summer had been unduly warm and Major Wilkinson was averse to hot weather. Such heat was trying enough in peacetime; fighting a war in it was impossible. One needed to be in a cool, clinical frame of mind to deal with a cunning fellow like the Hun. And the sun had a particularly bad effect on the British soldier. Made him leisurely in his movements, slack in his dress, a yawning gunner with a lazy aim. Major Wilkinson couldn't wait for autumn and prayed for a bitter winter to stiffen the sinews and summon up the direct hits that would blow the Hun to smithereens.

The entrance to the airfield sported a rustic arrangement that caused the Major to wonder if he was visiting a military establishment or a rodeo show in the United States of America. The sentry did not even trouble to stop the car, and in front of the first of three Bessonneau hangars two men in disgustingly greasy overalls were sitting on the grass munching apples. One of them without a cap on, would you believe. The Major was glad that he had made the hot dusty journey from Brigade HQ. It had not been necessary, of course. He could have communicated the order by telephone in the normal way. But he was curious. He had been co-operating with the Royal Flying Corps for close on six weeks, yet he knew very little about it. Oh, he'd seen their noisy machines drifting over the trenches as if they had all the time in the world to get to God-knows-where, but he'd never actually met the peculiar birds who flew them. Now, here he was, right in their nest. And a more disgracefully inefficient encampment he'd never seen.

A strong smell of manure came from somewhere behind a hedge and the Major waved the driver on another twenty yards or so to the side of a tumbledown barn that had been converted into three Flight Offices and an Officers' Mess, with the officers' quarters housed above. The door marked 'C Flight' looked much sturdier than the rest of the building and the Major wondered if the whole caboose might not cave in around him if he opened it too sharply. But he was eager to catch these birds in their natural state.

Sergeant Mills had just put his feet up on the desk and taken his first bite of one of the 'windfalls' Corporal Jones had picked in Monsieur Flemmard's orchard the night before, when the door burst open. Mills goggled, jumped to attention, and slid the apple into his tunic pocket.

'Where is your commanding officer?'

'Did you mean the Squadron Commander or "C" Flight-Commander, sir?'

'I've no idea. Captain Dornish. He's the chap I talk to on the telephone from Brigade HQ.'

'Brigade HQ' had a stiffening effect on Sergeant Mills' position of attention. 'Captain Dornish is "C" Flight-Commander, sir. He's flying this morning, I'm afraid.'

'Oh. What time does he descend?'

'Descend, sir? Oh you mean—We call it landing, sir. There's no telling, sir.'

'But surely you have times for ascending and times for landing?'

Mills swallowed nervously. He'd had this trouble before. How *did* one explain the difficulties to army officers who knew nothing about flying? They expected aeroplanes to fly to timetables, as if the place was Charing Cross station. He was relieved to hear the drone of an approaching machine.

'That might be Captain Dornish now, sir.'

The Major went to the window and watched the BE2 making its approach. It looked extremely high in the air in relation to its distance from the airfield. Suddenly the engine stopped. The Major's heart missed a beat.

'He's in trouble, surely. What does one do?'

Mills cleared his throat and explained that the pilot always switched off to make a landing, 'blipping' the engine as required, and the Major looked on in grudging admiration as the BE2 turned to lose height and floated over the hedge at the far end of the field, the wheels of the undercart and tail-skid settling on the grass in perfect unison.

A three-pointer always gave Alan Farmer a good feeling. When he could do it every time he'd be entitled to consider himself a good pilot. Still, he wasn't doing too badly. Two weeks in France, flying over the front lines every day, and he hadn't wrecked a machine. And the morning's work had been his best yet. Twenty minutes to knock out that HB. That would take some beating. Most of the credit went to his observer, of course. Mr Bravington had corrected their own battery's fire with the Aldis lamp and they'd got the Hostile Battery at the third attempt. A good chap, Mr Bravington, even if he *was* an officer. After all, it *could* be a sticky relationship; a sergeant pilot with an officer for observer. The pilot was really in charge of the machine, but if you were unlucky enough to be flying with an officer who insisted on you bowing to his authority . . . Mr Bravington wasn't one of those, thank the Lord, although their relationship had got off to a shaky start on Alan's arrival at Ste Marie. In trying to avoid the Squadron's 'favourite Hun' – a two-seater with a deadly accurate machine-gun – Alan had put them down on the wrong side of the lines and Mr Bravington had caught a bullet in the arm from a German infantryman. Alan's marksmanship with the Winchester, followed by a rather nifty take-off, had got them out of more serious trouble; like spending the rest of the war in a prison camp.

'No sign of our favourite Hun again,' Bravington said as they walked to the Flight Office to make their report. The Squadron had not sighted the troublesome Albatros for more than a week now and it looked as if the menace had been moved to another sector. 'See you in the Flight Office. Must pay a call. Forgot to go before we took off. Feel like a whizz-bang about to explode.'

The Flight Office door was inclined to stick. Alan gave it a healthy shove. This time it did not stick. It swung fully open, banged against the wall, and Alan found himself facing a startled Major. Alan snapped to attention. He was not wearing his cap, of course, so he didn't salute. He had removed his flying helmet but his leather flying coat was still buttoned up, and the Major assumed that because the man was a flier he was obviously a commissioned officer.

The Major looked at Sergeant Mills, gave him a curt nod, dismissing him, and Mills pulled on his cap, saluted, and hurried gratefully out.

'One can't be too careful these days.' The Major glanced outside before closing the door. 'Other ranks can't keep their mouths shut. And with all these spies we're rounding up of late. Area's infested with them it seems.' That was the trouble with fighting a war where so many different foreigners were allies. Hard to tell one from the other. Seeking out spies was a needle in a haystack job. Only thing to do was to keep everything under your hat. Give the information to commissioned ranks only.

The Major spread the map on the desk thinking, begrudgingly perhaps, what a fine, alert young chap this pilot was. Not at all the 'peculiar bird' he had expected to meet in this quite disgracefully untidy and disorganised establishment. The Major prided himself on his ability to assess the calibre of a man within seconds of meeting him, and this young officer was wasted here. They could have done with his obvious qualities in the trenches.

'I'm from Brigade HQ, by the way. Major Wilkinson.'

'Good morning, sir.' Alan didn't know what else to say. The Major commented on the lack of security at Ste Marie. Not even a decent bit of barbed wire around the airfield. 'Barbed wire could be a hazard to the machines, sir.'

The Major nodded. Chap had all the answers. And that leather coat he was wearing. Tailor's bill must have been pretty heavy. A wealthy father, no doubt. Probably had his own flying machine before the war. Lot of these RFC chaps came from that sort of background, so he'd heard.

'I understand we've no idea when Captain Dornish will be descending, or landing, or whatever, but I haven't got all day. In case I have to leave before he gets back, I shall explain the job to you.' He indicated the map. 'We've got a battery of eighteen-pounders along here. Because of the shell shortage, we can only fire a limited number of rounds a day. Now. The Hun has a couple of batteries of light stuff that pester our infantry . . .'

'We knocked one of them out this morning, sir.'

The Major blinked. Alan had deliberately made light of it; as if it was just one of those jobs they did in passing on to something quite important.

'The light stuff is no real trouble,' the Major said. 'But the Hun's got a howitzer – that *is*. We know roughly where it's sited. This area, here.'

'We've been flying over there, sir. I'm surprised we haven't spotted it.'

It was under camouflage, the Major explained. A methodical animal, the Hun. Same time every morning, camouflage off, and whoof! The Hun's bit of hate. Dead on five ack emma.

'Then that's the time to locate its position, of course,' Alan said brightly. 'If we're over the area when it starts firing, we can spot the flashes. The trouble is, we've never flown that early. It's a bit before our time. We can't take off until we've some dawn light, at least. And to be flying over that area at five ack emma — ' Alan consulted the map, estimating the distance and flying time – 'We'd need to take off at half-past four at the latest. It'll be dark then. And if we can't see the ground on the way there, and we want to be certain of being over the howitzer's area when she opens up . . .'

Yes, the Major understood the difficulty. He knew their flying contraptions couldn't fly in the dark. Why no one had yet found the answer to that problem was beyond him. These mechanical chaps in the Flying Corps had their brains in their hands and their heads filled with clouds. It had taken him exactly ten minutes to solve the problem of flying in the dark.

'Presumably you can get your aeroplane off the ground in the dark?'

'Yes, sir. The difficulty is finding our way to the target.'

The Major was unable to resist the little smile of self-congratulation.

'I've thought of that. I've arranged for the infantry to fire recognition flares at five-minute intervals.' He had marked the positions and times of the firing of the flares on the map. 'The last flare will be fired just here. Directly west of the target area. Presumably, you'll have some light by that time and you should be able to find your way to the howitzer by flying directly east.'

Alan nodded. It seemed workable. In theory, at least.

'I can't make the decision, of course. It's up to my Flight Commander, Captain Dornish.'

'Then where the devil is he?' The Major glanced irritatedly at his watch. 'I'd like the job done tomorrow.' He peered out of the window as if to be sure that no one was listening, then continued in quieter tones. 'You see, my eighteen-pounders can't reach that howitzer. So we've brought up a fifteen-inch naval gun. Runs on rails. As soon as we've got the location from you, we plaster the area. But we need an accurate map co-ordination. Obviously.'

Alan understood. If they didn't get the howitzer first time, the Hun would change its position and they'd have to repeat the whole performance.

'That's why we've kept quiet about our fifteen-inch,' the Major went on. 'If the Hun did get to hear of it, he'd pull his howitzer back. So I'd sooner we kept it to ourselves, you understand? Total security. No other ranks to know.' He saw Alan staring at him. 'These rumours of spying. Wise to play safe, I'm sure you'll agree. And after all, no need for other ranks to know, is there? I assume your ground staff don't need to know the details of your flying operations?'

'No, sir, the ground staff don't need to know — '

'Then that's that!'

'But the pilots do.' Seeing the Major's puzzled look, Alan went on: 'You said no other ranks to know, sir.'

'That's right.'

'But some pilots are "other ranks", sir.'

The Major looked at him in utter disbelief for a moment or two. 'You mean you have pilots who are not commissioned officers?'

'Yes, sir. NCOs, sir.'

'An NCO in command of an aeroplane?'

Alan explained, calmly and politely, that the ability to fly an aeroplane was not dependent on a man's breeding or schooling. The Major looked distinctly put out. 'You mean you have NCO pilots here in "C" Flight?'

'Just one, sir.' Alan looked steadily at the Major. 'Myself.'

'So he left with a flea in his ear, did he?' Captain Dornish studied the map the Major had left behind. 'A tricky one. All very well in theory. In practice, it could end up in an unholy mess.'

'I'd like to volunteer, sir.'

Dornish smiled faintly at Alan and limped to a door separating the Flight Office from an ante-room, beyond which was the Officers' Mess. He'd had a bad crash three months earlier and his leg still troubled him from time to time.

'As none of us have ever attempted flying in the dark before, I think I should fly this one myself. I have got a bit more experience than the rest of you.' He looked at Sergeant Mills, who had just come in from the airfield with a worried expression and a sheaf of greasy papers. 'Corporal Jones again?'

'He's still worried about the magneto.'

After lunch, Captain Dornish walked over to number

two shed where the gloomy Welsh mechanic had taken the magneto apart yet again.

'It's all right now, sir. Remembering the state it's in, anyway. I got 'em to patch the bullet-holes. They're strong enough. It's the rest of the machine I'm worried about. She needs a complete overhaul, I've told you that. She hasn't seen the Depot for months.'

Yes, Dornish knew that as well as anyone. But they just couldn't spare a machine at the moment. If Corporal Jones had his way the entire Flying Corps would be grounded. Was he reasonably confident the machine would get off the ground tomorrow morning?

'Oh yes, she'll get off the ground all right, sir. What worries me is what it might do when it gets up there.'

The new chap was unpacking his kit when Alan ducked into the tent. 'Jock' Guthrie was an observer; thin, delicate-looking, with sandy hair, and a trusting smile. He was older than average, Alan thought. A lot older, perhaps. He might even be thirty. The Scots accent was friendly, homely somehow, and Alan knew he was going to like Jock Guthrie. And he was glad to have someone to share his tent.

'Alan Farmer, eh? How long have you been here then?'

'Two weeks.'

'I'm just over from Blighty. I don't quite know what I expected France to be like.' He grinned. 'Tidier than it is, I know that. Incredible what a mess an army can make of a place. Like hens! Who owned this bed before me?'

'A pilot. Sergeant Merrigold. He went west, I'm afraid. On the day I arrived.'

'It's lucky I'm not superstitious.'

'How many hours have you done as an observer?'

'Two hundred.'

Alan could hardly believe his ears. Anyone with fifty hours was considered, in Army terms, an old campaigner.

'I was Lord Belfitt's chauffeur, you see,' Jock said, as if that explained everything.

'Lord Belfitt? He had about the fourth or fifth licence ever given to fly, didn't he?'

'The seventh, I think it was. He was sour about it, I know that. His family motto. It's in Latin but it means "I lead the way." So he resented being seventh.'

'You were his chauffeur?'

'Only on the ground. He flew the Farman himself. The trouble was he never got the idea of how to read a map. He used to fly around getting lost. It was my job to follow him in the Rolls and pick him up wherever he landed. I couldn't always find him, of course, then there'd be the devil to pay, so I learned how to read maps myself and he used to take me with him as his observer.'

'Is Lord Belfitt in the Flying Corps, too?'

'No. He's as old as God. Anyway, they'd never accept him. He's blind as a bat. I was his war effort, you see. He ordered me to volunteer.'

Late that afternoon, Charles Gaylion and his observer, James Favell, arrived back from the long reconnaissance. Charles, a 2nd Lieutenant and the son of Brigadier-General Gaylion, had transferred to the RFC from a Hussars regiment, having been interviewed at the War Office on the same day as Alan Farmer. The two young men had done their initial flying training at Beechwood under Captain Triggers, Charles going on to Upavon to complete his training on Avros and BE2s, whilst Alan underwent the basic army training required of all civilian entrants before being allowed to finish their flying courses. They had met briefly on the day before Charles flew to France and had quarrelled over Triggers' newly instituted lectures on air fighting. Charles had joined the Corps to fly, not to kill, and deeply resented Triggers' instruction in 'how to shoot down Huns'. But Alan stuck up for Triggers. The man was teaching his pupils to defend themselves in the air. His motive was to prolong their lives not merely to kill the Hun. Charles accused Alan of hero worship, and, of course, there was more than a grain of truth in the accusation, for if it had not been for Captain Triggers, Alan would not have had his chance to train as a pilot. The son of a Sussex blacksmith who had been killed crashing an aeroplane he had helped to rebuild, Alan had lied his way into the RFC by telling the interviewing officer that he had flown his father's machine. On their first training flight Captain Triggers, believing Alan to be an experienced flier, had allowed Alan to take the controls, and Alan, stubbornly determined to live up to the lie, had almost killed them both. Triggers had been furious and Alan had immediately packed his suitcase, convinced that his career in the RFC was over before it had begun. But Triggers, despite his anger, had recognised Alan's inherent ability and decided to forget the incident.

Eventually, Alan earned his 'wings' and was posted to Ste Marie, where Charles had arrived six weeks before. 'It seems our lives are inextricably intertwined,' Charles had quipped when they met. And he apologised for the quarrel on the occasion of their last meeting in England. 'All that nonsense I talked about joining the Corps to fly, not to kill. Triggers was quite right in teaching us to defend ourselves in the air. It's more than just the occasional pot-shot to show willing nowadays, you know. We're shooting in deadly earnest. A damned shame, really. But there it is. Watch out for a two-seater with a machine-gun. He's pretty deadly. We call him "our favourite Hun".' Then it had been Alan's turn to apologise. 'I as good as called you a coward,' he began, rather sheepishly. But Charles wouldn't let him finish. 'You were quite right,' he said. 'We're all cowards. You find it out the first time you fly over the Hun lines.' He smiled at Alan's disbelief, then recalled his own words on the occasion of their quarrel. 'I said that as you were a blacksmith, you'd know nothing of the conduct of gentlemen. But the surprising thing is, out here, the most unlikely chaps turn out to be gentlemen.' Alan didn't understand. 'You will do,' Charles said, quietly. 'Since I've been in France I've learned that being a gentleman has little to do with a chap's manners or the cut of his clothes.'

Alan was quite taken aback at this admission. It appeared that Charles's six weeks in France had broadened his outlook, made him more tolerant; miraculously, he'd lost the smugness that Alan had so disliked in the man. Oh, the arrogance was still there, the disdainful air of certainty, the supreme confidence of the son of a Brigadier-General who snapped his fingers to summon waiters and took the best of everything for granted. But that was the result of 'breeding', of course, and Alan could forgive that. Yes, on the whole this 'new French Charles' was a friend Alan could admire and respect and hold up as a model for his own ambition. On one of the other Squadrons a sergeant had been 'commissioned in the field' so Alan had hopes of being commissioned himself in the not too distant future. How proud his mother would be when he arrived home on leave with that pip on his sleeve. As for Lorna Collins, the girl he was to marry some day, he could just imagine her face when she opened one of his letters signed '2nd Lieutenant Alan Farmer'.

But the friendship between Alan and Charles was viewed with growing resentment on the Squadron, by commissioned officers and other ranks alike, and particularly by the other members of 'C' Flight. An NCO and an officer flying together, that could be borne as a necessary eccentricity of the Flying Corps. But a sergeant and an officer mixing socially was quite another matter. Hints were dropped, criticisms voiced, but to no avail. With his gift for smoothing out disturbing ripples with a twinkling smile and a smart remark, Charles remained impervious, whilst Alan, true to form as the 'iron man from Sussex', blinked aside warnings with stubborn indifference. On one occasion, however, he lost his temper. It had been one of those mornings when everything had gone wrong. A fruitless search for an HB that had obviously been wrongly positioned on the map, then, when they'd eventually found it, their own battery, for God only knows what reason – shortage of shells most likely – had failed to fire. To crown it all, they'd been caught napping on their way home by their 'favourite Hun', the German two-seater with the dreaded machine-gun, who had given them hell. 'Something to say to you, Alan,' Corporal Jones said when Alan came into the shed to see just how close the bullets had been. 'It's about you and Mr Gaylion. We've been having a bit of a talk, you see. Us NCOs, I mean. We think you should — ' That was as far as he got. Alan's fist stopped the rest. 'Only thinking of you, Alan, that's all.' Jones passed his hand across his lips and stared at the red smear as if he couldn't believe his eyes. The blacksmith was such a calm imperturbable fellow. You could try and provoke him all you wanted and he'd just smile in that easy cocksure way of his, and you'd end up like a madman yourself, wanting to dent his iron head with a swipe of the heavy spanner. 'Thinking of you, Alan, that's all. Someone's bound to clamp down soon. And you, a sergeant, you'll come off worst. Officers always get away with everything.'

The Hun made no such distinctions, Alan thought, as he examined the three bullet holes in the small section of fuselage between Mr Bravington's cockpit and his own.

Officer and sergeant alike had only just got away with their lives that morning.

'I hear our Flight Commander's taking off before dawn light tomorrow,' Charles said to Alan as they passed the estaminet that had been pronounced out of bounds since the altercation between the 'perfectly sober RFC personnel' and the 'drunken infantry'. 'And taking this new chap along with him. Rum, isn't it? A tricky job like that, I mean. You'd have thought he'd want an observer with a lot more experience.'

'Jock Guthrie's got more experience than the rest of the Flight put together. Two hundred hours.'

'Two hundred? What is he – an angel? Here, let's try this place. And don't talk to any strange soldiers. Or we'll find ourselves in another brawl.'

Charles insisted on paying for the first round. 'Just keep your eyes off her,' he said as Alan slid the photograph of Kate from Charles's wallet. 'For your own good. I've told you before. My sister would eat two of you country-bred lads before breakfast.'

'She's nothing like you, is she?' Alan said, admiring the delicate beauty of the features and the mass of dark, softly waved hair.

'Precisely. She has none of my generous good nature.'

'The No Conscription Fellowship. I really can't see a girl with a face like this getting up to speak before a lot of men, persuading them not to fight for their King and country.'

'Chaps like that don't have to be persuaded, do they? They're just gathered there to reassure one another. And my sister's one of them.'

'You call your sister a chap?' Alan laughed. 'She doesn't look like one to me.'

'Your opinion of her doesn't count,' Charles said,

snatching the photograph from Alan and putting it back in his wallet. 'You just stick to your little milkmaid and don't be greedy.'

Alan was stiffly silent for a time. Charles laughed and thumped him on the back. 'You're a sulky brute, aren't you? Why do you have to take everything so much to heart? Here, this wine's filthy. Let's go on to champers. And it's your turn!'

The BE2 lifted off the moist grass, roared over the paraffin flares on the west side of the field, and disappeared like a raging yellow ghost into the darkness beyond. In spite of the early hour, most of the Flight had dragged themselves from their beds to watch the unusual event. Corporal Jones, who had been working on repairs until well after midnight, shook his head in deep foreboding. But at least the magneto was working all right. 'You were a mug volunteering for it,' he remarked to Alan, who was gazing enviously into the smoky darkness above the light of the flames, trying to catch sight of the machine as it turned eastwards. 'Captain Dornish might have let you do it.'

'A feather in the RFC's cap,' Alan said, quietly. 'Finding a howitzer in the dark.'

'Won't be dark by the time they reach it,' Charles yawned. God, why on earth had he bothered? The spectacle hadn't really been worth leaving the cosiness of his bed. And he had a splitting head from the champers. 'Let's hope Brigade HQ don't make a habit of it.'

'Depends on the success of this job, doesn't it?'

Charles was too weary to reply. But he had the gravest doubts. Flying over enemy lines in daylight was bad enough, when you could see where you were going and what you were up against. But at least you were independent. Life, or death, rested on the responses of your hands and feet to whatever you saw with your own eyes. Captain Dornish and his observer (new, and cheerfully ignorant, poor devil, despite his two hundred hours) were flying blind, solely dependent on flares fired by infantrymen who regarded aeroplanes as a blessed nuisance and who were notedly envious of the comfortable lives their fliers led. God, fancy having to put your life in the hands of such fellows.

'Douse those flares,' Richard Bravington bawled at a group of mechanics. 'It's not November the bloody fifth.' And he turned to Charles. 'The new chap seems a decent sort. What's his name?'

Late that afternoon, when the last vestige of hope had faded, Charles asked Alan to see to Sergeant Guthrie's belongings.

'After all, you knew him better than anyone else.'

'I hardly knew him at all,' Alan murmured, looking at the field paybook. His name was Clarence. No wonder he'd been so anxious to introduce himself as 'Jock'. 'I haven't done this before. What do I do with his personal belongings?'

'Put them into store until we know something a bit more definite. I mean, as yet we've no reason to assume that he's — ' Charles forced a smile. 'It's quite likely he's having a meal in some German mess at this very moment. Who's his next of kin? I see. Mother. I shall have to write to her, too, as soon as we know something. Captain Dornish has a wife. Silly, but I didn't even know.' He looked rather sheepish. 'The Squadron Commander says I'm to be Flight Commander until – well – until we get someone to replace Captain Dornish.'

After dinner, Alan sat on his bed and read the unfinished letter to Lorna. It had been tucked away in his haversack for the past three days. The poor girl would be

27

anxiously awaiting it, he knew that, yet something had prevented him from finishing that last half-page. It was as if he'd had something important to tell her but couldn't quite call to mind what it was. Now, he knew it well enough. But how to say it? He looked at the two neat piles on Guthrie's bed. Personal belongings and property of the RFC. Personal and impersonal. Heartbreak and duty. The belongings might so easily have been Alan's belongings in two neat piles on *his* bed. He had volunteered for the job of locating that howitzer. If he'd been allowed to do it he'd have been wherever Captain Dornish was at this moment. It was all very well for Charles to say they'd been taken prisoner, but it was much more likely that they'd been killed.

Alan stared for a long time at the yellow flame, moving gently inside the glass of the hurricane lamp. Life, nurtured there, waiting to be snuffed out. A deep sadness pervaded him. He found it unsettling. He couldn't remember feeling like this before. Or could he? Yes. Just. When he was fifteen years old. The summer of 1912 when his father had been killed.

He read the letter to Lorna yet again, then lay back on his bed, utterly defeated by the blank half-page. How the hell could he explain to her how he felt?

'Excuse me, sarge.'

It was Miller, a diminutive Cockney 2nd AM. He'd called to collect Guthrie's 'stuff'.

'And get rid of that bed,' Alan snapped. Sergeant Merrigold. Now Sergeant Guthrie. Alan wasn't superstitious, not in the least, but why keep the bed there? After all, he could do with a bit more space. Miller looked worried. He knew exactly what to do with the stuff. He'd done it three times before. But what did one do with a bed? 'I don't care what you do with it,' Alan hissed. 'But damned well get rid of it.'

The CO at Beechwood Reserve Squadron was sorry to lose his best instructor. 'I can only wish you good luck and say that Ste Marie is jolly fortunate.'

'Thank you, sir. I hope the members of "C" Flight agree with your opinion.'

'C' Flight wouldn't agree, of course, the CO told himself two days later, as he watched the fair-haired, erect figure striding across the airfield to the brand-new BE2. Not on first acquaintance, at least. Captain Triggers would frighten the daylights out of them. But by God, they would come to respect and admire the man. Of that the CO had no doubt whatsoever.

Triggers followed the route he had outlined so many times to his pupils in the past months: the railway line to Folkestone, turning south midway between the two white crosses in the chalk fields, then, a simple matter of maintaining his compass course until the French coast was reached. He could not for the life of him understand why some of his pupils found it so difficult. Good God, his grandmother could have done it with the greatest of ease, and she was half-blind, poor woman. And she might even have made a better job of tuning the engine. It was running pretty rough. Disgraceful! After all, it was brand new!

It was a gloriously clear day, and long before he reached the French coast he thought he could see as far as St Omer, where he was to deliver the machine before going on to Ste Marie. He wondered what his new Squadron would be like. He'd been told their main duty was Artillery Observation; spotting enemy targets and ranging the artillery on to them. It was like that nowadays, of course. Squadrons being assigned to specific tasks. Very different from August 1914. A pilot was a jack-of-all trades then, carrying out any task that was asked of him.

As he crossed the French coast he mused on the number of times he'd been to France before the war and couldn't decide if it was three visits or four. There was the time of that flying display when he'd hared off back to England to take flying lessons, twice to Paris with his parents, and he was sure there must have been one other occasion, but he couldn't for the life of him think when it was. A waste of time pondering on it, really, for it was very likely some imagined visit as a naughty-minded schoolboy with wishful visions of la vie Parisienne. And – damn his eyes! – just like that dreaming schoolboy, he was flying much too far east. Of course, idiot that he was, he should have allowed for the stiff west wind. Good job his pupils weren't here to see him now. St Omer, that he'd thought he could see in the far distance, was much, much further west, and if he continued on his present course he might well end up landing at the Aircraft Park with a brand-new BE2 shot full of holes by Hun Archie. What a humiliating arrival for the new commander of 'C' Flight, Ste Marie. His cheeks burned with the imagined shame as he pushed right rudder and eased the stick over until she was heading almost directly into the strong westerly wind. Quite suddenly, the engine, as if in petulant objection to this unseen force, began a frightful clattering, like a gleeful madman with a can of old nails. A few seconds later, just as abruptly, the clattering ceased, and was followed by a series of rapid gunshot-like cracks. A volley from an amateur firing squad. And the engine fell dead. Triggers had not the faintest idea what had happened, and in the relative silence that followed, with only the moaning of the commiserating wind in the struts and the wires, he had no time or inclination to try and fathom it out. He had to prepare for a crash landing. And in terrain with which he was totally unfamiliar.

How he managed to miss both the trees *and* the farmhouse Triggers would never know, and as the high-walled barn shot towards him he knew he wouldn't live long enough even to consider the matter. He could not turn without severe risk of a wingtip scoring the grass – but no, it wasn't grass, it was corn, or some other crop, so he'd risk it. Push rudder, stick right over.

The BE2, almost vertical, suspended in the air by some momentary miracle, skidded along the barn wall – or so it seemed to Triggers – partly straightened out as he tore the stick over again in the opposite direction, and crunched down, sliding disastrously along the furrowed earth, to nestle, content in her ruin, several yards short of an evil-looking pond. If only she'd managed to come down in the crop of whatever-it-was, Triggers mourned as he surveyed the badly-wrecked machine. But there it was. With crash landings, you could hardly pick and choose.

Overcoming difficulties that might have defeated lesser men, even those who spoke French with more clarity and less vehemence, Triggers managed to find a telephone. Judging by the way his bad news was greeted at the Aircraft Park, the future of the Flying Corps had been utterly dependent on the safe arrival of the brand-new BE2, and after a long and extremely trying conversation about who should collect the wreck, and when, with yard and metre descriptions of the width and narrowness of a maze of lanes and cart-tracks that had obviously been designed to frustrate all hope of access, Triggers ended up swearing and blinding at a 'Corporal' who turned out to be a Major. He was informed that someone would have to guard the wreck until whoever-was-available reached the God-forsaken machine, and finally – the matter of least concern, it seemed – something would have to be done about getting the pilot to Ste Marie. 'Don't worry about me,' Triggers snapped, feeling very much the idiot who had no regard whatsoever for the tireless efforts of the Royal Aircraft Factory in trying to maintain a supply of the much-needed new machines. 'I'll find my own way there.'

Half an hour later, hot, angry, and humiliated, with a vision of the Royal Aircraft Factory blazing merrily away as a result of a match struck by his own skilful hands, Triggers paid two farm-labourers the equivalent of three litres of wine apiece, and with a veiled promise of médailles for their vigil, left them standing by the wreck with sharpened pitch-forks. After walking fiercely southwards for almost two hours, he was grudgingly given a lift on a cart that reduced the speed of his progress by almost fifty per cent. He fell asleep, waking to find that the cart had taken him miles out of his way, and, after walking for another hour, found his way to a railway station.

'Ste Marie? That's near Béthune, isn't it?' Without waiting for a reply, the RTO turned away to the telephone. 'Yes, I know that, but there are twenty-seven men who were supposed to report to . . . yes, but isn't there a lorry or something? . . . I've tried them . . . yes, I know I could tell them to make their own way but I also know they'll make that an excuse to drift all over France . . . all right, if you do hear of anything, ring me back.' He hung up and looked wearily at Triggers. 'In the last twenty-four hours I've had six thousand men pass through here.'

'Six thousand and one,' Triggers said, pointedly. 'Yes, Ste Marie is near Béthune. There must be something going that way.'

The RTO glanced at the wings on Triggers' tunic breast. 'I thought you chaps flew everywhere?'

'Not in an aeroplane with a connecting rod in four pieces we don't.'

'Ten o'clock in the morning, I'm afraid. That's the next for Béthune. But if you've nowhere to stay for the night, there's a train due in half an hour. But it's only goods wagons.'

'I'll take that one.'

The waiting-room reeked of stale tobacco. Triggers recalled the RTO's words. Six thousand men in one day. War was an incredible business. When you thought about it. But he was much too tired. He noted the officer's greatcoat on the slatted bench. The owner would probably want to stretch himself out, so Triggers settled on the bench opposite, and finding it chillier in the place than it was outside, blanketed his flying coat about him. Twenty-five minutes. He'd better not doze off or he might go and miss the train. Hardly likely though. Goods wagons made an unearthly noise.

He was just slipping away into a blissful nap when the owner of the greatcoat came in. Infantry. A 2nd Lieutenant. Very young, yet somehow, oddly, old-looking. Ah yes, the set expression of pain, the careful manner in which he lowered himself on to the bench, the bulkiness at the hips betraying the bandages beneath the uniform; wounded, and most likely on his way home. Triggers introduced himself. The man seemed unwilling to talk. His name was Clarke, and yes, he *was* on his way home.

'To spend the rest of the war at the regimental depot, I imagine. Trying to instil a proper spirit of enthusiasm into those too inexperienced to know better.'

'You got a Blighty one then?'

'Yes. The one thing I determined when I first came out here was that, whatever the statistical evidence, I at least would remain unscathed. I was wrong.'

Triggers looked suitably sympathetic. 'What happened?'

'I caught a whizz-bang.'

'No, I mean – how are you wounded?'

Clarke winced as he pulled his legs up onto the bench

33

and endeavoured to make himself comfortable. 'Put it this way,' he said, his eyes studiously avoiding Triggers' gaze. 'I shall never be a father.'

'I'm sorry,' Triggers murmured, immediately regretting the fatuity of the remark. But to say nothing at all would have made the poor man feel even more uncomfortable. God, what a bloody awful war it was.

'I suppose a lot of people in England will find it funny. But I'd rather have lost a leg, or an eye, or something. When's your train?'

Triggers held up his wrist. He could just discern the hands of the watch in the fading light. 'Five minutes ago.' There was a whistle and the rush of escaping steam. The train at the platform started to move out. 'No, it's not that one. Going the wrong way.'

'Right way for me. But not far enough. Anyway, they've promised me an ambulance from here. If they remember. I can't walk much yet. And lying's better than sitting. What's your regiment?'

'Not a regiment.' His uniform and 'wings' were hidden beneath the flying coat blanketed about him, of course. 'Royal Flying Corps.'

'Oh.'

Triggers sensed the hostility behind the pain-racked eyes. 'You obviously don't think much of us?'

Clarke was silent for a time. Then, as if something inside him urged him to reply, he said: 'Just that the rest of us wonder whose side you're on.'

'What do you mean by that?'

'We've enough trouble with the Germans without your lot.' He turned away from Triggers' enquiring gaze and leaned back, painfully, on the bench. 'It's the middle of the night. I'm tired. I'm in pain. Let's shut up and pretend the other one of us isn't here.'

'I'm sorry about what's happened to you,' Triggers

said quietly. 'But I'd like to know what you mean.'

Clarke sighed sharply. 'If you insist. For the rest of the Army, this war's spent in trenches. It isn't an hour or so buzzing around where the fighting is, then back to a nice safe airfield miles behind the front lines. It's day after day, stuck in the same place, and any moment something can happen that means you get killed.'

'You don't have a monopoly of casualties, you know.'

'No, but at least we're relevant. Wars are won on the ground.'

'And you'll be stuck in the same blasted bit of ground for years unless someone finds a way of changing the way this war's being fought.'

'And you seriously think the RFC can do that?'

'I don't know what air power can do. Nobody does. At least, not yet. But I do know that air power gives the Generals the chance to try something new. They need never again be taken by surprise. Get overrun by an enemy they didn't know was there.'

'Generals don't get overrun,' Clarke said, bitterly. 'They're too far back. Like your airfields. It's the rest of us who get overrun.'

Incensed now, despite his sympathy for the young lieutenant's plight, Triggers explained that air power had already saved France. In September 1914 it was an aeroplane that had reported the German army's wheel away from Paris, enabling the French army to attack the German flank.

'From my particular trench, we don't deal in armies,' Clarke retorted savagely. 'We deal in companies. Platoons. Sections. Infantrymen. It was infantrymen saved France, not aeroplanes.'

'But the infantry wouldn't have known the flank was exposed if an aeroplane hadn't spotted — '

'I'm perfectly aware that from my trench I can't see

the wider perspectives, or the grand design, or anything else they care to call it. All I know is that every time an aeroplane comes over us – one of yours or one of theirs, it makes no difference – I know that we're going to suffer. You see – we survive by trying to be inconspicuous. Those of us who *do* survive. We ask only to be left alone. But then buzz, buzz, over comes one of your aeroplanes. God only knows what you're supposed to be doing.'

The door opened and the RTO looked in. 'Ah, there you are,' he said to Triggers. 'Next train in should be your one.'

'Thanks.'

'No news of my ambulance yet, I suppose?' Clarke enquired.

'Not yet. I'll try again.'

The RTO went out and the two men sat there in silence, each giving the impression that the argument was over and done with, and waiting for the other to reopen it.

'One day they may find a use for your lot,' Clarke said, with an embittered half-laugh. 'Then I'll just have been the result of an unsuccessful premature experiment.'

'You mean – your injury?'

'We were east of Béthune,' Clarke explained. 'The other side of the town there's an airfield called Ste Marie. I see you've heard of it.'

'Yes, I've heard of it,' Triggers said, rising from the bench and putting on his flying coat. He had heard his train approaching; the clank of eased couplings and the wheezing iron wheels screeching for oil as the wagons slowed down. 'What happened?'

'We were told there was an aeroplane coming over from Ste Marie. Just before dawn. We were ordered to send up flares. All along the line. At five-minute intervals. God knows why.'

'Before dawn. The flares would be the only way it could navigate.'

'Really.' Clarke could hardly conceal the hatred as he caught a glimpse of wings on the tunic breast before Triggers buttoned up his flying coat. 'Anyway. The aeroplane came. We sent up our flares as ordered. And all the little Huns, with their compasses and their rangefinders, they lined up on our flares. If they didn't get it right the first time it didn't matter. They only had to wait five minutes and up went another flare. And another. And another. And those of us who did what we were told, in due course, we were shelled to pieces.'

The goods train, hissing steam, jolted and clanked to a stop. Triggers was curious.

'You mean, some of you *didn't* do what you were told?'

'No. They did the alternative.'

'And what was that?'

'The usual thing. Open up on the aeroplane with everything they had. To persuade it to go away.'

'And what happened to the aeroplane?'

'The last I saw of it, it was still heading east.' There was a venomous satisfaction in Clarke's tone now. 'On fire.'

Triggers could hear the horrifying screams of the two burning men as he watched the steam rising from the platform. He bent down to pick up his kit, the holster of his Webley revolver squeezing against his arm and conjuring up that other monstrous vision – the time when he'd been forced to shoot his burning observer through the head. He moved to the door and looked back at Clarke. He quite understood the man's hatred. His heart wept for the man's pain and raged against the murderous minds that led nations to war and urged men to kill and maim.

'It's a small world, isn't it?' he said to Clarke before he went out. 'I am the replacement for the pilot of that machine.'

# 2

Triggers had not even passed through the gates of Ste Marie before the impact of his arrival was strongly felt.

'Have you ever seen me before?' he barked at the sentry. 'If not, then what the hell are you doing allowing me on to this airfield without establishing my identity?'

'But – well – you're in uniform, sir.'

'So is the Kaiser!'

In the Flight Office a nervous and smartly dressed Sergeant Mills, who had been forewarned about the new Flight Commander's 'insane rages' by a 'victim' on a nearby Squadron, was told to assemble 'C' Flight for a little chat in the hangar.

'The *Daily Express*,' Triggers said, waving a crumpled newspaper at the bewildered faces of the assembled airmen. 'An article here by a writer called H. G. Wells. I'm glad some of you seem to have heard of him. He says that at present, three hundred miles of Frenchmen and thirty or so miles of Englishmen and perhaps a score miles of Belgians are confronting three hundred and fifty miles of Germans. But the way to the left is barred by the sea, and the way to the right by Switzerland. There is a way, however, to the rear of the Germans – to their ammunition factories. He believes we could win the war if we had enough aeroplanes now.'

'Does that mean the Royal Aircraft Factory are turning out more machines, sir?' someone asked, hopefully.

'No, it doesn't,' Triggers snapped, leaving everyone more bewildered than ever. 'But H. G. Wells goes on to say that every aviator we have in the air now is worth one hundred men saved from death below. So. There's one man who disagrees with the opinion of certain generals that the role of the aeroplane is negligible in this war.'

'It's all very well for H. G. Wells,' James Favell grumbled as he walked out to his machine the next morning. 'He's never been artillery spotting over enemy lines, with frozen feet and fingers, Archie blasting away at you, and that damned Hun with the machine-gun breathing down your neck. Still, as our new Flight Commander, I suppose he had to make a jolly start by trying to stiffen our morale. What did you make of it, anyway? He was your instructor in England, so you should know.'

'I hadn't thought about it, really,' Charles yawned. 'I suppose he believes that the longer this war goes on, the better chance the Flying Corps will have of proving its worth. Something like that, anyway.'

Favell climbed into the front cockpit and tucked his map beneath his left thigh where it would be handy. 'Our Captain Triggers is not very popular with me, I can tell you. Switching me to fly with the new chap.'

'Thank God I've got rid of you.' Charles gave an exaggerated sigh of relief. 'Perhaps I'll get a decent observer now.'

'Heaven knows where you'll end up if you don't,' Favell quipped. 'You can only find your way when there are railway lines to follow. Thanks.' He took the Winchester and slid it between his knees, inwardly cursing Charles for leaving the Mess in the middle of his breakfast in order to accompany him out to his machine; as if he was seeing his friend for the last time. 'Why the hell couldn't he put the new chap with someone else?'

They watched 'Burlington Bertie' emerging from Number Two shed. A gangling young man with a faintly apologetic air, Bertie Evans had seemed at first meeting to be painfully shy, but had blossomed on his second evening in the Mess, delighting them all with some absolutely corking conjuring tricks.

'I jolly well hope he can make our favourite Hun disappear,' Favell said mournfully, as the sleight-of-hand expert looked wonderingly around the airfield. 'You know, I think he's short-sighted.'

'Don't be ridiculous. How on earth could he manage to become a pilot?'

'You could ask that question of any of the chaps they're sending out these days. God knows how they pick them.'

'It's not their ability. Most of them would be good pilots, average anyway, if they were given enough flying hours. But they're sending them out now with even less flying hours than I had when I came over. Surely he can see us? He can't be *that* short-sighted.'

Bertie Evans waved, grinned, and hurried towards them, like a lost boy at the seaside, reassured at the sight of his parents' deckchairs.

'Good luck, Bertie!'

'Thanks. I reckon I shall need it. My first flight over enemy lines.'

'A bit of fatherly advice,' Charles said, with a sneaking suspicion that he was younger than Bertie. 'If you do run into our favourite Hun, don't hang about on a parallel course. That's his best position for firing at you with that machine-gun of his. Get directly beneath, behind, or in front of him. Those are the positions that make it most awkward for him.'

The mechanic called to check that the engine was

switched off. 'Switch off!' Bertie called back and the mechanic pushed the propeller in quarter-turns to suck in from the carburettor. 'Petrol on!' Bertie pressed down the switch, confirmed that it was on, and the mechanic swung the propeller. 'Contact!'

Sounding like a giant venetian blind caught in a tremendous wind, the engine clattered into life and rose to a thunderous roar, the wing struts, flying and bracing wires thrumming in the rush of air. The chocks were pulled away and the BE2 hurtled forward, curved into the air, turned, and went on climbing towards the front lines. A rather flashy take-off Charles considered as he waved to Jim Favell; he hoped it wouldn't be Bertie's last. He wandered back to the Mess to finish his breakfast, musing on whether a chap with short sight would ever find his way through the Pearly Gates. 'Getting hard-boiled myself,' he remarked to Dick Bravington, when the orderly brought the eggs to the table.

In a field eleven miles to the east of Ste Marie, Leutnant Stein climbed into the rear cockpit of his Albatros and checked that his Parabellum machine-gun was moving freely on its mounting. The Feldflieger Abteilung near the village of Templeuve was equipped with six machines; an Aviatik B1, two LVGs, and three Albatros two-seater biplanes. There were now seventy-one Field Aviation Units in the German Air Service and the number and variety of their tasks had been steadily increasing since the outbreak of the war. Stein's unit covered a sector of roughly ten miles of battle front, stretching from Neuve Chapelle in the north down to just beyond the la Bassée canal, and its tasks were long reconnaissance flights to report on the British strength of troop concentrations, dropping bombs on enemy installations and railway junctions, and more recently, harassing British machines engaged in artillery reconnaissance in the sector. This last-named duty had become the most important and pressing function of the Field Unit at Templeuve. The British observers were becoming much too expert at the job of ranging the big guns on to their targets, and the German High Command were very concerned.

Stein, an observer and the best shot in his unit, had been permanently assigned to this task of harassing British machines. Having served in a regiment of Uhlans (cavalry lancers specialising in reconnaissance), he had requested a transfer to the Air Service soon after the outbreak of war and was now the most experienced air observer at Templeuve. On transferring, it had not occurred to him to train as a pilot. Pilots, as everyone knew, were just chauffeurs, mostly sergeants, whose job was merely to take the observer wherever he wanted to go. The observer, of course, was the really important chap. Or so Stein had thought at the time. But during these last few weeks he had begun to regret his decision not to train as a pilot. He had heard talk of a new German machine, a monoplane, with a fixed machine-gun that fired forward, through the arc of the propeller. It was all very secret at the moment; indeed, so secret that Stein's commanding officer had scotched all talk of it and Stein's pilot was of the opinion that the new monoplane and its magical forward-firing gun was a rumour put around quite deliberately in order to raise the morale of the German fliers. Not that it needed raising. Of course not. It was just that the British fliers in the sector were such a foolhardy lot and their antics could be rather unnerving at times. But rumour or not, the talk of the monoplane with the forward-firing gun had made Stein think about the future of the war in the air, and in particular the part he was to play in it.

Firing forward with a fixed machine-gun was such a

simple and logical innovation, it puzzled him why no one had thought of it before. 'Pusher' machines were able to fire forward, of course; with the engine behind the pilot, the observer could sit in the nose with a machine-gun on a swivel mounting. And Stein had heard of a French gun-mounting whereby the pilot was able to fire over the propeller arc with a machine-gun fixed to the top of the upper wing. But these ideas were no more than gestures of aggression when compared with the attacking possibilities of a single-seater machine with a gun that could be fired through the arc of the propeller; a flying gun, as it were, flown and fired by one man. This was surely the way the war in the air was destined to go. It had begun with aeroplanes being used purely for reconnaissance. Then the armies had realised the value of the 'flying eyes' in seeking out targets for the artillery and ranging their guns on to those targets. Now, machines like Stein's had the job of shooting down those flying eyes. The next step would be to 'attack' the 'attackers', and, eventually, the object of protecting the reconnaissance machines would be conveniently forgotten, and 'attack' would become an end in itself.

Stein was so convinced of this, and so excited and inspired at the prospect of flying alone in a machine for the sole purpose of entering into deadly combat with a lone enemy, that he had applied to his commanding officer to recommend him for training as a pilot. Stein's CO had been rather unhappy at the thought of losing his best observer but had reluctantly passed on the recommendation, and now Stein was eagerly awaiting news of his posting for pilot training.

'Shall we fly our usual course, sir?' Stein's pilot enquired as he went through his cockpit check. Stein nodded and swung the Parabellum so that it pointed almost directly downwards. He was seated behind his pilot and aft of the wings so that he had an almost unobstructed view of the ground below. The mounting of the Parabellum – a lightweight modification of the Maxim machine-gun – enabled him to fire into almost the full three hundred and sixty degrees of airspace above him, and because of his position aft of the wings, he could fire with reasonable freedom into the airspace below. At least, to port and starboard of his machine. An aeroplane flying directly beneath the Albatros would be in Stein's 'blind spot' of course, and therefore safe from the fire of the Parabellum. In this event, he could count on his pilot to bank the Albatros enabling him to fire directly downwards.

Stein and his pilot had flown together for the past five weeks and had reached the stage of mutual understanding where such manœuvres became automatic reactions. In situations where a decision was required – and Stein, as commissioned officer *and* gunner, made all the decisions – they relied on a series of hand-tap signals. For instance, a tap from Stein on the back of his pilot's neck and the Albatros would immediately begin to climb. Stein found this useful when an enemy was directly behind him, a position in which he was unable to fire his Parabellum without risk of hitting his own tail. As soon as his machine began to climb, however, the angle gave him the necessary margin for safety and, incidentally, a 'larger' target as the enemy machine passed beneath him; coming into 'plan view' as it were. Indeed, it was such a gloriously opportune moment it irked Stein that it didn't occur much more frequently. But because of the inability to fire forward, there was little point in a British machine coming on to Stein's tail, unless, of course, he found himself there quite by accident. This had happened on two occasions. Once when Stein had taken cover in cloud following some wickedly accurate Archie fire, and emerging from the cloud found a British two-seater just some thirty yards behind him. The tap on the shoulder to his pilot, the immediate climb, and Stein had fired his gun on a target he couldn't possibly have missed. But the damned Parabellum had jammed. On the second occasion, the British pilot of the 'sitting duck' had produced what had looked to Stein like a small cannon. Stein had been so confounded by the sudden appearance of what must surely have been the surprise introduction of a startling new aerial weapon that, by the time he had recovered, the British machine had passed beneath him and was heading for its lines. 'As far as I could see, it was just a speaking trumpet,' Stein's pilot said dolefully when they had landed. 'What he's using it for, God only knows. And I doubt if even He knows what goes on in an Englishman's mind half the time. After all, they do have some very strange methods of communication. Most of them don't work. But that doesn't deter them in the least. Being English, it's not the communication itself that is important – but the novelty of the method.'

Stein had laughed and agreed. The English certainly were a most eccentric enemy. Nevertheless, you had to respect them. They were very brave men. Ridiculously so, when one considered that although the British lagged behind the French and German air forces, it was the foolhardy English pilots who had committed the first acts of aggression in the air. Wasn't it an Englishman who had thrown a brick at a German machine soon after the outbreak of the war? And yet another of the madmen had flown with grappling irons attached to a length of rope in the vain hope of entanglement with a German propeller. What peculiar element pervaded the climate of those two foolish little islands to make its inhabitants so insanely aggressive when the odds were weighted so heavily against them? 'It's their love of sport,' Stein's pilot had spent a lot of time in England before the war as a representative for Bosch spark-plugs. 'It's a wonder they don't give their observers cricket bats to defend their machines.' They might just as well have done, Stein considered, because a rifle was no match for his Parabellum.

James Favell watched the shell burst north of the target, carefully noted the position, marked it on his map and slid the clock-code disc from the back of his map case. The circular piece of celluloid, with concentric circles marked alphabetically and its outer edges numbered like a clock, was used to convert the position of a shell burst into a letter-number code. Favell placed the transparent disc on the map with the centre spot over the target and studied the pencilled position of the shell-burst. It had been very close. Inside the inner circle of the disc, in fact. 'A' battery were damned hot gunners, no doubt about that. The next shell would be dead on target. It was just a matter of giving them an accurate map-reference for the last shell-burst so they could make the small but vital correction to their ranging. As he carefully adjusted the north-south line on the disc and considered whether the shell-burst was fractionally nearer to one o'clock than two o'clock, Favell marvelled at the power in his numbed, gloved fingers, and in the minute calculation being shrewdly pondered. In a few minutes time the earth beneath the lead pencil point would erupt in a massive explosion. And with a bit of luck would cause further explosions over the radius of something like a quarter of a mile. Favell was quite looking forward to the spectacle. He had never 'blown' an ammunition dump before. Indeed, he was so taken by the vision of the firework display in the offing that the thump jolted him around as if it had exploded on his shoulder.

'The Hun!' Bertie shouted.

The Albatros was diving towards them, on the port side. It could have come out of the dark layer of cloud that hung a thousand feet above or perhaps Bertie Evans really was short-sighted and hadn't spotted its approach. Damn the man! Damn all new pilots! And damn the Albatros! Why did it have to come now, when success was only seconds away? Annoyed and stubbornly unconcerned, Favell groped for the Aldis, motioning to Evans to turn to starboard. The port lower wing was obscuring Favell's line of sight to the battery.

'Keep turning!' he bawled at the hypnotised Evans, who was seeing an enemy machine for the first time, the German pilot's face oddly reminding him of a chap he knew at school. And why was the man smiling? 'Steady! Hold her steady, for God's sake!'

The Albatros turned onto a parallel course. The familiar form of attack. Stein aimed his Parabellum and willed it not to jam. Why didn't the English fools turn away? What the devil were they up to? Was it some sort of trap, or were they both stone blind? The observer, stupid fellow, was signalling with his lamp, and leaning so far over the side he was practically falling out. Muttering the terrible fate that lay in store for his armourer if the gun jammed this time, Stein pressed the trigger.

The stream of bullets raked the pilot's cockpit diagonally, killing Bertie Evans outright. Favell spun around, pointing his lamp at the Albatros in a gesture of defiance. 'A two . . . A two' the lamp flashed. The BE2 stalled. The port wing dropped, heralding the awful flutter that preceded the terrors of the spin. 'A two . . . A two' Favell shouted at the revolving earth. He could hear the gramophone in the Mess, the needle stuck, the snatch of melody insanely chasing itself and Charles laughing and winding. 'A two . . . A two!' A shame he had to die before seeing the result of his signal. But there, it would be a magnificently noisy epitaph. And he was glad about Bertie Evans's sightless eyes, God rest his new pilot's soul. At least he didn't have this agonising wait for the earth to come up and end it all.

Stein felt strangely sick at heart as he watched the BE2 hit the ground and burst into flames and was glad the horror was so diminished by distance as to appear no more frightful than the striking of a match. It had all been much too easy. Ignoble, somehow. A degrading success that made one yearn for failure. He tapped his pilot on the shoulder and motioned 'home'. As the starboard wing glided down into the turn, the Albatros rose sharply, as if violently offended at the sight of something on the earth below. Stein looked down. His pilot was pointing, having already spotted the gigantic eruptions directly beneath. He switched off his engine to enable himself to be heard. 'The dump at Gernville,' he called out. Stein nodded and cursed the British observer's signal. If only Stein had fired his burst just a few seconds sooner. He no longer felt sick at heart. Just plain annoyed. But an an hour later, he was quite pleased with himself, when his fellow officers toasted his 'kill' in the Mess.

'It certainly is your lucky day, Leutnant Stein', his commanding officer told him over lunch. 'I've just received permission to grant your request to train as a pilot. You leave on Friday. So tomorrow is your last day of service with the unit.'

And Stein determined to make it a memorable last day by shooting down a second British machine. His appetite whetted by the previous day's victory, he had a proud vision of himself arriving for pilot training with two 'kills' already to his credit.

He spotted the British two-seater descending from the

cloud layer just a mile or so from the lines and heading west, for home, and he decided that on this one occasion he would forget the strict rule forbidding him to fly beyond enemy lines. It was too good an opportunity to miss. He knew exactly how the British fliers would be feeling at this particular time, being all too aware of his decreased alertness at the end of a patrol. The occupants of the two-seater would be at their lowest ebb; physically exhausted by an arduous artillery spotting run, they would be cold and hungry, and already enjoying in prospect their bacon and eggs and endless cups of tea that were, after all, only a few minutes flying time away. In body and in mind they would be totally unprepared for what was now only a faint possibility of an enemy attack.

Stein motioned to his pilot to alter course for the front lines and to remain concealed inside the cloud layer until he gave his signal to attack. He wanted the surprise to be complete.

The explosion came perilously close and Alan eased his BE2 out of the shallow dive. The Archie shellburst had taken him unawares. He had made his descent in what he considered to be a 'quiet' spot; that was, out of the range of Archie guns. Obviously, this was a new Hun Archie gun, and he ought to report its position for the rest of the Squadron's benefit. He banked his machine to enable him to see the ground beneath, and awaited the tell-tale flash.

'Ess! Ess!' Bravington shouted, waving his hand in a snaking motion. Alan nodded and pushed into a steepily-banked turn to begin the 'essing' movement that would make it harder for the Archie gunners to range on to them. Poor old Bravington! He hated Archie more than most on the Squadron. He had once seen a direct hit. They were not common, thank the Lord, but once seen, never forgotten. So getting the new gun's position would have to wait until tomorrow.

The second shell exploded directly beneath the turning BE2, blasting it skywards, and Alan suddenly found the earth above his head. Something cracked against his windscreen and fell away. God, what the hell was it? Alarming tales flashed through his head – nightmare jokes of 'bits falling off'. But he had never met anyone who had actually *seen* a piece of his machine fall off and he regarded the tales as a mythical contribution to the grumbling campaign against their rotten old death-traps. Then, suddenly, a twist and a bob, and the clouds were back where they should be. His machine had righted itself without any help at all from the chap 'in charge'. But of course, why shouldn't she? Wasn't the BE2 reputed to be inherently stable? Whatever position she was in – at least, according to the theory – if you centred her controls she would right herself and return to flying straight and level. And that's exactly what had happened. Being a prim, right-way-up-minded lady, she had taken offence at finding herself upside-down and had got herself out of that undignified position with no prompting at all from her pilot.

'My rifle!' Bravington bawled, leaning over the side and staring at the earth. 'It's fallen out!'

Alan grinned. So that was the 'bit' that had 'fallen off'. A moment later, his right leg jerked away from the rudder bar and he felt a searing pain in his knee.

'Enemy!' Bravington cried, his eyes fixed on the diving Albatros, its machine-gun chattering.

Alan pushed his left foot on the rudder and swung the control lever over, glancing back to see the enemy already turning after them. The Hun pilot was no sluggard. But Alan knew that all he had to do was to keep in front of the

Hun for another mile or so and they would be safe enough. The German observer could not fire forward, and once the BE2 had crossed the lines the Hun machine would turn back. They never flew over British territory, everyone knew that. As Bravington once commented, 'The German commanders have a sensible regard for the lives of their fliers. And why not? Fliers are in short supply. Why let them bumble up and down over enemy lines, like we idiots have to do, for all and sundry to take a pot at?'

As he crossed the British lines, however, Alan was dismayed to see the enemy showing no sign of turning back, and as it came on to a parallel course in the familiar attacking position, Bravington gestured in despair. Having lost his rifle, they were completely unarmed. Not that a rifle was much use against a machine-gun, but it gave one the illusion, at least, of making a fight of it. It was better to die with your finger on the trigger of a Winchester than waiting for your Maker with a pair of twiddling thumbs. He looked anxiously at Alan. It was all up to him now.

Stein swung his Parabellum on its mounting, preparing to aim. Alan unbuttoned his flying coat and slid his Webley from its holster. Bravington groaned in disgust. He might have raised a laugh if it had not been for the feeling that it might well be his last. If a rifle was a pretty useless weapon in the air, then a revolver was an absurdity. Pilots only carried the thing for comfort. If the eternal nightmare became reality and you found yourself going down in flames, then a bullet from a Webley was infinitely preferable to being roasted alive. But as an aerial weapon, the Webley was no more than a futile gesture of defiance.

Stein pressed the trigger of his Parabellum machine-gun. Alan fired his Webley twice and turned away. A bullet tore through the fabric of the cockpit just above his throttle hand, and as he pulled out of the turn, two tremendous explosions rocked the BE2 from side to side and left her shuddering from the impact. British Archie this time, damn them, Alan muttered angrily, seeing the drifts of distinctive white smoke. God, hadn't they already had enough from the Hun Archie guns? What did the British gunners think they were doing? Firing on a Hun machine was all very good and proper, but not when a British machine was in their line of fire. Couldn't they see the roundels? Of course they could, but they damned well didn't care. Their clumsy great feet safely on the ground, smacking their lips over mugs of tea, and very likely betting on who would cop it first.

A third explosion sent him jolting and cursing, with Bravington glaring as if it was all *his* fault. Then came the fourth! Whoomph! A giant fist crashed down on the nose, and as the earth came rushing up, Alan fought to regain control of the crazily diving machine. Then he remembered! Leave it to her, you idiot, just leave it to her!

He centred the controls and – lo and behold! – she rode out of the certain-death dive in a long graceful curve. Alan looked around for the Hun. It was turning back to the lines.

'With his tail between his legs!' Bravington called out, grinning all over his face. 'Good old British Archie gunners!'

Bless their rotten-aiming hearts, Alan murmured. And the danger having passed, he gave himself up to the agony of his leg.


'Nothing to write home about,' Charles quipped as they lifted Alan on to the stretcher. 'But you'll get leave out of it, you lucky dog.'

Alan forced a grin. In normal circums̶ have been delighted at the prospect of leave̶ that letter to Lorna? Now he would have to ex̶ he certainly didn't relish the prospect of that.

# 3

Careful not to wake old Tom and his wife, Harry Farmer left putting on his boots until he'd closed the back door, then he walked with mindful tread down the gravelled slope into Haverton Lane. At the end of the Lane, the smithy looked stone cold in the grey dawn light but Harry knew that the ashes would still be warm on his hands when he came to clear them out in an hour or so's time. Away from the sleeping village he walked with freer step. Harry was fond of a walk in the morning; and in a warm summer like this one, an hour in the open air satisfied his mind and made him less tetchy in the ten or eleven hours in the stifling heat of the smithy. And this early there was no one about, not even the landwomen; according to old Collins, they always turned up late and couldn't work for toffee.

At the bottom of the curving hill Harry stopped, shocked to see the bloated body of a dog in the slowly moving waters of the stream. For an instant, his mind cast back to the trenches; but there'd been no cleansing waters there, of course. Crossing Lovell's Bridge, he dropped over the low wall and sat on the big stone beside the stream to eat the bread and cheese he had slipped into his pocket the night before. Harry liked this spot. Here, there was so much to consider, reflect upon, smile at the emory of; the school yard where he and Will used to play strong horses and weak donkeys, busting their muscles to boast their reputation as sons of the blacksmith, and the hill they used to race 'backwards' up and where they'd first seen Conway Starke, the squire's son, whizzing down on his new bicycle – the first they'd ever seen in Becket's Hill. (Strange that one of Conway Starke's contraptions should have been responsible for Will's death.) Across the way, beyond the stretch of wild shrubbery and twisted trees they called 'the wilderness', Harry could see the steeple of the church, the reminder of the woman he had never known. His mother lay buried there in the churchyard. She had died when Harry was born. His father's grave was alongside hers, and brother Will's just a few yards away. But it was the wilderness that held Harry's fondest memory. He'd had many a smile over that April afternoon when he and his brother Will had gone shooting with Molly Grayson. How the girl had screamed at the very first flutter, clutching Will's arm as he pressed the trigger, and watching with relief and joy as the partridge flew safely on. How strange Harry had thought the girl then, shaking his head in despair at his brother for marrying a contrary-minded creature from the town, and grumbling at the dance she had led them both when she first came to live in the house. But looking back on it now, who could blame her? Leaving her comfortable home in Lewes to keep house for two brothers who scraped a bare living in a country smithy and whose only knowledge of the feminine touch came from old Aunt Nell who wore her late husband's socks, smoked a clay pipe on the sly, and came in twice a week to do the brothers' washing and bake their bread. Oh yes, Molly Grayson had been a startling new experience for the seventeen-year-old Harry, and naturally enough, he supposed, he had fallen in love with his brother's wife.

Now, twenty years later, quite *unnaturally* he felt sure, he still had the same secret longings and fond reverence ('love' was a word he had grown too old for, surely?) for the woman who lived alone in the 'old house' next to the smithy. Molly Farmer was now his employer and paid Harry's wages each Friday for working in the smithy that had been in the Farmer family for four generations. Not that this situation bothered Harry one whit. He had no relish for ownership. And he had forfeited any right to the family business when he'd left Becket's Hill at seventeen to join the cavalry just before the start of the South African war. With the reorganisation of the British Army, he'd been placed on the Reserve, working in smithies in Oxfordshire and Wiltshire, and then, when the war with Germany had begun, he'd gone to France with his regiment. As a farrier, of course. He'd worked as a farrier all his days, even in his time in the Army. He knew nothing else. There was nothing else he *could* do, or wanted to do, so 'what to do with my life now?' he had asked himself over and over in those dark days at the base hospital in France. A blacksmith with one arm. At that time he could think of no more useless creature on God's working earth and he had reached a depth of despair so alien to his sturdily cheerful nature that he could only look back on the time with a deep sense of shame and self-disgust. After all, he had suffered no injustice. During all those years on the Reserve the British Army had paid him each week for the risk of such a happening, so what right had he to complain when the pound or two of flesh was eventually extracted?

By the time he was invalided out there was no vestige of self-pity or bitterness in him, but he had an overwhelming urge – for the first time since he'd left Becket's Hill all those years ago – to see the old home again. When he arrived, his nephew Alan was just off to join the Flying

Corps, and Harry had been persuaded by Old Tom to stay on and run the smithy until Alan came home again. Harry's last visit to Becket's Hill had been in the summer of 1912 to attend his brother's funeral. He had been shocked by the news of Will's death, and further shocked and bewildered to learn that he'd been killed in an aeroplane crash. Colonel Starke's son, Conway, had bought the remains of a crashed machine and had persuaded Will, who'd always had a bent for 'contraptions', to help him rebuild it. Will, catching Conway Starke's enthusiasm for the new sport, decided to learn to fly. He had crashed the machine on his first solo flight and had burned to death. 'A terrible sight for young Alan to see,' Old Tom had said to Harry after the funeral. 'Yes, the lad was down there with us, on Collins's big field, when it happened. The missus is worried. How it might affect him. Seeing his own father die like that. One thing's for sure. It'll put the lad off aeroplanes and such for the rest of his life, thank God.'

Old Tom could not have been more wrong, Harry mused as he walked along to Rudkin's shop for the shaving soap and tooth powder for his contribution to Alan's parcel. It was strange – an enigma, really – that the lad should have been so keen to join the Flying Corps after witnessing the horrifying manner in which his father had died.

'It seems silly sending him gloves in this hot weather,' Molly said as she placed the newly-written letter alongside the socks, khaki gloves, and two tablets of Coal-tar. 'But he said in his last letter how cold it was up there. You still haven't heard from him then?'

'I'll bring the scarf tonight,' Lorna said, evading the subject of 'why' she hadn't heard from Alan for ten days. She had been reading the casualty lists in Mrs Edwards' paper five minutes before. She just couldn't think of any other reason for Alan not writing. 'I've only got another ten rows to do, so I'll finish it dinnertime.' She dipped the pint measure into the urn and poured the 'drop extra' into Molly's jug. 'And I've bought him a fountain pen.' She hoped it wasn't too much of a hint. 'And my mother's sending up two bars of chocolate. She'd heard it's always welcome and very nourishing.'

'That's kind of her,' Molly said, feeling a bit tight in the throat. 'He's a lucky boy, all thinking about him like this. You'll stop for a cup of tea, won't you?'

Lorna was silent as Molly fetched the cups and poured the tea. Three weeks since Alan had left for France and she'd still not brought the subject up. She really ought to tell his mother how things were. 'Did Alan mention anything to you before he left?'

'Mention what?'

'Well. He said we might become engaged when he does come home on leave.' She could hardly bear to watch Molly's reaction to the news. 'Would you mind?'

Molly laughed. 'Mind? Why should I mind?'

'The war's taken him away from you. Now I'm planning to take him away as soon as he gets back. And my mother says . . .' She hesitated, not quite sure how to put it. She glanced at the photograph of Will Farmer on the mantelshelf. 'Your husband passed on. And now your son away in France. It's different when you're living in a town, my mother says. But living alone in a village . . .'

'You get used to it,' Molly said lightly, not wishing to go into the subject of her loneliness. 'We need a box, really. They say you should send things to France in a box to save damage.'

'My father says you're still young,' Lorna persisted.

'That's nice of him,' Molly grinned. 'I'm thirty-seven, if he'd like to know.'

'He knows already. And that's what he means. You're still young enough. On the other hand, you shouldn't wait too long.'

'I see. And has your father got someone in mind for me?'

'I'm sorry,' Lorna said, anguishedly. 'We don't mean to interfere.'

'No need to be sorry. I'm flattered you all talk about me so much. Now, let's find a box, shall we?' She looked earnestly at Lorna as they scrabbled about in the cupboard. 'All those gloves and socks I've been knitting for the men at the front. Perhaps I should have put my name and address inside them and hoped for the best, eh?' She laughed at Lorna's agonised features. 'Only joking, girl.' And she touched back the wisp of light brown hair from Lorna's forehead; a gentle movement, approving the girl's concern and at the same time assuring her that it was not at all necessary. 'I'm very happy for you both. And thanks all the same, but you don't have to find a man for me in exchange for my son.'

Harry came in from the smithy with the stick of shaving soap and the tin of Calox tooth powder.

'Well, that's sensible,' Molly said. 'Now why didn't I think of things like this?'

'I remember the things I was always needing when I was over there,' Harry said quietly. He smiled fixedly at Lorna. He was always more conscious of Molly's nearness in the presence of others; afraid they might suspect his feelings for his dead brother's wife. 'Morning, Lorna. You heard from Alan yet?'

'No, not yet.' And she had to be going or she'd never finish her round. 'Arthur Rudkin'll have a box,' Harry said, when Lorna had gone. 'A tin one's best.'

But everyone was asking for the tin ones, Arthur Rudkin said, and they'd all been taken. However, he'd have a look in the back of the shop to see if he could find one. 'Just over the half pound, that all right?' He slid the butter from the scales, wrapped it with a deft little flourish, and surveyed the assembly of small packages on the counter, sensing perhaps what Molly was thinking. 'The bills are smaller, anyway, with no man in the house.'

'I'll answer that when you've totted it up,' Molly said, glad of the excuse to smile. Watching Arthur Rudkin always made her want to laugh. The absorbed way in which he patted the butter, weighed the sugar, slid around behind the counter reaching for this and that, while shouting to his mother, who was an invalid, that he'd be there just this minute. His father had kept the shop before him, and his son must have been born in that long white apron Molly thought, for she'd only ever seen him without it on Sunday mornings going to church.

'Three and tuppence-ha'penny,' he said, and seeing Molly's tut-tut, explained that the sugar and flour had both gone up again. 'The war will ruin us all, eh? Oh. The tin. I'm sure to have one there somewhere.'

When he'd gone into the back of the shop, Molly looked at the poster again.

'The Electric Theatre'
An Unusual and Startling Entertainment
'LOVE AND PAULINE LESTRANGE'
Continuous Performances
Seat Prices 3d 2d 1d

The picture palace in Caxton was something of a wonder to her. She'd not seen one of the moving pictures that were now all the rage and the posters displayed in the shop for the past three months had begun to make her aware of how 'old-fashioned' she'd become. Even that phrase – all the rage – made her feel behind-the-times, forgotten, life going on for everyone else in the village, her own having stopped three years before on the day Will had died. The irony of it was, when she'd married Will Farmer and come to live in Becket's Hill, she'd been regarded with envy as the 'lady from the town' who had been educated at a school for girls only and could talk on matters other than the harvest and the weather. Perhaps Lorna was right. Thirty-seven. Not young, but not too old. Perhaps she *should* start looking around for another man. Putting it that way made her want to giggle; yet she felt strangely guilty.

'It's very good this week, they say,' Arthur Rudkin said, nodding at the poster as he put the tin down on the counter. And he wondered if this was the moment to ask her. He'd been trying to summon up courage for more than a month. After all, it was full three years now; the woman was well and truly widowed, so there was nothing improper in asking her to go out with him, whatever the rest of the village might think. 'I go of a Wednesday night. That's tonight.' Fearing the rebuff he felt certain to come, he sent his regards to Alan instead and helped to put her shopping in the basket. 'Good morning, Mrs Farmer.'

'Good morning, Mr Rudkin.'

'Just a minute!' She'd forgotten the tin. 'Don't go without it.'

'Oh, no. Thank you.'

'You wouldn't care to come, I suppose?' He retied the string of his apron as she stared at him uncomprehendingly. 'The Electric Theatre. There's an omnibus leaves at six.' Seeing her waver, he added: 'And one back at half-past nine, so you'd be home before it's dark.'

Harry was jiggling the cross-piece on the back of the armchair when Molly came downstairs with her best frock. 'It's simple enough,' he said. 'A spot of glue. And one of the joints needs packing. A job I can manage.'

'It's been like it for years. I've got used to it.'

'Worry me. Things not properly joined.' It was a good excuse for him calling round that evening. They wouldn't say much. They never did. But he'd be there in the kitchen, near her. 'I could call in this evening if you like.' Molly smiled, vaguely, as she fetched the iron from the cupboard. 'If it's convenient, of course.'

'Yes. Whenever you like.' She seemed in another world as she smoothed out the frock. 'I'll leave the key in the place.'

'You going out?'

'The house won't fall down, I hope?'

Harry stared at her. Then at the frock as she laid it out on the table. 'Where are you going?'

'The Electric Theatre. With Mr Rudkin. Wasn't it kind of him to ask?'

'It's a thirsty place, I find,' Arthur Rudkin said once they had settled in their seats. He had brought along two oranges from the shop. Seeing Molly's anxious little smile, he offered to peel it for her. 'That's Mrs Lloyd,' he murmured through the applause for the wax-faced, fluffy-haired pianist who had materialised beside the potted palm. 'She used to live in Egerton Street, three doors along from the shop. No, Molly didn't remember her. 'Before you came to live in Becket's Hill, no doubt. Her husband went off to Brighton on an outing and never came back. Sad for her, really.' Mrs Lloyd began to pound the keyboard with a force and exuberance that belied her frail appearance. 'The whole family was musical.'

Molly thanked him for the peeled orange and tried to look as casual, as bored, as disinterested, as everyone else seemed to be, but her heart was beating like old-fun and she was reminded of that silly, excitable girl attending a theatrical performance with her father to celebrate her eighth birthday. It was quite ridiculous to feel this way at thirty-seven years of age. She couldn't see anyone she knew, thank God.

'Excuse me,' the bustling nurse said, and Molly rose from her seat to allow them to pass. The man was in hospital blue and his head was heavily bandaged. Molly felt a sudden pang of guilt. For the first time since Alan had left for France, an hour or more had passed without her giving him a single thought. Was it right for her to be out enjoying herself like this when he was over there, fighting in that frightful war and, perhaps, at this very moment, facing mortal danger?

The lights went out, the curtains were drawn back, and an oblong of flickering light appeared on the screen. 'Are you comfortable, Mrs Farmer?' Arthur Rudkin enquired politely, as the words on the screen requested Ladies Under Forty to Remove Their Hats. Yes, she was, Molly said, her voice somewhere under her seat, and for the next sixty-five minutes all thoughts of Alan and the war were black-and-whited-out by the goings-on at 'Gilbert Ransome's homestead in old Wyoming', a ricketty building that threatened collapse whenever yet another motor-car rattled up in clouds of dust and screeched to a halt, its occupants falling out and jerking like lunatics all over the place. Molly wondered why everyone was in either a terrible rage or grinning all over their faces; it seemed there was no happy medium in old Wyoming. Once inside the homestead (which could have done with a good sweeping, as there was even more dust flying about than there was outside), everyone started rushing about again, looking at their watches and having qualms about a fellow called Luke Lestrange, who arrived in the biggest cloud of dust of the lot and had the thickest black eyebrows Molly had ever seen. He stamped up and down the stairs as if to prove they'd been made by a very poor carpenter, thumped his fists about the back rent for a place no decent person would have been found dead in, and threatened to jail the nice young man who'd gone down the road to ruin through no fault of his own and whose poor mother had died in a very skimpy dress in a snowstorm in Alaska. One minute everyone was upstairs, then, for no apparent reason, everyone was downstairs; then Black Eyebrows and the nice young man started fighting and the rotten old stairs collapsed altogether. But there, it all ended quite happily, with Black Eyebrows being hurled through an upstairs (or downstairs?) window, the back rent was forgotten, and the nice young man fell down on the sofa with the fair-haired girl with the blackest eyes on God's earth.

But it was all a wonder, really Molly considered, when the lights came on and the apparition from Egerton Street played the King.

'Did you enjoy it, Mrs Farmer?' Arthur Rudkin enquired, picking up the bag of orange peel from under the seat.

'Yes, indeed,' Molly said, noticing how white everyone was now that the lights were on. 'It was ever so real.'

On the omnibus home, Arthur Rudkin leaned across to point out where an aunt lived, and Molly thought he looked quite reasonable when he wasn't in the shop. Anyway, a lot nicer in a suit than in that ridiculous long white apron.

'It looks very good next week,' Arthur Rudkin commented, after a mile or so of silence. And he cleared his throat. 'If you'd like to go again, that is.'

Harry was at the range stirring the gluepot when Lorna arrived with the scarf. 'She's gone out,' he said casually, as if his sister-in-law was always gallivanting off with someone or other. 'To the picture palace in Caxton with Arthur Rudkin.'

'Fancy that,' said Lorna, astonished. Molly had certainly lost no time in taking the advice Lorna had given her that morning. 'Gosh! Wouldn't it be nice if she and Mr Rudkin got married?'

Harry was grimly silent as Lorna unfolded the fawn, green and brown striped scarf. 'D'you think Alan will like it?' she enquired.

'Just the thing for morning parades,' Harry said dourly.

'Alan says fliers wear all colours. They're not like the soldiers in the trenches.'

'No, they're above all that, of course.'

Lorna thought she understood why he sounded so bitter. The poor man had lost his arm in the trenches, of course. Harry was struggling to fit the glued crosspiece on to the back of the armchair. 'Here, let me help.' And she kneeled on the chair seat, holding the uprights steady as he fitted the crosspiece. 'You know, you *do* look like Alan's father. As I remember him, anyway. Mrs Farmer says you look nothing like him at all.'

'Are you helping or hindering?' Harry said sharply.

Lorna was silent until the crosspiece was fitted and the joints pressed home. 'Do you think it's wrong? Going to the picture palace, I mean?'

'No business of mine where she goes, is it?'

'The places themselves, I mean. My father says they're a worse evil than the drink. It's the darkness he doesn't hold with. Men and women sitting there together, he says ...'

'Hand me that rag,' Harry rasped. He snatched it from her and wiped the surplus glue from the joints.

'Tom says you're not too fond of women,' she smiled tentatively.

'If you're fishing for compliments ...'

'Oh no, it wasn't that.'

'I'll give you one, all the same,' he said, taking a deep interest in the gluepot. 'Alan is a lucky young fellow.'

Lorna felt warm inside. They were all wrong about Harry. He *did* like women. She wondered why he'd never married. An unhappy experience long ago, no doubt. 'I'll tell Molly you left the scarf,' Harry said curtly, hinting that it was time for her to go home. But Lorna didn't take it. She had to tell him. Who else *could* she tell? She was worried about Alan. He'd promised to write regularly, promised faithfully, and Alan never broke his word, Harry must know that. Yet she hadn't had a letter for ten days.

'Molly would have had a telegram if anything had happened to him,' Harry explained. 'So. You're wasting your time fretting.'

'Thank you, Harry,' Lorna said, her eyes shining. And just before she went out: 'I'm glad you came back to live in Becket's Hill.'


'Oh, it's you,' Molly said, on her hands and knees and moving away from the smithy door to allow Harry in. He'd found a good stout piece of string. 'Oh, for Alan's parcel. Would you believe, I'd forgotten all about it.'

'Enjoy the picture?'

'Oh. Yes. A wonder, really. Now it's back down to earth with a vengeance.' And she dipped the brush into the pail and resumed scrubbing vigorously. Had Mr Rudkin enjoyed it? Oh yes, he'd enjoyed it, and yes, she'd noticed that Harry had put the door key back in its place when he'd left the house, and yes indeed, he'd made a very good job of mending the armchair; and if Harry could move his feet because she wanted to scrub just there. Then something occurred to her. Something she'd been thinking about the last few days. 'This house is your old home, and here I am living in it, and you in lodgings over at Tom's.'

Harry was curious. What was she leading up to? 'I don't think of this house as mine any more, if that's what you mean.'

'But it was your father's house. And his father's, before him. And that smithy out there in the family for four generations. Will was always proud of telling me that. So. You've more right to be living in the house than I have.'

'Nonsense that. When I left the place at seventeen, well, that was that. You're Will's widow. So the house is yours. I've never thought of it any other way. Why?'

'I thought I ought to bring it up, that's all. To see how you felt about it.'

Harry was even more curious now. Why had she brought the subject up *now*? Was it something to do with Arthur Rudkin? 'You're not thinking of moving out, are you? I mean, going to live – well – somewhere else?'

Molly laughed. 'Whatever gave you that idea?'

'Did Arthur Rudkin enjoy the picture?' Harry enquired, hardly daring to look at her.

'You've already asked me that once,' Molly said, wringing out the floorcloth. 'He asked me if I'd like to go again next week.'

Harry tightened the string around the tin box as if it was Arthur Rudkin's neck.

'He's a very kind man,' Molly went on. 'But I had to say no. If I'd said "yes" the poor man might begin to think – well – you know. And there couldn't be anything like that between us. Not as far as I'm concerned, anyway.'

Harry whistled about the smithy for the rest of the morning, though he didn't quite know why he was so happy. 'There couldn't be anything like that between us' Molly had said, referring to Arthur Rudkin. But her words held even more truth where Harry was concerned. He could never ask Molly to marry him. His brother's widow. The law was against it.

'It's from Alan, right enough,' the postman called. Lorna had seen him pushing his bicycle up the cart-track and she'd put down the pig-food and run like the wind. 'You've been waiting long enough, eh?'

'Oh, I've been thinking all kinds of terrible things,' she said, breathlessly. 'Thank you, Mr Wadham.'

She ran into the long grass behind the cowshed and opened the envelope. The officer had censored it again, blow him! – but only two and a half lines, and the little cross was in the left-hand corner, the code they'd agreed upon before Alan had left for France; it meant that he was still stationed at the same airfield. Her eyes skimmed over the first page. The news was practically the same as in his previous letter – flying most days, the village looking not unlike Becket's Hill from the air, more trouble with a farmer over stolen fruit and a vanished chicken, how friendly he'd become with Charles Gaylion who was an 'absolutely splendid fellow' – but there, Lorna understood how it was. What else could the poor boy say if he wasn't allowed to write about his part in the fighting? She knew 'what else', of course, and in joyous anticipation of reading the words he had spoken to her, here in the seclusion of the long grass on the day before he had left for France, she turned the page over. Her eyes were instantly drawn to the lower half. Here, the pattern of the handwriting differed from the rest, the margins wider and the lines sloping downwards. Mildly curious, she read what was written there. Unable to believe the words, she read them again.

'Lorna?' It was her father, standing by the pig food, wondering where she'd got to.

'Leave me alone,' she cried. 'Just leave me alone.' He stared after her bewilderedly, as she ran down the cart-track.

'I just don't understand the boy,' Molly said, when she had read the letter. It made her quite cross. Her own son, yes, and risking his life for his country, but he needed a stiff talking to, upsetting the poor girl like this. 'I'm sure he doesn't mean it.'

'I think he does,' Lorna said.

'Saying here that you haven't had time to get to know each other, when you went to school together down at Lovell's Road? I shall give him a piece of my mind next time I write.'

'I'd rather you didn't,' Lorna said, anguishedly. 'I don't think it would help matters. But thank you, all the same.'

'Come on now,' Molly said, putting a comforting arm around her. 'It'll all come out in the wash.'

Which came sooner than either of them could have imagined. Old Tom very nigh dropped his tongs when Alan hobbled into the smithy. 'Good God, boy,' the old man said. 'What on earth have they done to you? Harry! Look who's here!'

'It's nothing much,' Alan said, embarrassed by the fuss as they held open doors, puffed up cushions, and brought a stool to put his leg on. 'Just a flesh wound, that's all.'

'Someone's made a poor job,' Old Tom said with an eye on the crutches. 'We had no idea, o' course.'

'Thank goodness,' Harry commented. 'Molly would have been in a state if she'd heard he was wounded and not known it wasn't serious.'

'She's over with my Alice,' Tom said. 'I'll go and tell her you're here.'

'Indeed, you will not,' Harry said firmly. The old man was always putting his foot in it. He'd mention the wound and frighten the life out of Molly. 'She'll be along in a minute or two.'

'Well, I never,' Molly gasped when she saw Alan sitting there. 'And we've not long sent off a parcel to you. And no food in the house. Not food for a man, anyway.' The boy was so thin. She had heard all about the bully beef and knew it wouldn't suit him. Then she saw the leg. 'How did it happen?' she cried, reminded of the bullet-riddled body in the nightmares she'd been having.

'It was getting out of my aeroplane,' Alan lied. 'I fell a bit awkwardly.'

Harry saw Molly's questioning look and quickly changed the subject. 'I'll fetch whatever you need from the shop,' he said welcoming the opportunity of pursuing the campaign of menacing glances that he'd been giving Arthur Rudkin whenever he called there for his half-ounce of Three Nuns.

After bustling about with bedclothes to be aired, and preparing the baking of enough to feed a regiment, Molly asked when Alan had to go back.

'On Friday,' Alan lied. He wasn't due back until Saturday, in fact, and he wasn't at all sure of the reason for this second lie to his mother.

'You're glad to be home, I expect.' From the way she expressed the question, Alan knew his mother sensed how he was feeling. 'It's not easy to explain,' he began. And when they sat down to eat: 'It's all come so suddenly. I've had no time to look forward to coming home. I can hardly believe I'm sitting here. If you know what I mean.'

They ate in silence for a time.

'Is it because of Lorna?'

Alan didn't know what to say. He thought Lorna must have shown her the letter, of course. 'It's not easy to explain . . .' he faltered.

'You've just said that,' Molly said, tartly. 'Mixing with your officer friends. Home's not good enough for you now, is that it?'

No, it wasn't that at all.

'Anyway, whatever it is,' Molly said, spooning a second mountain of potatoes on to his plate, 'the poor girl's in a state down there. The least you can do is to talk to her.'


'You'd better come through, I suppose,' Mrs Collins said grudgingly, as if Alan were the coalman. 'Lorna's in the parlour playing the piano.' And she eyed the crutches as if they were infectious as Alan hobbled over the polished tiles towards the diffident notes of Spring's uncertain awakening. Mrs Collins had betrayed no surprise on seeing him, Alan thought, so the whole of Becket's Hill must have known he was home on leave.

'It's Alan Farmer,' Mrs Collins announced, and Lorna turned on the stool, trying her best to look surprised. Alan knew they must have seen him coming up the cart-track. Been waiting for him, no doubt. Seen him fall when one of the blessed crutches had slipped away from him. He shouldn't have allowed his mother to persuade him to come. 'I'll leave you to talk then.' Mrs Collins glanced at her daughter, then at the clock, and left the room, leaving the door ajar.

'I'm sorry,' Lorna said. 'But I showed her your letter.'

'And my mother as well.'

Lorna got up from the stool. 'I didn't know it was supposed to be a secret,' she said petulantly, and she picked up the music from the stand, studying the triplets in the seventh bar as if they were to blame for everything. Alan was taken aback. He'd expected to find her in floods of tears. Yet here he was, standing on his crutches, an awkward, uncomfortable hero, and she hadn't even asked him to sit down. 'My mother said we shouldn't let you in.'

That was no surprise to him. Mrs Collins had never been struck on him, Alan knew that well enough. Though he didn't know what the woman had against him. Apart from the fact that he was taking her only daughter away from her. Well. She could heave a sigh of relief, because it was all over between them. He'd made up his mind about that.

'You'd better sit down, hadn't you?'

'No, thanks. I can't stop. I'm meeting Harry.'

'How did it happen?'

Oh. His leg, of course. 'Our favourite Hun. A German aeroplane with a machine-gun.' He was overdoing the discomfort a bit, though he didn't know why. He hadn't come here for sympathy, dammit. 'I told my mother I did it getting out of my machine.'

'I see. A white lie.'

Her expression had suddenly softened and Alan sensed the yearning behind her eyes. The tremor in her voice when she'd said 'a white lie' told him that she now expected a confession of other white lies; the ones he had written in the letter.

'Are you sure you wouldn't like to sit down?'

'I'm sorry I wrote that letter.'

Her eyes lit up and he cursed himself for raising her hopes. 'What I mean is, I didn't know I'd be coming home on leave when I wrote it. If I had done, I wouldn't have written it. It wasn't easy to put down on paper.' But there, he *had* put it down on paper. He'd explained to her how it was, so what was he doing here trying to explain it all again? 'Anyway, there it is.' She was waiting for him to go. And by the look on her face she was going to cry. And he hated the thought of her crying. Her mother would come barging in accusing him of God-knows-what. 'You understood what I said in the letter?'

'No, not really. I understood about our knowing each other in school all those years but that not really counting. So that we hardly knew each other before you went to France.'

'Well, it's true, isn't it? When I first asked you home to tea I'd already volunteered for the Flying Corps. We only saw each other – what? Three times – '

'Four!'

'Four times then, before I went to France. It's daft, when you come to think of it.'

'What is?'

She *was* going to cry. He *knew* she was. Well, it was no use. He wouldn't be changing his mind. Not to save a few tears and a few accusing black looks from her mother. 'It's daft thinking we feel the way we do when we hardly know each other.'

'You still think you feel the same way then?'

She was trying to trap him. 'No, I don't,' he said, shifting uncomfortably on the crutches and wincing at a stab of pain from his leg.

'I wish you'd sit down,' she said, her eyes glistening and filled with concern for him. She affected a smile. 'There's no charge, you know.'

'It might have been lies for all I know,' he said harshly. He ought to be horse-whipped for sounding so brutal. She looked so fragile, so bewildered, her love for him so painfully evident, that he wanted to put his arms about her, to comfort her, to tell her that she must forget him, put him out of her mind. But that would ruin it all. 'Not deliberate lies may be, but lies all the same.'

'I don't know what you're talking about.'

'The things I said to you before I left for France. I even believed them myself, I suppose, because – I was going away to the war and I must have thought it would be a fine thing to have a girl back home and — ' he broke off, confused and angry. 'I told you in the letter it wasn't easy to explain.'

'I'm sorry,' she said, timidly.

'There's nothing for you to be sorry about. It's my fault. For saying things like that – important things – without giving them too much thought. Thought for you, that is.'

They stood there in silence for what seemed an age to Alan. His leg was giving him hell now. And he *knew* her mother was listening outside the door. That's why she'd left it ajar. She was waiting with bated breath for the juicy upshot of it all; the talk of 'renounced love' and all the rest of the twaddle that the gossips in the village would make a bean feast of.

'I have to be going now,' he said, casually. 'I promised to go to The Plough with my Uncle Harry.'

'I'll see you again, won't I?'

'Oh, yes.' He turned the knob of the door and pulled it wide open. Her mother wasn't there, after all. 'I'll see you about the village no doubt.'

She hurried over to hold the door open for him. She was going to cry buckets the moment he'd left the house, he knew that. But she was determined not to shed a drop in front of him.

'I've no need to tell you, of course,' she said. 'But I still feel the same about you.' And after he had gone: 'I always will.'

'Good riddance,' Mrs Collins sniffed, shaking the curtain into place once Alan was lost to view. 'The Flying Corps has turned his head.'

'You don't understand him,' Lorna said, when she had stopped crying. 'He doesn't want to hurt me.'

'Doesn't want to hurt you? What's he done already then?'

Lorna shook her head defeatedly. She didn't understand Alan's reasoning, but she knew that it was something to do with war. Going to France. Something had happened to him. Or was happening to him. 'But whether he believes it or not – I know he's still fond of me.'

'He's fond of himself, that's for sure.' Her mother swept up a few crumbs of earth left by Alan's boots and went prowling for more. 'He'll end up like his father, that one. Will Farmer went flying high. Mixing with the gentry and building that aeroplane. He came down to earth soon enough. And so will that son of his.'

# 4

Outside the railway station, two sailors were seated on their kitbags smoking cigarettes. There was a sprinkling of khaki in the jostling crowds and somewhere in the vicinity a band was doing its brassy best to remind young men in two minds where their first duty lay. Yet it was still hard to believe that a war was raging just a hundred miles away. The noise of the traffic, the hollow chatter of the ladies in 'all the latest', the shouting newsboys and flower-sellers, all contrived to make people forget the mud and the blood, and the cries of the wounded and the dying. And why the hell not, Alan thought. Just because he was standing there, marooned on his crutches, with no idea of how to enjoy all this pandemonium, he could hardly expect the bustle of the city to come to a halt in sympathy. It served him right for telling his mother he had to be back at Ste Marie on Friday instead of Saturday. At first, the thought of twenty-four hours on the loose in London had conjured up wildly exciting visions of the seven-day leave that Charles Gaylion just couldn't wait for; seven days of sleep, and seven nights of wine, women and song. But Alan, alas, had no idea where to begin. And in truth, it made him feel guilty to even contemplate the excesses of a Gaylion week of whoopee, let alone partaking in a twenty-four-hour slice of it.

The alternative was to find his way to one of the services hostels, where benevolent ladies would insist on doing their bit by making him feel 'at home', which was the last thing he wanted. He'd end up retiring to a sober bed, where he would lie awake all night thinking about his mother – lying in *her* bed in Becket's Hill thinking of her son 'journeying across France'. Why the dickens had he told the needless lie? But he knew the answer to that well enough. It had been no more than a vague idea at the time, but since then he had planned it all very carefully. Yet here he was, without the courage to make the first move; which was simply a matter of hailing a taxi-cab and asking the driver to take him to Percival Square. Number twenty-four. And whoever answered the door, he knew exactly what to say. He'd rehearsed the three little speeches over and over in his mind in the long, long evenings of the past eight days, sitting in the silence of the kitchen with his mother. One speech for the butler, one for Charles's mother, and one for the marvellous girl herself. If the butler answered the door, Alan would say: 'Please forgive me for calling on the hop like this (Charles said "on the hop" quite a lot), but I happened to be passing (they wouldn't ask *why* he was passing; it wasn't good manners), and as I'm a friend of Charles and in the same Flight, I thought I might call and pay my respects.' It was all so simple, really. And quite in order. Charles would have called at Alan's home if he'd been passing through Becket's Hill, Alan was certain of that.

'Where was it you wanted, soljer?'

The taxi-cab had pulled up in front of him and the driver was already opening the door.

'I – er – I'm not going anywhere, thanks. Just – waiting for a friend.'

'Thas' all right then,' the taxi-driver grinned. 'An' don't look so worried. Just doing my bit, thas' all. You pick up one or two o' those poor wounded boys, the wife says, an' take 'em where they wants to go. Won't let me join up, see. It's me chest. Some other time, eh, mate?'

'Just a minute,' Alan said, as the driver leaned over to close the door. 'I don't think my friend's going to turn up, after all. Percival Square, please. Number twenty-four.'

'If you'll come inside, sir,' the butler said. 'I'll see if madam is still at home.' He motioned to Alan to take a seat and went off up the stairs. Alan sat stiffly and uncomfortably in the large oak armchair, his hands resting on the carved heads of the two ferocious lions.

He had a sudden vision of a furious Charles Gaylion. 'What the devil were you doing in Percival Square? I mean, where were you going? Where had you come from?' Rather foolishly, Alan hadn't considered what excuse he was going to make to Charles when he got back to Ste Marie. But there was plenty of time to think of that. A whole day. He hoped to goodness Kate *was* at home now he'd gone to all this trouble.

'You must forgive me, Mr Farmer, but I'm just on my

way to Carrington Hall. A most important meeting, so I mustn't be late. So you're a friend of Charles? I am Evelyn Gaylion, his mother. No, please don't get up. Levin told me about the crutches. Are you in pain? No, good. Tell me, is Charles behaving himself?'

Alan didn't know what to say. He knew from Charles's conversation that the family discussed their personal lives quite openly and that Charles's mother and sister would have been considered 'very forward' by the women of Becket's Hill; but surely Charles hadn't mentioned his visits to brothels?

'Oh yes, he's behaving himself,' Alan said, hoping to God that would suffice.

'I'm so glad. Tell me, are you boys getting your parcels regularly?'

Yes, they were, Alan replied, remembering Charles had told him that his mother was 'extremely active with brown paper and string' and that in the event of the allied armies failing to stem the German advance, the Hon. Evelyn Gaylion's parcels would certainly stop their gallop.

'I do hope you won't think it rude of me, but I really must be off. Time and the Women's Emergency Corps wait for no man. Goodbye, Mr Farmer. Thank you so much for calling. And do see that Charles behaves himself, won't you?'

Alan's heart sank. He wasn't going to see Kate, after all. Drawing on her lace gloves, Evelyn Gaylion strode to the foot of the stairs.

'Levin?'

The butler appeared like a wearily patient genie. 'Yes, madam?'

'Take Mr Farmer up, would you? Oh dear, I quite forgot. Can you manage with your crutches?'

Yes, he could, Alan said, wondering why on earth he

was being asked upstairs. But he hesitated to question it. He didn't want to show his ignorance.

'There's a meeting in the drawing-room, d'you see,' Evelyn Gaylion explained, nodding towards the pale cream double-doors. 'It's Charles's sister Kate.'

Levin showed Alan into 'the study' where there were a great many books, mostly belonging to 'Miss Kate', 'Mr Charles not being one for reading overmuch'. A few minutes later he brought in some tea on a silver tray, was concerned that Alan was seated in a draught, and closed the window.

'Will the meeting downstairs be going on for long?' Alan enquired, deciding to wait until Levin had left the room before attempting to pour the tea from the tiny bone china pot.

'One never knows with Miss Kate's meetings,' Levin replied, with an expression of barely concealed disgust. 'It's the No-Conscription Fellowship, you understand.'

'Good Lord!' Alan heard her cry out as she came running up the stairs. 'Why on earth didn't you tell me? I could have sent them all home.' And she breezed into the room, hand extended, to welcome Alan as if she'd known him for years. 'Sitting here all alone, I don't know what you must think of us. I'm Charles's sister, Kate. Oh, Levin made you some tea, at least. That's something. Are you staying the night?'

Tongue-tied, stunned by her dark-haired beauty and the vivacity of the impish smile, Alan struggled to his feet.

'No, please,' she said, catching sight of the crutches behind the chair where Levin had placed them. 'Don't get up.'

But it was too late. In turning to reach for the crutches, Alan's knee caught the occasional table. The silver tray and its bone china contents slid to the floor with a crash.

'Don't apologise any more,' Kate said, her eyes twinkling with mock severity. 'Or there'll be nothing of you left.' She looked at Levin, who was on his hands and knees, sweeping judiciously with a little silver-handled brush. 'Oh, leave it now, Levin. And don't mention it to mother. She's bound to blame it on Desmond.'

'Who's Desmond?' Alan asked, after apologising yet again.

'He was speaking at the meeting just now. You wouldn't like Desmond. And he'd loathe and despise you, I'm afraid.'

'When he hasn't even met me?'

'You're in uniform, aren't you?'

'And he thinks I shouldn't be?'

'Desmond thinks everyone should refuse to fight for their country. Then there'd be no wars.'

'And what about you?' Alan said, realising how easy and confident he felt in her presence. He thought he'd be much more nervous; awed by the girl when he met her in the flesh. But it seemed that he'd been much more in awe of that photograph in her brother's wallet. 'What do you believe?'

'I'm not sure I believe anything,' Kate said. 'I suppose I just like taking opposite views of everything. Everyone's so dashed patriotic, intent on doing their bit, so I go around preaching pacifism and putting everyone's backs up.'

'But – why?'

'Oh, for Heaven's sake, don't look so serious,' she laughed. 'Let's talk about you instead. Why are you a friend of Charles, anyway? You're a sergeant, aren't you?'

'Charles has been very good to me,' Alan said, his confidence waning now that she had made him newly aware of the very different worlds they lived in.

'Tell me, what do you do?' she asked. 'What *did* you do, that is, before the war?'

'I was a blacksmith.'

'Gosh! Arms like iron bands and all that. Where do you live?'

'In Sussex. A village called Becket's Hill.'

'Are you married?'

'No.' But he would be, Alan resolved. One day. To *her*. 'Can I ask you something?'

She laughed. 'What if I said "no"? Wouldn't you ask, just the same? You're very timid, aren't you? For a blacksmith, I mean. Well? What's the great question?'

'Your mother said something I didn't understand. About Charles. She asked if he was behaving himself.'

'Oh, that. He drinks. But surely you know that?'

'He drinks, yes. But not that much.'

'He's turned over a new leaf, I suppose. He used to drink a lot. Even when he was at school. Whenever there was anything he couldn't face up to. He'd never let on, of course, but I'm afraid my brother is – well – he's not as brave and carefree as he tries to make out. When do you have to go back?'

'Tomorrow.'

'Are you going home tonight?'

He dithered undecidedly and before he could say 'yes' she had already decided he should stay the night in Charles's room.

'I can't do that,' he protested.

'You're blushing like a country maiden,' she hooted. 'Oh, I think you're lovely. I do, really. I'm so glad you came. Anyway, Desmond will be splendidly furious when I tell him I've been entertaining a gentleman in uniform. A brave flier, gladly suffering his wounds for his King and country. Don't look so frightened. I shall wait until you've left the house, of course.'

'I can't stay. Really I can't.'

'Nonsense. We'll have dinner together. I'll get Levin to bring it in here. It's cosier in here, don't you think?'

'What about your mother?'

'Oh, she won't be here. She's rushing about all over Kent for the next three days. No! No excuses! You're under orders. You're a sergeant, so you must know how to take orders. Unless, of course . . . ah yes, that's why you're so anxious to go home. There's a girl of course.'

'No. There isn't.'

'Liar!'

'It's no lie. There was a girl. But I broke it off.'

'Oh? Why?'

'It may sound daft to you.'

'I'm sure it won't.'

No, it wouldn't sound daft to her, Alan thought. She would understand. If he could manage to explain.

'Do you know how long a pilot reckons to last over there? Six weeks. Two months, if he's lucky.'

'I see. So you want to save her the hurt, is that it?'

'Now you're laughing at me again.'

'No, I'm not. I think it's rather sweet. I feel sorry for her though. What did you tell her?'

'I'm not quite sure now. Anyway. It's all off. So that's that.'

'Cruel to be kind, eh? If it had been me, I'd have seen right through you, of course.'

'Perhaps Lorna did. For all I know. Anyway. It's not just that. I'm not sure now that we're right for each other. In fact, I'm certain we're not.'

'Not sure. Then you're certain.' She laughed. 'It sounds to me as if you're terribly in love with her.'

'No, I'm not.'

'That's more like it. Now you sound as if you mean what you say.'

'I do. I know I don't feel that way about her any more because – well – I've met someone else that I know I could be very fond of.'

'Gosh, you're quite a Romeo, aren't you? For a blacksmith, I mean.' She had pulled on the bell-cord to summon Levin. Now there was a discreet little tap on the door and Levin came in. 'Ah, Levin. I'd like dinner served in here.'

Levin looked at her in surprise. 'In here, miss?'

'That's right, in here. And Mr — ' She clapped a hand to her cheek and gave a little shriek. 'Great Heavens, I've asked you to stay the night and I don't even know your name.'

Alan's face reddened and Levin turned his poker-face in the direction of the top shelf of the bookcase. 'Alan Farmer,' Alan murmured.

'Alan Farmer. How deliciously simple. Don't you think so, Levin?'

Levin nodded in agreement, and at eight o'clock he served dinner in the study as requested, reappearing three hours later with a pair of Mr Charles's pyjamas.

'They have been aired, sir.'

'Oh. Thank you,' Alan said. And when Levin had wished him a comfortable night and left the room: 'Shall I see you again?'

'Not tonight, you won't,' Kate giggled.

'You like trying to shock me, don't you?' Alan smiled. He knew it wasn't just the wine. He was head over heels in love with the girl. 'I'd like to meet you again.'

'Would you, indeed?' Kate said, with a tantalising smile. 'Why?'

'You like asking me awkward questions, too. I want to meet you again because – well – because I think you're nice.'

'God! No one's ever called me nice before.'

'Then I'm glad I'm the first. Shall we meet again?'
'I should like to think about it.'
'And when you've thought?'
'I shall drop you a little note.'
'Promise?'
'I promise!'

'Our favourite Hun has reappeared,' Charles said, as Alan stepped down from the tender. 'We've not seen a hair of him since you left. He must know you're back. How's the leg? Here, give me your haversack. Lord, I don't want to sound dismal but you look worse than when you left.' He gave Alan a meaning nudge. 'Where have you been sleeping, eh? If that's what leave in Blighty does for you —'

'I feel fine,' Alan snapped.

'Oh, we're that glad to be back, are we?' Charles grinned. 'What news on the milkmaid Rialto? No, don't tell me. I already know. I had a ghastly vision of you taking one look at each other, falling into each other's arms, and deciding to get married on your next leave.' And he winked. 'And I bet I'm not far out.'

'Afraid you are. It's all over between Lorna and me.'

'Well, well! Living up to your reputation, eh? The iron man of Sussex.'

Alan decided not to mention his stay at Charles's home until later. He had been unable to think of a reason for having been in the area of Percival Square, and anyway, whatever reason he gave, Charles wouldn't believe it. Like his sister Kate, Charles could see right through him. Besides, he'd done with telling lies. The two lies he had told his mother were still running the gauntlet of his conscience. And Charles had greeted him with such delight. No, it wasn't the right time to bring up what might be a touchy subject.

'I thought we might have a little homecoming spree this evening,' Charles said, as Alan unpacked his haversack. 'I didn't expect you this early. You must have left home at the crack of dawn.'

'I left yesterday,' Alan said, and quickly added: 'The bicycles are out, with my leg as it is.'

'Thought of that,' Charles said, with a little smug smile. 'I've commandeered the tender for the evening. How about that? Cost me two packets of cigarettes though.'

Alan changed his mind. After a few drinks, Charles was not always in the best of moods. His reaction to the news could be – well – unpredictable, to say the least. It was better to tell Charles now.

'I left yesterday, as I say. Went up to London. Oh. While I was there, I called on your mother.'

Charles looked stunned. 'What? You went to my home?'

'That's right.' He whistled as he went on unpacking, as if that was the end of that. But he knew from the dangerous light in Charles's eyes that it was only the beginning. 'I thought that as you might not be getting leave for quite some time, I'd tell her you were well and getting on fine. She was on her way to a meeting, so we didn't have much of a chance to talk.' He took a shirt from the haversack and shook out the creases. Charles snatched it from him and threw it aside. 'Here, hang on — '

'Look me in the eye, damn you. What the devil d'you mean by sneaking into my home, talking to my mother about me?' He was white with rage, his fists tightly clenched, and Alan shifted his weight on to his good leg to be ready for the blow that was sure to come. 'What did my mother tell you?'

'Tell me? She didn't tell me anything. She asked if you were behaving yourself, that's all.'

'Oh, you're so bloody honest and upright, aren't you? But underneath you're just a two-faced, sneaky little —'

'You're not in school any longer, Charles,' Alan said, immediately regretting having mentioned 'school'. Hadn't Kate told him about Charles drinking at school when he couldn't face up to things? 'Anyway, I'm not interested in what your mother and your sister think of you —'

'My sister? So you spoke to my sister, too, did you?'

'I've got my own opinion of you, thanks very much,' Alan said. And it was changing, rapidly. He was beginning to wonder why he'd ever looked up to this raging lunatic.

'*That* was why you called there, was it? To see my sister?'

'No use making any bones about it. Yes. I called there to introduce myself.' He might as well get it all over and done with. 'And she asked me to stay the night.'

It was fully half a minute before Charles could find the words : '*Where* was my mother?'

'She wasn't in the house, if that's what you mean.'

'You dare to stand there and tell me that you and my sister —'

'Don't talk so daft. I slept in *your* room. And in *your* pyjamas.'

'That's what *you* say!'

'And you know it's the truth.'

'You dirty little guttersnipe. You wheedle your way into my confidence, into my friendship, and then use it to take advantage of my sister.'

Alan sighed wearily, wishing he'd waited, after all, until Charles was drunk. His reaction couldn't possibly have been any more ridiculous than it was when he was sober. The only thing to do was to hit back. Make him sit up.

'Don't judge everyone by yourself, Charles. *I* don't go to brothels, remember.'

'You little prig,' Charles sneered.

God, it really was like school, Alan thought, and sat despairingly on the bed. 'I'm sorry, Charles. But if I'd known you'd make this much of a song about it, I'd never have called there.'

'It's my fault,' Charles said, at last. 'I realise that. I've had enough warnings from my fellow officers, God alone knows. But I thought I knew best. I was wrong. From this moment, our friendship is at an end.'

Poor old Charles, Alan reflected, as he made his way to the Flight Office. Whatever Brigadier Gaylion's ambitions were for his son, Charles was obviously incapable of fulfilling them. Charles's mother was anxiously sympathetic, and in Alan's view, that must have made matters worse. Alan should have been angered, he supposed, by Charles's accusations; but the thought of any man, let alone 'a country innocent', trying to seduce a girl like Kate only made him smile. Charles was merely making a show of protecting his sister's virtue, Alan was certain of that. And he guessed it was part of Charles's eternal act of putting on a brave face. If anyone in that family needed 'protecting', it was Charles, not his sister, Kate.

Alan felt a vague sense of disappointment as he sat in the Flight Office awaiting the arrival of Captain Triggers, who had heard of Alan's return from leave and had sent for him. Alan had always looked up to Charles, using him as a model for the man he would like to become. But the charming manners, the air of total confidence, the way in which Charles brushed aside problems as if it was beneath him to grapple with them, was all a shield. It seemed that there was no real substance to the man. But that wasn't true. Alan was sure of it. To hell with the gloomy opinions of Charles's family. Yes, dear sweet Kate's included. Alan knew Charles better than they did. Kate had said her brother couldn't face up to things and so took refuge in drink. But she knew nothing of the hazards Charles had faced over here. And faced them without flinching.

He paced around the office for a time, punishing himself for ever having conceived the 'sneaky' idea of calling at Charles's home. The least he could have done was to warn Charles of his intention. Yes, Charles had been right to fly off the handle. And now their friendship was at an end. Whatever Charles was, or was not, the fact that they were no longer friends saddened Alan deeply.

'So the leg's still a bit stiff, eh?' Triggers said, when Alan had bent it with the 'greatest of ease' and said he was desperately keen to fly again. 'Oh, we shan't disappoint you. You'll be artillery spotting, starting tomorrow.'

'Thank you, sir,' Alan beamed.

'As an observer. No, don't argue, Sergeant. That leg's not ready for a rudder bar. Give it another week or so. Anyway, we're short of observers at the moment.'

'Very well, sir. Who am I flying with?'

'Mr Gaylion.'

Charles ignored Alan's signals throughout the whole of the long reconnaissance trip, and when they landed went off without a word to make his flight report. Fifteen minutes later he ducked into Alan's tent wearing that supercilious little smile that Alan had come to know so well during the week following the 'blow-up' over Kate. He'd have given anything for the freedom to plant the knuckles of his right hand into the taunting face.

'Hello, Charles.'

'Mr Gaylion, if you please.'

'Mr Gaylion,' Alan said patiently, picking up his scarf

from the bed and folding it with extra care. He knew his neat methodical ways annoyed Charles intensely. 'Just heard some bad news in the shed. New chap in "A" Flight. Our favourite Hun — '

'Have you been writing to my sister?'

Alan was taken aback. No, he had not been writing to 'Kate'.

'I've just had a letter from her. She enclosed a note for you.' He waited for some comment but Alan refused to bite. 'I've burned it, of course,' Charles said, as if it were quite the normal thing to do in the circumstances. Alan went on folding his scarf. 'That milkmaid of yours knitted that for you. Have you no finer feelings at all?' Alan was genuinely perplexed. 'I thought you'd broken off with her,' Charles explained. 'So how can you possibly be so callous as to go on wearing the thing?'

'Waste not, want not. Where I come from we make the best use of everything.'

'Not my sister, you don't.'

'That's not what I mean and you know it – *sir*.'

'You're a little prig, d'you know that? It makes you feel noble, does it?' Alan had no idea what he was talking about. 'Making that girl of yours suffer because you think you might be killed.'

Alan was stung. But his face betrayed nothing. He smiled like someone who has just solved a rather unimportant puzzle. 'I've been thinking about that. My reason for breaking it off with Lorna, I mean. The truth is, I don't feel the same way about her any more. As simple as that.' He knew exactly what Charles was thinking. 'And it's nothing to do with your sister, Kate,' he added. Although he knew very well that it had everything to do with it. He had never met anyone remotely like Kate and one day he would marry her. For a moment he felt like flinging his ambition in Charles's arrogant face but he knew that however determined he was to marry the girl, if Charles objected so strongly then Kate's parents would certainly share their son's objections; by voicing his intention he was simply starting a war in which he was bound to be the loser. In any case, there was Kate herself to be reckoned with. He had yet to win the girl's respect and affection before taking on her family. 'I was trying to tell you when you came in – our favourite Hun shot down "A" Flight's new pilot this morning.'

'Don't change the subject.'

Alan put one glove on top of the other and placed them alongside his goggles and helmet.

'A methodical chap the Hun,' Charles said icily, with a meaning glance at the neatness and order of Alan's bedspace. 'Tell me – do you fold your socks when you take them off at night?'

'Something ought to be done about that Hun, I suppose.'

'Done? Like what? He has a machine-gun. He flies faster than we do. Can fly higher, so he always has a height advantage. On top of that, he waits until we're on our way home. Tired. Our fingers too numb to pull triggers. Anxious about the possibility of running out of petrol. That's his cowardly method.'

'Cowardly? Sensible, I'd say.'

'Yes! You would!' Charles exclaimed, disdainfully.

'Look at it from his point of view,' Alan said, beginning to wonder which of his enemies was the worst – the Hun or Charles Gaylion. 'The most efficient way of shooting us down is to attack us when we're at our weakest. When we're on our way back from the long reconnaissance. Or wrapped up in our job of ranging for the artillery – popping up unnoticed when we least expect him.'

'You know, sergeant, I think you're on the wrong side

in this war,' Charles said, venomously.

'You once told me we were all on the same side. Fliers, I mean.' Alan pulled off his boot with a little triumphant flourish and dabbed the Cherry Blossom on the toe-cap. 'Back in England, before we came out here, remember? All that about fliers being different from the soldiers on the ground. Not wanting to kill each other. The brotherhood of all who fly. You once condemned Captain Triggers because his observer had shot down a Hun machine while it was taking off.'

Charles made no reply. He was on sticky ground. It was wiser to remain silent, giving the impression that it was useless for someone of his intellect and breeding to try and reason with the iron-bound mind of an ill-bred son of a blacksmith. He turned to duck out of the tent. But his curiosity got the better of him.

'You said something ought to be done. What were you proposing?'

Alan went on polishing his boot. Someone had to do something about their favourite Hun and as he was flying with Charles until his leg was properly mended it seemed too good an opportunity to miss. Charles looked astonished. Surely Alan was aware of their Flight Commander's orders? 'You should be. All Triggers' rules are burned on your chest.' 'C' Flight's business was reconnaissance and ranging for the artillery and they were not to engage the Hun unless it was absolutely unavoidable. The rule was especially applicable to the Albatros with the machine-gun. 'You're not suggesting we deliberately engage him, are you?' He waited for some comment. Alan spat in the Cherry Blossom. 'I'm just a sergeant, aren't I?' he said cagily. 'As you keep reminding me. So it's not my business to go suggesting anything at all. I just take orders.'

'You cunning devil,' Charles hissed. Alan blinked innocently over the top of his boot. 'So the onus is on me to make the decision, is it?'

'No need for anyone to know but me. Back from the long reconnaissance tomorrow. Lunch. And if there's nothing else on, a little nap and we'd be as fresh as daisies. And according to Dick Bravington — '

'*Mister* Bravington, if you please — '

'According to Mister Bravington, I *am* the best shot in the Squadron.'

'With a rifle! And we all know that a rifle is absolutely useless against that machine-gun.'

Alan put on his boot and stood up. 'If you're not up to it, Charles – sir! – then that's that. *I* can't give the order. But I intend going after that Hun. As soon as my leg's better and I can fly as pilot again — '

'You *are* a little prig,' Charles sneered.

Alan was stung. 'I intend going after that Hun. And I intend writing to your sister, too.' He turned away from Charles's hard eyes. 'Don't worry. I shan't tell her you burned her letter to me.'

'I shall tell her myself,' Charles rasped, and ducked out of the tent. A moment later, he popped his head in and said, with a fierce glare: 'Right then! Tomorrow! After lunch!'

Charles's BE2 climbed steeply over the village of Ste Marie, the stiff west wind urging her on towards the front lines. His Winchester held 'at the ready' in the crook of his left arm, Alan gazed down at the Gothic spire of the church and the clay-coloured roofs of the simple buildings that huddled around it in supplication, praying for God's protection against the terrors of the war. On days like this, the merciful power of the strong west wind carried the murderous pounding of the big guns away to the east and the war receded in the minds of the villagers.

But they knew, of course, that the awful monster was still only seven kilometres distant and that they might well wake up the next morning to find the fearful jaws engulfing them. And the west wind, however strong, could do nothing at all about that.

Three miles north-east of la Bassée, when at last they were clear of a most persistent Archie gun, Charles spotted the Albatros. It was still climbing, having just taken off from its base at Templeuve, and if it continued its present course across wind, Charles's BE2 with the strong westerly still behind it would surely intercept the German machine.

A few minutes later, the Albatros' observer Leutnant Lanz, the replacement for Stein, saw the BE2 through the interplane struts on the starboard side. Lanz was curious. He had not seen a British machine this far north for some three or four weeks. British machines on long reconnaissances were by this time all too aware of the threat of the machine-gun-armed two-seater and flew further south, avoiding the area around Templeuve. Perhaps this one had lost its way or was being flown by a new and inexperienced pilot who had not been warned or was foolhardy enough not to heed it. Lanz motioned his pilot to climb away to port, intending to take the Albatros on to a parallel course above the 'victim', whose pilot and observer, inexperienced or otherwise, could not have failed to see the enemy machine. Apparently, they had not yet noticed the threatening presence of the Parabellum machine-gun, for they were still maintaining their course.

His eyes fixed on the turning German two-seater, Charles throttled down to enable himself to be heard above the noise of the engine. Alan was wiping the oil from his goggles; seeing clearly might mean the difference between life and death in the coming minutes. 'Don't forget!' Charles shouted, and proceeded to remind Alan of a tactic they had discussed – or rather, had argued over – before taking off. 'I shall turn into him. Climbing to get above him.' Alan nodded and murmured, 'You hope!' He considered the tactic flamboyant and suicidal. The moment the machine-gun started firing the sensible thing to do was to turn away. Whatever one did after that was a matter of personal choice. But it was essential in the first instance to avoid the murderous fire of the Hun's machine-gun. However, Charles had insisted that turning away was just what the Hun would expect them to do; turning in and climbing above him would have the value of surprise. 'A surprise for him, or for us?' Alan had asked. If Charles had any doubts himself about the proposed manœuvre, this laconic remark of Alan's appeared to dispel them utterly and he was fiercely determined to carry out the unexpected 'turn in'. 'We'll be climbing across him, so it'll give you a good angle for the Winchester. Clear of that damned obstructing wing of ours. And remember – go for the pilot. Never mind hawk-eye Hans with the machine-gun. Get the pilot, and you get them both.' Alan had drily reminded him that he wasn't on the ground shooting at barn doors from twenty yards. He was aiming from a moving platform at a moving target and the odds of hitting the Hun machine were hundreds to one, let alone hitting the pilot. And Charles's ridiculous manœuvre would be trebling Alan's difficulties. 'Your job is to hold her as steady as you can,' he told Charles. 'In order to give me a chance to take aim.' Charles argued that the steadier he held his machine the better target they made for the Hun machine-gun. 'And whose idea was it in the first place, anyway?' he went on furiously. 'Tackling him with a rifle, I mean? You suggested it. And you keep going on about being the best shot on the Squadron. So now's your chance to prove it.'

Alan tried in vain to keep his sights on the riding Albatros as it came on to a parallel course about three hundred yards away and several hundred feet above. The man in the rear cockpit was aiming his machine-gun. Alan glanced quickly towards Charles, who had seen the German observer preparing to fire. Charles put the BE2 into the climbing turn a fraction of a second before the machine-gun opened up. Alan strove to keep his sights on the Hun machine, which, from his point of view in the turning, climbing BE2, flashed diagonally from left to right, leaving Alan staring along his sights at the dark greys and browns of the battle-scarred earth. Damn Charles Gaylion and his smug-faced daft ideas

Charles was shouting, wanting to know why Alan hadn't fired. Alan glared at him and turned to watch the Albatros, now climbing after them. Leutnant Lanz had been so dumbfounded by the British machine's manœuvre that he'd missed the glorious opportunity of firing as it had passed directly above him, and he was now grimly determined to make the Englishmen pay for their audacity. Besides, he had to try and live up to the reputation of his predecessor, Leutnant Stein. Lanz's pilot was for ever singing Stein's praises and so Lanz was intent on proving that he was certainly as good a shot as Stein, if not better.

The BE2 levelled out, the Albatros still climbing in pursuit. Charles waved to Alan, signalling his intention, then kicked left rudder and pulled the stick over, putting his machine into a steeply banked left-hand turn. Lanz, preparing to fire his machine-gun on the starboard side the moment he came on to a parallel course, suddenly found his quarry was nowhere to be seen. Lanz's pilot was pointing to port. Lanz turned to see the BE2 coming directly towards him. He cursed and heaved his gun on to the port side. But before he had time to take aim, the

BE2 had passed overhead. Lanz's pilot blinked around at him, wondering why his observer had not fired. Lanz had missed a second glorious opportunity. Lanz's pilot was obviously thinking that Leutnant Stein would not have missed such 'sitting ducks'. Lanz was now convinced that this English pair were set on humiliating him. The thought was punctuated by a whine and a plopping sound as a bullet passed through the fabric somewhere in the region of Lanz's feet. Lanz motioned angrily to his pilot and once again the Albatros turned in pursuit of the BE2.

Flying straight and level, Charles watched the Albatros climbing once again to come on to a parallel course. 'Hold her steady this time!' Alan bawled and sighted his rifle on the climbing enemy.

With vicious intent, Leutnant Lanz slammed his Parabellum on to the starboard mounting. The BE2 was no more than a hundred and fifty yards away. He couldn't possibly miss. He'd teach them to make a fool of him. He heard a bullet whine overhead and cursed the English observer who was certainly a deadly marksman and deserved to die. Lanz aimed, eagle-eyed, and pressed the trigger of his Parabellum.

The BE2 turned violently away, began to climb, hung in the air for a second or two, then fell away, fluttering downwards out of control. Lanz stopped firing, held up a hand in acknowledgment of the cry of congratulation from his pilot, and gazed down at the spinning machine as it carried its occupants to certain death. They had tried to make a fool of Lanz and now they had paid for it. However, as he watched the machine approach the moment of impact with the earth, Lanz shared the agony of the waiting men whose bodies would soon be broken and burning. Foolhardy men. Stupidly brave. Their motive had not been just to make a fool of him, of course, Lanz knew that well enough. They had died in an insanely gallant attempt to deal with a superior weapon and a superior marksman.

Just when Lanz decided not to watch the hellish moment of impact and was on the point of motioning his pilot to fly southwards in search of further prey, something very strange happened. Indeed, as far as Lanz was concerned, it was much more than strange – it was little short of a miracle. As for Lanz's pilot, he simply refused to believe it was happening. His eyes were playing some sort of trick. Everyone knew that once a pilot got into a spin like that one – well! – he was a dead man!

But whether the pilot was dead or alive, the BE2 looked healthy enough as it flew low over the brown earth and into the west wind, heading back to the front lines and home.

Corporal Roberts looked up as Charles walked into the armoury. 'Any luck with our favourite Hun, sir?'

'Yes, indeed,' Charles said, meaningly. 'I'm still alive.'

'Gave you a bad time, did he, sir?'

Charles was looking thoughtfully at the Lewis gun in its place in the gun rack. The machine-gun had remained there unused since Corporal Jones had made that abortive attempt at mounting it on the interplane struts where the vibration caused by its firing had practically torn the bottom wing off. 'No one's come up with a decent mounting for that thing yet, I suppose?'

'Nor likely to, neither.' Corporal Roberts stared balefully at the Lewis. 'The BE2 is a reconnaissance machine. The chap who designed her didn't give a thought to the fact that we might want to arm her some day, did he?'

'He'd have been inspired to give it some thought if he'd had my experience this afternoon,' Charles muttered. 'The riggers have just counted the bullet holes. Twelve of the blessed things. Grumbling about having to patch them. I told them – I'm just glad the holes are in my machine and not in me.'

Alan took off his flying coat and threw it on the bed. 'I say, that's rather sloppy,' Charles said as he ducked into the tent. 'Not putting it on a hanger? My word, what on earth would Mum say?'

Alan bit back an angry retort and sat on the bed. His leg was troubling him. It always ached after flying. It was having to sit in that one position, unable to move it about.

'You look done in,' Charles said. He sounded suspiciously cheerful, Alan thought, considering the fiasco they had made of tackling the Hun and the number of times they'd both died in the hair-raising minutes of that spin. 'And rather down in the mouth. So unlike you, Alan.'

'Sergeant, you mean, don't you? And you know you broke the most important rule of all this afternoon, do you?'

'Going into that spin, you mean?' Charles's tone was rather too offhand. He was obviously very pleased with himself. 'Well, as we seem to be in the mood for breaking rules . . . anyway, the rules are made to save our skins, aren't they? So if we can save our skin by breaking one now and then, who's to argue?'

Alan had to admit that the spin had got them out of trouble. Up to that moment they'd been lucky; Alan was forced to agree with Charles that if they hadn't ducked out of the scrap when they did they'd have been badly mauled if not shot down. Charles had put her into the spin quite deliberately and the experience had certainly put the wind up Alan.

'It put the wind up me, too,' Charles grinned. 'But an interesting way of losing height rather quickly, what?

D

Fooling the Hun into thinking he'd got us and giving us time to get away.'

'How's it done? Pulling her out of, I mean?'

'Nothing to it, really. Control lever forward. Hard opposite rudder. Engine on as soon as she starts to pull out.'

Alan regarded him with reluctant admiration. 'When did you learn to do it?'

'This afternoon!'

'You mean — ?' Alan swallowed hard. 'You mean that when you put her into that spin you had no idea how you were going to get out of it?'

'Oh, I wouldn't go as far as saying "no idea". I mean we all have our pet theories about getting out of spins, don't we?'

'Theories yes, but we don't know that they'll work in practice.'

'I know mine does,' Charles grinned. 'What are you looking so glum about? I *did* get us out of it, didn't I?'

'Just don't try it again, that's all. Not while I'm flying as your observer. Risking your own neck to prove your theories is all well and good. But risking the life of your passenger is another matter.'

'You ungrateful wretch,' Charles said lightly. 'I saved our lives with that spin, you know. And after all, it was your idea. Going after the Hun, I mean. Still, I suppose you're right. I shan't try it again. Anyway, it won't be much use. The Hun will be wise to it next time.'

'What d'you mean – next time?'

'The next time we have a shot at him. We should be on the long reconnaissance again in three or four days time. Same routine, eh? Lunch. A little nap. And off we go.'

'Why are you suddenly so keen to have another shot at him?'

'You said it yourself. Sooner or later, someone has to

do something about that Hun. And knowing how brave and daring you country lads are ...'

'We cling to life, too,' Alan said sullenly, beginning to regret having ever persuaded Charles to go hunting the Hun. 'Country people live longer than townsmen, did you know that?'

'Here, you're not getting cold feet, are you? Ah, but of course, I was forgetting. It was our favourite Hun who put that bullet in your leg, wasn't it? Afraid it might be your head next time, what?'

'All right, all right,' Alan muttered, testily, 'I admit I was wrong in deciding to go after him. That's what you want from me, isn't it? I was wrong – and you were right. A rifle *is* useless up against that machine-gun.'

'Indeed it is. That's why we're taking the Lewis gun next time.'

Alan stared at him. 'The Lewis gun? But there's no mounting for it. We've tried various mountings and none of them work.'

'We haven't tried mine.'

'Yours? You've made a mounting?'

'Not made it, no But I've had a brilliant thought. And you're a blacksmith, aren't you?' And with a slyly challenging air, he added: 'Of course, making a horseshoe is one thing. Making a mounting for the Lewis is quite another.'

That evening the replacement pilot arrived. Second-Lieutenant Palmer was just over from Blighty with fourteen hours flying time and desperately keen for action. 'You'll need a few more hours yet before going over enemy lines,' Charles explained when he had introduced Palmer to his fellow officers in the Mess. 'You'll need to get to know the sector, where our batteries are placed, Hun Archie and so on. Archie is our pet name for anti-aircraft fire, by the way.' Oh yes, Palmer knew that. There was very little he did *not* know, in fact, and he surprised them all by announcing, rather smugly, that Captain Triggers had already singled him out for a 'special task'.

On the following afternoon Alan enlisted the help of Corporal Jones, the stoop-shouldered Welsh engine-fitter who had earned himself the title of the Hunchback of Notre Hangar, and started work on Charles's mounting for the Lewis gun. 'Not exactly Leonardo da Vinci, is it?' Jones said, studying Charles's drawing of what was virtually two triangular brackets converging on a small square of metal. The brackets were to be bolted to the side of the observer's cockpit so it meant making two mountings, one for the port side and one for the starboard. Alan had made no comment when Charles handed him the drawing but he was impressed by the very simplicity of the mounting. 'So simple it's almost bloody moronic,' said Corporal Jones, whose hobby was reading a dictionary his Aunty Gladys had given him for his seventeenth birthday. 'And he doesn't mention how we're supposed to fix the Lewis gun to this here square of metal. I mean, after all, the gun's got to be movable, hasn't it?' And Jones stood there in the observer's cockpit, arms akimbo, gazing bleakly at the interplane struts and wires. 'And even then you got problems of some magnitude, I'd say. Firing through this lot. Like trying to make love to a woman through a chickenwire fence.' He looked uneasy as they measured and cut the iron tubing to the required lengths for the brackets. 'And Captain Triggers knows what you're up to, does he?' Alan made no reply, consoling himself with the thought that all would surely be forgiven when they announced the triumphant news of the shooting down of the troublesome Hun.

The arrival of the French two-seater created something of a stir. Its passenger, a bearded man in a Norfolk jacket, was holding on his deer-stalker against the wind, and when the gigantic figure emerged from the cockpit, Dick Bravington wondered how on earth the machine had ever managed to take off. After ordering the inquisitive Sergeant Mills to take a walk around the hangar, Captain Triggers introduced 'Mr Woods' to the new pilot, Palmer, who had already been alerted by Triggers that his 'special task' was in the offing.

'Second Lieutenant Palmer is our new pilot, just over from Blighty and I'm sure he's just the man for your purpose, Mr Woods.'

Mr Woods smiled, nodded, doffed his deer-stalker and shook Palmer's hand warmly. Palmer murmured 'How d'you do, sir,' and stood proudly to attention, keenly aware of an atmosphere of hushed importance.

'Mr Woods is a Belgian,' Triggers explained, as if to dispel any feeling that the genial giant with the tell-tale stains of air-sickness down the front of his Norfolk was completely dumb.

'He *does* speak English, however . . .' And Mr Woods bade Palmer a very good morning to prove it. 'To business then.' Triggers looked levelly at Palmer, who by this time was almost bursting with serious intent. 'Mr Woods needs to learn how to swing a propeller,' Triggers said. He gave the shattered Palmer a consoling pat on the shoulder. 'There's a very good reason for it, of course,' he went on, and without troubling to say what it was took Mr Woods off to lunch.

'Orders are orders,' Corporal Roberts said, flicking the ash from his cigarette with an air of officialdom. 'The Lewis gun is only to be handed out for use on the long reconnaissance.'

'But no one bothers to take the blessed thing on the long reconnaissance,' Charles said impatiently. The NCO's attitude was bordering on downright impertinence but Charles knew he had to play his cards carefully. 'It's more nuisance that it's worth, having no proper mounting. And that's the very reason I want it. You see – I've devised a new mounting for it and I want to try it out.'

'I understand, sir.'

'Of course you do,' Charles beamed. As he'd told Alan, he'd have no trouble at all in getting hold of the Lewis. 'And I'll want four drums of ammo, of course.'

'You've mentioned it to Captain Triggers, have you, sir?' Roberts gave a sourly superior smile. These young officers, they thought theirselves so clever, but he could read 'em like a blinkin' book. 'As I said, sir – orders is orders, I'm afraid.'

'What about no smoking in the armoury?'

The cheeky young blighter! Roberts gave a jerky little smile. 'Well, sir– I mean we all do it, don't we, sir?' But his old pals' smile crept uneasily away under Charles's heavily accusing stare.

'But smoking's not all you get up to in here, is it, Corporal?'

Alan was sawing a length of piping for the starboard mounting when Charles dumped the Lewis gun down on the bench. How on earth had Charles managed it?

'You'd better ask Corporal Roberts in the armoury. Lord knows what he gets up to in there at nights.'

'Blackmail, eh?' Alan grinned. He nodded towards the mounting on the port side of the cockpit. 'Got the first one made and fitted. It'll take the weight of the Lewis all right.'

'Good. Here – what's this hole for?'

'You hadn't considered how to make the gun movable on the mounting, had you?'

'One can't be expected to think of every minor detail,' Charles said airily. 'Obviously, from the smug look on your face, you've surmounted that little problem.'

Alan had attached a spike on to the underside of the Lewis gun. The gun could then be 'dropped' into the hole bored in the mounting, enabling the gunner to switch the gun quite rapidly from port to starboard simply by lifting it out of one mounting and dropping it into the other. Charles nodded, climbed into the observer's cockpit and asked Alan to hand him the Lewis gun.

'It beats me why we don't put the observer in the rear cockpit like the Hun does. Here in the front cockpit one is severely hampered by all these damn struts and wires.' And he traversed the gun, noting the 'safe' lines of fire. He gave Alan a warning look. 'Seems to me you can only fire with safety on the aft quarters. Any other direction you're likely to hit the propeller, the wings, the tailplane – or *me*. So don't get too enthusiastic, will you?'

The British two-seater was barely a thousand yards away and heading directly towards him. Lanz had no reason to suppose it was the same machine that had cheated him out of his 'kill' a few days earlier. But he had a hunch that it *was* the same machine. Instead of turning away and staying out of harm's reach, this pair were showing the same foolhardy lack of respect for Lanz's machine-gun as the pilot and observer of that previous encounter. But they wouldn't make a fool of him this time. And if they staged that show of spinning to their deaths again, they'd have a nasty surprise. Lanz had told his pilot that in future they would follow spinning machines down in order to make sure they were not feigning 'dead'. 'Turn on to a parallel course,' Lanz shouted to his pilot, and he fired five rounds from his Parabellum to make sure it was not jammed. He was not going to take any chances whatsoever with this pair of English madmen.

Alan watched the Albatros turning, noted the observer's machine-gun on the starboard side, and dropped the spike of the Lewis into the hole on the portside mounting. Charles continued to fly straight and level, his eyes on the Albatros as it came on to a parallel course, above and ahead. Alan gestured to Charles to 'get her up'. Charles eased back the stick and the BE2 nosed upwards, slowly and reluctantly, as if it was all too much of an effort. The engine should have gone into St Omer for an overhaul weeks ago, but as there was such a shortage of machines, the Depot had been unable to lend them a replacement, and the Flight just could not cope with the amount of work to be done flying three machines instead of four. 'So your engine's a bit rough,' Triggers had snarled when Charles complained. 'When you're flying a BE2, if the engine's running rough or sweet as treacle, it makes very little difference to its damned awful performance.'

So here they were, Charles considered, preparing to engage the enemy in a machine that was hardly capable of taking on a decent-sized moth, let alone the much vaunted German two-seater. And armed with a machine-gun with a severely limited arc of fire, mounted on an assemblage of scrap-iron that would very likely shake to pieces once the Lewis opened up. It would be downright hilarious if it were not for the fear that hung inside him like a great shameful stone.

'Bring her up, bring her up!' Alan raved, struggling to sight the Lewis. The port upper wing obstructed his view and he gestured wildly to Charles to bank to starboard. Charles eased the stick over and Alan aimed the Lewis at the Albatros, now slightly above and ahead. Damn! The struts and bracing wires were right in his line of sight.

Coolly, and with deliberate care, Lanz aimed his Parabellum at the climbing British machine. He was about to press the trigger when he saw the barrel of the Lewis gun jiggling between the struts of the BE2 as Alan strove vainly to find a safe line of fire. Astonished at the sight of the spidery contraption on which the British observer appeared to be lying so precariously whilst waving some instruction to his pilot, Lanz raised his eyes from the sights of the Parabellum to make sure he wasn't just seeing things. At that moment, Alan fired the Lewis. The German pilot, expecting to hear the sound of the Parabellum's opening burst, was disconcerted by the distant chatter of the Lewis. Realising they were not firing but being fired upon, he jerked the Albatros into a climbing turn. Lanz, standing in his cockpit, surprised by the burst from the Lewis and certainly not expecting his pilot to execute the violent evasive manœuvre, was thrown to one side, the vertical drum of the Parabellum catching him full in the mouth. He cursed his pilot. But the man's prompt action had saved their lives, for the bullets from the burst had come uncomfortably close. The damned English madmen had surprised them yet again. Now they too had a machine-gun. But what a ridiculous place to mount it; one wing above the gunner, another wing below, and a forest of struts and wires on either side. One needed to be a contortionist *and* a trapeze artiste in order to aim and fire from such a mounting. Why did the English like to make things so difficult for themselves? Lanz sucked the blood from his cut lips and watched the BE2 circling below. He came to a decision and signalled to his pilot to switch off his engine so that he could hear what he proposed to do about the threat of the machine-gun. 'We must fly above him, of course, as we normally do. But we must keep *ahead* of him. That makes it more difficult – if not impossible – for him to fire at us. We mustn't allow him to draw ahead of us. That gives him a wider arc of fire.'

Charles climbed his BE2, endeavouring to come on to a parallel course. But the Albatros continued to climb ahead, and as Alan strove to aim his Lewis through the struts and wires of the banked machine, the Parabellum opened fire. Charles veered away in a diving turn, the BE2 losing yet more valuable height.

After flying in a wide circle, the BE2 once again climbed doggedly to the attack. Alan cursed the upper wing that came between the muzzle of his Lewis and his target. Once again Alan heard the clatter of the Parabellum. But just as Charles went into the steep-banked turn to evade the stream of bullets, Alan caught a glimpse of the Albatros, hanging just above him. He pressed the trigger.

Charles heard an ominous thudding sound accompanying the stuttering fire of the Lewis. What the hell was happening? Another sound answered. An agonised cry that floated past, borne on the turning wind of banking mainplanes. Christ, no! Not a cry, but the tortured creak of straining wood. Charles stared at the buckling strut between the port side wings. Alan had seen it, too, and as they both looked on in horror, the strut, partly severed by the burst from Alan's Lewis gun, snapped. As if signalling a frantic distress, the two bullet-ridden ends of the severed strut fluttered wildly in the thrusting wind.

'Get her down!' Alan bawled. But Charles had already thought of that. He eased the stick forward, pushing the nose down to maintain flying speed, and switched off the engine. As they glided earthwards, the two young men stared anxiously at the port-side wings where the ends of the severed strut clack-clacked above the urgent sounds of rushing air, the ripple and stretch of loosening fabric, and the west wind singing in the wires. The wing sections near the severed strut, now unsupported, were bending ominously. Alan glanced up at the Albatros, circling like a vulture far above them, then stared into the distance, towards the front lines, still several miles away. Anxiously, he turned to warn Charles not to lose height too quickly.

'You've done your bit for today,' Charles shouted accusingly. 'Just leave it to me from here on.'

'We don't want to land behind enemy lines, do we?'

'I just want to get my feet on the ground,' Charles raged, his eyes riveted on the bending wings. 'I don't much care who owns it.'

'Speak for yourself. I don't want to spend the rest of the war in a prison camp.'

'At least our necks would be safe. You and your idiot ideas.'

'My ideas? I like that! Whose idea was this useless gun mounting, anyway?'

'Shut up, will you? I'm trying to put this lame duck down — ' He gave a cry of alarm as Alan appeared to dive over the side of the cockpit to reach the Lewis gun, lying parallel to the fuselage on the outer end of the mounting.

'What the hell are you doing now?'

'Guess what I can see?' Alan heaved the Lewis off the mounting, lurched across the cockpit, slammed the spike into the starboard mounting and pressed the handle of the Lewis downwards, swinging the barrel end up towards the diving Albatros.

'Good God!' Charles shouted savagely. 'We've got enough trouble without him.'

'He doesn't know that, does he?'

Lanz certainly did not. As far as he was concerned this annoying English pair were ducking out of the fight again. He didn't like the way they called the tune, soaring blithely to the attack when it suited them, and then, when things got too hot, waving goodbye and heading for home. This time they weren't going to find it quite so easy.

The burst from the Parabellum raked the bending port-side wings and Alan heard his windscreen shatter just before he pressed the trigger of the Lewis. The Albatros pulled out of the dive barely thirty yards above and the fine target it presented caused Alan to transgress the limits of safety once again. Sliding out across the mounting until his knees were on the edge of the cockpit, he swung the Lewis inboard continuing to fire the traversing machine-gun until the stream of lead was uncomfortably close to Charles's right ear.

'For God's sake!' Charles roared.

'Shut up and give me a hand.'

Charles reached for the belt of Alan's flying coat and hauled him back into the cockpit. Alan, his eyes on the turning Albatros, changed the Lewis to the port mounting.

'Here he comes again.'

'Shoot at *him* this time, will you?' Charles shouted. 'I'm rather fond of my ears.'

The Albatros came on to a parallel course, slightly above the BE2, and Lanz aimed his Parabellum. But this time Alan fired first. The German pilot heard an unfamiliar bell-like sound as a bullet nicked a wire close to his head. Instinctively he turned his machine away from the line of fire, much to Lanz's chagrin.

'Again, again!' Lanz shouted, waving his pilot to circle into another attacking position. But no sooner had the words left his lips than a great orange flash appeared just ahead of them. Whoomph! The impact of the explosion was like a giant hand thrust full in the nose of the Albatros. Archie fire! Lanz, in his determination to shoot down the BE2, had been unaware that they had flown so close to the front lines, and he had strict orders from his Commander that under no circumstances whatsoever was he to fly over enemy territory. There was no point in taking unnecessary risks. Pilots and observers, to say nothing of the machines, were much too valuable. As a second Archie shell burst on their port side, Lanz signalled his pilot to turn for home.

'Thank God!' Charles muttered, easing back the stick to clear the trees that loomed ahead. Then, fearful of stalling, he pushed the stick forward again and heard a tearing sound. Alan dived to look down over the side, his look of alarm confirming Charles's fears. They had hit the trees and torn off the undercart. 'Brace yourself,' Charles yelled. 'I'm putting her down.'

It was a perfectly executed landing, and they might have got away with remarkably little damage, apart from the loss of the undercart. That is, if it had not been for the shell crater. Fortunately, the grass was long and acted as an effective brake, so that by the time they reached the crater the BE2 had almost stopped. She nosed down the side of the crater like a maimed, hunted animal, crawling gratefully into hiding.

'Well done, Charles.'

'Just presence of mind, that's all.'

Their gratitude to Mother Earth for putting herself beneath their feet once more was short-lived.

'Toss you for which of us recovers the undercart from the top of that tree,' Charles said mournfully, as they surveyed the snapped propeller, the crumpled wings and the engine buried in the side of the crater. 'We won't exactly be the toast of the repair depot, will we?'

'At least we're alive.'

'That's the trouble,' Charles said. 'I've a strong feeling we're going to wish we weren't.'

Triggers was furious. Hadn't he told them not to go look-ing for trouble with the Hun? Yes, he understood that sooner or later something would have to be done about the one with the machine-gun, but that was a matter for his decision, not theirs. They were not to go taking mat-ters into their own hands like this. Who the hell's idea was it, anyway? Alan said it was his idea, but Charles insisted that the blame lay entirely on his shoulders. The mount-ing for the Lewis had been his brainchild.

'But I *made* the mounting, sir,' Alan said, determin-edly. 'And without troubling to get permission.'

'I drew the Lewis gun from the armoury, sir.'

'Well, well, both so anxious to take the credit.' Trig-gers looked fiercely from one to the other. 'Are you so proud of yourselves, then?' They waited in silence. 'Who fired the Lewis?'

Alan came stiffly to attention. 'I did, sir.'

'I see. According to Mr Bravington you're the best shot on the Squadron.' His tone was brutally sarcastic. 'You're certainly the most original. You must be the first flier in the RFC to shoot himself down.'

Alan now looked shamefaced under Triggers' wither-ing gaze. 'The arc of fire is so limited in the front cockpit, sir.'

'A gunner! Want to be a gunner, do you?' Triggers stabbed a threatening finger at Alan's 'wings'. 'You won't be needing those then, will you?'

A sudden chill came over Alan. Surely Triggers wouldn't strip him of his 'wings'— 'I'm very proud of my wings, sir. But I *am* flying as Mr Gaylion's observer at the moment. Until my leg's properly healed.'

Triggers said nothing. Alan waited, agonised, for his Flight Commander's decision. 'Does that gun mounting work?' Before Alan could reply, Triggers added: 'When there's not an idiot using it, I mean?'

'Yes,' Charles said firmly. 'It does work, sir.'

'Good! Then in future we can take the Lewis gun on the long reconnaissance. That's when it's most needed.' And he looked dangerously from one to the other. 'On the long reconnaissance only. Understood?' He gave a curt nod to Alan, who saluted and went out, then he turned to Charles, his manner a little more relaxed now, an attitude of pained reproof, as a fond father to an erring son, 'Do you and Sergeant Farmer *have* to live in each other's pockets?'

Charles's reply was almost too positive. 'We don't, sir. Not any more.'

Triggers nodded slowly. He had sensed some personal trouble between Charles and Sergeant Farmer. He was mildly curious, but there, it didn't really concern him. He was relieved that the tiresome problem had resolved itself. 'Mr Gaylion. This Lewis gun incident. You're not just a flier, you know. You're a commissioned officer in the British Army. So you'd be wise to rid yourself of the quaint little notion the General Staff have of the Flying Corps. We are *not* a bunch of irresponsible grease-faced mechanics. If you insist on thinking along those lines, then you'd better transfer to another Flight, where they might subscribe more to that point of view.'

'I'd rather not transfer to another Flight, sir. I've got used to the chaps in "C" Flight.' What else could Charles say? To admit that he respected and admired his Flight Commander would be laying it on a bit and – well – he could hardly say he'd become 'fond' of the blighter; in spite of Triggers' vicious tongue in these pi-jawing sessions. And so he said, with a half-apologetic smile: 'I'd miss these little chats, sir.'

Two days later a new machine arrived from the Aircraft Park at St Omer and Charles and Alan flew off, midmorning, to silence a particularly troublesome enemy gun. After searching in vain for an hour and a half they were forced to the conclusion that the gun had either been moved or was heavily camouflaged. In any case, is wasn't firing or they'd have spotted the orange flashes. In order not to waste the trip entirely they directed the battery's fire on to some heavy transport moving towards what appeared to be a rather important road junction and flew back to lunch secure in the knowledge that a gang of German road-builders would be kept very busy for quite some time. The business of the Lewis gun mounting was now totally forgotten. Triggers put forward his suggestion that the mounting might be used on the long reconnaissance flight, but the tale of Charles and Alan's alarming experience had got so twisted in the telling that the mounting itself had become the villain of the piece. Consequently, the pilot and observer on the long reconnaisance flight took one look at the ominously bent remains of the mounting and flew off with renewed faith in the Winchester repeating rifle.

After lunch Alan stretched out on the warm grass outside his tent and wondered if the sky was as blue over Becket's Hill. He imagined Lorna as Mrs Somebody-or-other in some future time – after the war, perhaps? – in a wifely pinafore cooking a dinner that was deliciously different from the heavy, unappetising mess that was settling, oh, so slowly, under his braces. But she wouldn't be Mrs Alan Farmer, that was for sure, so why was he thinking about Lorna instead of Kate, who called it lunch not dinner? And that brought him back to 'the question' again. What had Kate said in that note, the one that Charles had burned? She had promised to write and tell him whether or not she wanted to see him once again. Damn Charles Gaylion for burning the answer to a question that was so important. Had Charles read the note,

Alan wondered. Perhaps Kate had said yes, she wanted to see Alan again, and that's why Charles had burned it. But no, Charles hadn't read the note, of course. He wouldn't. Not Charles. But damn him for burning it, all the same. He couldn't write to Kate without knowing what she'd written in that note. She'd fully expect him to refer to it. He could hardly pretend to ignore it, and he certainly couldn't tell her that her brother had burned it in a fit of pique. If he did, he'd never hear the end of it from Charles. Why, oh why did the girl put a note for him in with the letter to her brother? Could she have guessed, perhaps, that Charles would burn the note? But why should she do that? To amuse herself at his expense? She seemed to be the sort of girl who liked to toy with men's affections. Well – she wouldn't toy with his. She was going to marry him. She didn't know it yet, but he'd be getting his commission. So let her laugh at him all she wanted for the time being. She'd take him seriously enough in the end, he knew that for sure.

'Who the 'ell's this then?' The corporal rigger sucked noisily at the mug of tea. 'One of your lot, serge? There's no one flying from A and B Flights.'

Alan cursed the man for intruding on his vision of the brand-new second lieutenant arriving on Kate Gaylion's doorstep for lunch with a bunch of flowers that had cost at least five shillings. And couldn't the damned man tell by the droning that she wasn't one of theirs? 'Not a BE2 at all, a machine from another Squadron'. Alan sat up, shading his eyes from the sun, and studied the oncoming aeroplane. Good God! It couldn't be, surely? He'd never seen one this far inside the lines. He jumped up and ran to the 'lookout', a home-made instrument consisting of a telescope attached to the top of a bicycle wheel and mounted on a revolving stand, so enabling it to be turned in both horizontal and vertical planes.

'A Hun! She's a Hun!' Alan cried, running back to his tent for his Winchester. The rigger ran to the shell-case hanging on a rope, beating it furiously with the stick. Men stumbled from tents and emerged from hangars, staring at the diving Albatros. Alan dropped on one knee to steady his aim and sighted on the pilot of the machine. As he put the preliminary pressure on the trigger, a fluttering object caught his eye. He fired and the Albatros turned, climbing away in the direction of the front lines. 'Cor, it's a message!' someone cried. Alan looked on in amazement as the little leather bag with its guiding streamers plummeted on to the field.

With the exasperated air of a man receiving a bill for goods already paid for, Triggers unfolded the sheet of buff paper and read the contents aloud. 'We wish to renew the duel with our gallant enemy — ' He looked at Alan as if that was a distinct untruth for a start, then went on: ' — tomorrow at dawn. Good afternoon.'

Triggers looked at the note with some distaste, tore it up and dropped it in the waste basket. Alan, who had rushed into the flight office in a fever of importance, the message bag intact for his Flight Commander to open, now wished he hadn't bothered. Triggers was treating him as if he'd trumped up the whole business.

'When the war is over, sergeant – *then* you can go home and play your games on the village green, or wherever it is you play them. But while you are here, your job is reconnaissance and artillery spotting.'

Alan licked his lips and took the plunge. 'That particular Hun *is* becoming rather a nuisance, sir.'

'He's not the only one, sergeant.' Triggers' tone implied that there was no more to be said on the subject. He picked up the message bag with its streamers, icy disdain in his manner. 'Take this with you. I'm sure you'd like to hang it on the wall of your blacksmith's shop.'

Alan glanced at the torn notepaper in the waste basket and dropped the message bag on top of it. 'Refusing the challenge is of no importance to me, sir.'

'What do you mean by that?'

'I'm a sergeant, sir. Matters of honour don't concern NCOs, do they, sir?'

Triggers looked dangerous. But before he could reply there was a knock on the door and Mr Woods came in, followed by Second Lieutenant Palmer. Alan saluted and went out.

'Mr Woods has mastered the art of swinging a propeller, sir.' Palmer said, glad that the chore was done. The huge Belgian was totally unco-ordinated and his fear of the BE2's 'four-bladed guillotine' had caused a great deal of amusement amongst Palmer's fellow officers, with quips galore on the subject of the 'special task' for which Palmer had been selected. However, having spent several days in the company of the Belgian, Palmer sensed from the man's careful conversation and his unwillingness to talk about himself or his occupation that the propeller-swinging was merely a prelude to something pretty important. Palmer was eager to learn what the next stage of his special task entailed, and he couldn't wait to see his sniggering tormentors laughing on the other side of their faces.

'Thank you, Mr Palmer,' Triggers said. 'That's all.'

Palmer gaped. Triggers smiled pleasantly. 'Now you can start putting your hours in. You'll need quite a few before you're ready to fly over enemy lines.'

'You didn't think Triggers was going to let *you* fly Mr Woods over the lines, did you?' chortled Bravington, as Palmer fumed up and down the tiny room they shared above the Mess. 'Important job like that when you're still wet behind the ears?'

'One of you might have told me he was a spy,' Palmer ranted. 'I feel such an idiot. Everyone knowing except me.'

'But we don't know,' Bravington said with aggravating innocence. 'I mean, we haven't been told. Just a process of elimination. What else could he be? And learning to swing a propeller – well – the pilot who lands him will want to take off again, won't he? One can keep the engine ticking over, yes, but you never know what's going to happen in a situation like that. So the chap who's being landed needs to be able to swing the prop, just in case.'

Palmer was silent for a time. 'I've made a priggish ass of myself, haven't I?'

Yes, he had, Bravington said. And served him damned well right. Palmer looked sheepish as he combed his hair to make himself presentable for dinner.

'Any advice to offer?'

'Yes, I think so.' Bravington counted his meagre loose change. 'After dinner, wish Mr Woods Godspeed on his venture, with a suitably veiled "whatever it may be", implying to all and sundry that you know very well what Mr Woods is up to.'

'That's jolly clever,' Palmer said gratefully. 'Thanks!'

'Not at all.' Bravington gave him a little fixed smile. 'And for the Godspeed bit – I suggest you treat all and sundry to large brandies.'


'It's a wonder Triggers didn't chop your head off,' Charles remarked when Alan had recounted his conversation with Triggers. 'Matters of honour don't concern NCOs? Did you really say that to him?'

'Well, it is a matter of honour, isn't it? A challenge like that?'

'So you thought you'd goad Triggers into changing

his mind and allowing us to go off and meet the Hun at dawn tomorrow?'

'Something like that, yes,' Alan said tightly. 'But it didn't work.'

Charles gave a short, harsh laugh. 'Did you really think it would? You're so heavy-handed, that's your trouble. But there, you are a blacksmith, of course. In future, if you simply can't resist a dig at your superiors, then try and do it with a little more subtlety.'

'You may be my superiors in rank,' Alan said hotly, 'but that's as far as it goes.'

'Oh dear,' Charles smiled maddeningly. 'Now we're taking it all personally, are we?'

Triggers kept the engine idling, so there was no need for Mr Woods to swing the propeller. Triggers gave him a consoling smile. 'Never mind, perhaps you'll get a chance to swing her on your return flight.'

'Thank you for a pleasant journey,' Mr Woods replied, after arranging to meet Triggers in the same spot on the following Wednesday. Then he shook his pilot warmly by the hand and hurried away. Triggers smiled to himself as the burly figure turned and waved before disappearing into the trees; here they were, twenty miles behind enemy lines, having arranged a meeting fraught with dangers in the casual manner of two London club members planning another merry evening on the town. Triggers pushed the throttle lever forward, turned away from the trees, and took off into the stiff wind blowing from the west. The cloud had thickened since he'd left Ste Marie and now hung in a dark blanket as far as the eye could see. Triggers climbed to a thousand feet or so below the cloud layer and turned thirty degrees south in order to avoid the area around the Hun airfield at Templeuve. He was flying alone, armed only with a Webley revolver. So he was taking no chances.

Twenty minutes later, a dozen miles from the front lines, he saw a German two-seater descending from the cloud and coming obliquely towards him on the starboard side. The occupants had obviously spotted him and intended giving fight. Triggers pulled his stick back, hoping to reach the cover of the cloud before the enemy machine came close enough to open fire. In the German two-seater, Lanz, seeing the BE2 commencing to climb, signalled to his pilot to maintain their height advantage and the Albatros nosed up to the cloud.

Triggers cursed the BE2's rotten rate of climb as he watched the Albatros coming on to a parallel course just above him. By this time he had spotted the observer's machine-gun and knew the machine to be the 'favourite Hun' that was giving the Squadron so much trouble. He drew his Webley and glanced anxiously up at the dark blanket that appeared to be rising as he climbed, remaining tantalisingly out of reach, as if refusing to give him refuge.

The Albatros settled on its parallel course and Lanz swung his Parabellum on to his target. Without troubling to take aim, Triggers fired two shots from his Webley. A gesture of defiance, no more. Only by a miracle could he have hoped to score a hit. A rifle was a poor enough weapon in the air, so what chance did one have with a revolver? It was kept in one's holster as a comfort. Like a flask of brandy to a man facing execution. If you happened to be shot down, trapped in a burning machine, the Webley would be worth more than all the prayers ever made by man. But in a situation like this one, it was absolutely useless.

As he heard the Parabellum open fire, Triggers instinctively pushed away to port. But he kept her climbing. He either had to remain a sitting duck for the time it took him to enter the cover of the cloud layer or play tag with that deadly machine-gun for the dozen or so miles to the front lines. And he didn't fancy the latter. Flying into the stiff west wind, which had freshened considerably since his take-off, plus the time taken up in evasive manœuvring, might mean pitting his wits for the best part of an hour with the combined skills of this noted pilot and determinedly deadly gunner. On top of all that, there was the ever-present risk of running out of petrol. He had no desire to land in Hunland twice on the same day. He looked back to see the Albatros turning after him, crossing above him and coming on to his port side, the damned Parabellum again swinging down to point – or so it seemed to Triggers – directly into his eyes. The two machines were flying at approximately the same speeds and so the Albatros appeared to be stationary above him and he, fool that he was, simply hung there, waiting to be killed. Sacrificing the urgency of the climb for a bit more speed, Triggers eased the stick forward.

A second before he heard the burst from the Parabellum he felt a searing pain in his right shoulder. He'd been hit! He swung his machine violently over into a steeply banked turn, away from the deadly stream of fire. As he levelled out, he looked around for the Albatros. It was nowhere to be seen. It had been several hundred feet above him and must have flown into the cloud layer. His cunning enemy intended to take him by surprise. At any moment the Albatros would materialise from the cloud with its damned machine-gun blasting away at him before he had a chance to take evasive action. Like hell it would! The burning pain in his right shoulder flared up like a fanned flame as he pulled the stick back sending the BE2 into a climb so steep that it was almost standing on its tail. Half a minute later, she entered the white darkness of the strato-cumulus. As Triggers levelled out, something flashed overhead. A formless black ghost against the whiteness. It was several seconds before Triggers realised that it must have been the Albatros. A near collision! His mouth went dry at the thought. Small wonder pilots hated flying in cloud and avoided it at all costs. But in this situation there was no alternative. He had to stick it out and fly blind for five minutes at least, if he was to succeed in shaking off his attacker.

He glanced about him, below and above, in the practised manner of the professional pilot. But there was nothing to be seen but the dense grey-white vapour. How he hated it! It concealed him from his enemy, yet threatened him with other dangers; unseen. unrealised, unaccounted for. At this very moment death might be lurking just yards ahead, looming up, giving him no chance whatsoever to avoid it. He could do nothing but sit there and trust to luck, hoping against hope that some other pilot in the vicinity wasn't doing the same damned cowardly thing. The odds against colliding with another machine were thousands upon thousands to one, he knew that well enough. But it wasn't in Triggers' nature to trust to chance, however high the odds were in his favour. His eyes strained through the arc of the whirring propeller, into the vaporous wall, the remnants of the parting shrouds condensing in droplets on his face. If death ever came in liquid form. Triggers mused, it would come in just these damned icy drops. God, they were even finding their way down inside his clothing. Then he realised that the hateful warm-cold dampness was the manifestation of fear. The fear of the unknown. The invisible, the intangible; the awesome mysteries of nothingness, that were only given substance by the clouds in which they lay concealed. What gibberish, he thought, and a few seconds later, his heart stopped as the final shroud parted. The cloud had come to an end. What the hell was it directly in front of him? A hill? He'd never seen a hill in the area. He surely could not have come *that* far off course. And it was hardly a hill; more a mountain. Good grief! He yanked back the stick and watched the misty horizon ride obliquely down through the slanting rain.

There had been no hill, of course. And certainly no mountain. Just the flat earth, which was now beneath him. And the cloud – that he had 'come to the end of' – still above. He had been, quite unknowingly, diving earthwards. That, indeed, was the holiest of all the holy terrors of flying in cloud. With no horizon as a guide (and God having neglected to endow all newborn fliers with a psychic plumb-line), one had no means at all of gauging the angle of one's machine in relation to the earth. A pilot had once told Triggers that, whilst flying in cloud, he had gradually turned into the inverted position and had carried on flying, quite unaware that his face was 'looking at hell instead of Heaven'.

But there it was, Triggers had emerged from the damp treachery of the cloud and there was no sign whatsoever of the Hun. And small wonder, for the rain was teeming down. All that was left to him now was to find his way home. Which was easier said than done. First, he had to find out where he was. He knew where he *ought* to have been, of course, based on the assumption of straight and level flight whilst in the cloud. But in considering the alarming manner in which he'd made his exit from the black brooding mass, that was too much of a miracle to hope for. So he had to find a landmark and find his way home from that. But the landscape, its features blurred in the darkness of the storm, and further obscured by several thousand feet of driving rain, was no help to him at all in locating his position. He was forced to go down and take a much closer look. He'd be a nice big target for Archie, of course, and any other keen gunners who'd be ready to fire away even in rotten weather like this, in the hope of shooting down one of the hated flying contraptions. But by this time Triggers was feeling so very wet, wearily wounded, thoroughly miserable and alone that a bursting Archie shell might have seemed companionable. Bravery, he considered, as he nosed earthwards through the drenching torrent, was more often than not just sheer desperation.

Just before he levelled out, the bullet in his right shoulder began giving him hell, and he cursed the Hun for his ignominious plight. And he went on cursing him long after he had sighted the comforting spire of the church of Ste Marie.

Alan listened to the rain spattering on the canvas and swashing into the grass at the foot of the tent walls and wondered if the same rain was falling on Percival Square. He had almost finished the letter and was unable to decide between 'best wishes to your mother' and 'kind regards to Mrs Gaylion'. If he had been writing to anyone but Kate he could have asked Charles; they were no longer friends, but at least Charles was talking to him now. Still, he'd solved the problem of the burned note by thanking Kate for it and then going on to write of other matters. But he wished he knew what she'd written. She'd promised to tell him whether or not she wanted to see him again. However, looking on the positive side of the situation, if Kate had said she didn't want to see him again the fact that he'd made no reference to it in his own letter would show her that he was determined to make her change her mind.

He decided, finally, on 'kind regards to your mother', and was just in the act of writing the words when the flap was torn aside and Triggers stepped into the tent. His flying gear was drenched, the sodden woollen scarf serving as a makeshift sling in which his right arm hung life-lessly. His lean features, wet with rain and gleaming with an almost spectral whiteness in the sombre light of the hurricane lamp, were contorted in pain and frozen rage.

'About that Lewis gun. I told you it was to be used only on the long reconnaissance.'

Alan came respectfully and bewilderedly to his feet. 'Yes, sir. You did, sir.'

'I've changed my mind,' Triggers hissed. And tore out.

Charles was dozing in the one comfortable armchair in the mess, drifting wishfully light-headed through a noisy haze of London streets, winging his way from restaurant to supper dance, a girl on either arm, when a fist pounded the arm of the chair.

'Sorry, sir,' he said, sitting upright and bold, as if his father had been standing there awaiting an explanation for his son's drunken behaviour. It was Triggers, of course, and holding the largest brandy Charles had ever seen.

'That note from the Hun. You and Sergeant Farmer will accept the challenge. You'll engage the Hun to-morrow at dawn.'

'I've given it some thought overnight,' Charles said, clearing the tools from the workbench and motioning to Alan to fetch the lamp from the hook. 'Hell, where's the chalk?' Alan handed it to him; an irony, a fatalism in the gesture, to which Charles took exception. 'And I'll brook no argument this time, sergeant. Whether you agree or not, this is what I intend to do. This is the Hun.' He stabbed a white cross on the workbench top. 'And this is us.' This time, the chalk snapped.

'I see,' Alan said, as if to underline the fact that even the chalk didn't agree with Charles's harebrained manœuvres.

'Instead of veering away from his fire,' Charles went on determinedly. 'I shall turn in and pass underneath him – like this.' He waited for some comment, but Alan remained dutifully silent. 'Well?'

Alan shrugged. 'As you say, whether I agree or not, that's what you're going to do. So. Off we go then.'

'You really are an unimaginative oaf,' Charles said testily, as they walked out to the waiting machine. 'Passing underneath the Hun and firing up at him gives you a much freer arc of fire.'

'You've no need to worry,' Alan said dourly. 'I've learned my lesson. I shan't chance firing through the struts again.' He settled in his cockpit and gave a significant glance at the upper wing, situated right above his head. 'A freer arc of fire, eh?'

Charles could not resist the obvious retort. 'If you put a few bullets through the top wing, at least you won't shoot us down again.' And when the mechanic was sucking in, he added: 'If we don't get the Hun this morning, I strongly advise you to keep out of Triggers' way.'

'We won't need to,' Alan replied, determined to have the last word. 'Because if we don't get the Hun, it'll mean the Hun's got us.'


Leutnant Lanz waved and smiled at the approaching BE2 with the vigour and warmth of someone greeting a long-lost friend. For the past twenty minutes the Albatros had flown in wide circles five or six miles east of the front lines, and Lanz had gazed morosely into the murky western skies, becoming more and more convinced that the British pair had not accepted his challenge. 'You see? I was right!' he shouted to his pilot. 'I knew they would turn up.'

Lanz's pilot looked sourly at the British observer, who was waving to acknowledge Lanz's enthusiastic greeting. On the previous day, when Lanz had announced his intention of issuing the challenge, his pilot was certain that the British machine was not from Ste Marie but from some other airfield further south. 'You've no reason at all for supposing that,' Lanz had replied scornfully, implying that his pilot had cold feet. But there, what else could one expect of a sergeant. 'We'll be flying over a hornet's nest,' his pilot had retorted disgruntedly. 'And in venturing beyond the front lines, we'll be disobeying orders into the bargain.' And the very idea of taking the risk of being shot down by ground fire in order to drop a message on an enemy airfield smacked of the insanities of the British. 'That's exactly why we're going to do it,' Lanz had snapped back. 'We shall play them at their own ridiculous games. And we shall win.' He didn't care to admit to his pilot how peeved he was that the British pair had twice outwitted him. On the day of their last encounter, Lanz had searched the skies in vain for almost five hours, thirsting for revenge.

But Lanz's desire for revenge had cooled somewhat since he had issued the challenge, and now, as he watched the BE2 coming on to a parallel course five hundred feet below, Lanz felt vaguely grateful to the foolish pair for accepting his invitation and for proving to his surly and ill-bred sergeant pilot that gentlemen were gentlemen, even when they were the eccentric English variety. Indeed, Lanz considered as he settled down to business at the butt end of his Parabellum, it was rather a shame to have to kill them. He took careful aim and was just about to fire when the BE2 skidded out his sights and passed beneath him. His hand traversed the Parabellum, but his mind, still partly preoccupied, was not functioning with the swift precision vital to the life-or-death situation, and before he could pull the trigger the bullet from Alan's Lewis had passed into his brain. He felt no pain. Just a warm streak through the clouds of his mind. The flash of a bright red streamer thrown towards him by his mother on the day he was so proud to be no longer seven but eight years old.

'You got him!' Charles whooped. 'You got him!'

Alan's reaction was confined to a little twisted smile. He had stopped firing but his eyes were still fixed on the Albatros above. The German pilot looked anxiously at his dead observer. He was alone and defenceless now. He had to duck out of the fight. There was nothing else he could do. He glanced bewilderedly about him, searching for the 'vanished' enemy. By the time he spotted the BE2 it was climbing towards him on the port side, and so close that he felt he could see the gloved finger on the trigger of the Lewis gun.

'Fire, for God's sake!' Charles bawled. 'Fire!'

But no sound came from the Lewis gun. The Albatros turned away. Charles turned after him. What the devil had happened? Why hadn't Alan fired? He pushed the stick savagely forward and the BE2 dived beneath the fleeing German machine. 'Now!' Charles raged. 'Now!' Alan was seemingly oblivious, his eyes on the Albatros, once again directly above them. He aimed the Lewis and pressed the trigger. 'Blast!' he muttered, viciously.

'Bad luck, sir,' Corporal Roberts said when Charles returned the hated weapon to the armoury. 'That's the trouble with the Lewis. She's prone to jamming.'

Alan was folding his scarf when Charles ducked into the tent.

'She didn't jam the first time though, did she?' Charles said, angrily. 'You didn't pull the trigger. And we had him at our mercy.'

Alan looked at him. 'Sorry I let you down,' he said, and went on folding his scarf. Charles took out his cigarette case. He was more curious than ever. The iron man of Sussex. But there was a flaw in the metal. A minute fracture. At last it had been revealed.

'Cigarette?'

'No thanks.'

Charles lit his own. 'Triggers is going to be unbearable for the next few days.'

'I have apologised,' Alan said testily. 'D'you want me to go on my knees?'

'No. But I think I'm entitled to an explanation.'

Alan sighed impatiently and sat on the bed. 'I thought of my father,' he said. 'I was there, in Collins's field, on the day he crashed.'

Charles nodded and wondered why on earth he hadn't guessed. After all, he knew that Alan's father had burned to death, and that Alan had witnessed it when he was fifteen years old.

'Ah well,' Charles said at last. 'Triggers will have to lump it. Here. Don't be uppity. Have a fag.'

And he tossed his cigarette case on to Alan's lap.

# 5

Leutnant Oswald Stein completed his basic training and passed the strict German Air Service tests in what must have been a record time of eleven days. After gaining his pilot's certificate at the pilots' school at Doberitz, he was recommended for further training at the Kampfeinsitzer Abteilung. Stein was greatly excited when he heard of the recommendation; it confirmed his own opinion of his exceptional gifts as a pilot and put him firmly on the path to achieving his cherished ambition of becoming a 'fighting pilot' instead of a mere 'chauffeur' to an observer, for the newly-formed Kampfeinsitzer Abteilung trained carefully chosen pilots to fly the new single-seater monoplane fitted with a fixed machine-gun that could be fired through the arc of the propeller. The secret of this devastating device was to be jealously guarded, hence the reason for choosing pilots whose skill would minimise the risk of it falling into enemy hands. The story behind the invention of the device and its subsequent adoption by the German Air Service was told to Leutnant Stein by his flying instructor, who had been present at the interrogation of Roland Garros, a French pilot of record-breaking fame in prewar days, who had been shooting down German two-seaters with apparent ease in his Morane monoplane. Forced down behind enemy lines, Garros' machine had been captured and the secret of his success revealed. A machine-gun had been fixed to enable Garros to fire forward through the propeller, on which metal wedges deflected the estimated seven per cent of bullets that failed to pass through the whirring blades. Anthony Fokker, a Dutch aeroplane designer working for the Germans, examined Garros' machine and the armoured propeller and immediately set about perfecting his own forward-firing gear, a mechanical system stopping the action of the machine-gun when the blades of the propeller came into the line of fire. Fokker fitted the gear to his new single-seater monoplane and demonstrated it to the German generals at an airfield near Berlin. But the generals were distinctly unimpressed. They needed proof of this 'revolutionary weapon' in actual war conditions.

And so, donning the uniform of a lieutenant in the Air Service, Fokker flew from Douai, a German airfield fifteen miles from the front lines, and searched for a victim to substantiate his claim that the fast new monoplane with its fixed machine-gun could sweep the enemy from the skies in the space of two or three months. After a few disappointing patrols, Fokker found his potential victim – a two-seater Farman pusher biplane, ahead and below, and utterly at the mercy of his forward-firing gun. Even when the pilot and observer of the Farman spotted Fokker's machine it was highly unlikely that they would take evasive action, being firm in the belief that they were 'safe' when the enemy was behind them; the German monoplane was a 'tractor', its propeller whirring in front of the nose, so it could not possibly open fire during its dive. They would simply watch and wait until the monoplane came abreast or passed beyond them and then manœuvre accordingly, to attack or defend.

Fokker dived on his unsuspecting victims, their cumbersome Farman an easy target in his sights. At point-blank range his finger curled around the trigger of the murderous Parabellum. Then he turned sharply away and flew towards Douai, leaving his 'victims' shaking their heads in puzzlement. Landing at Douai, Fokker explained to his superiors that as a Dutchman he was unable to kill in order to prove the value of his invention. His brief career as a fighting pilot was at an end and he was returning to his factory. However, he would leave behind his monoplane and his forward-firing gun for someone else to prove the worth of the marriage of his two brain-children.

The 'someone else' was an Air Service pilot named Oswald Boelcke, who was delighted with the performance of the monoplane, and his enthusiasm for the fixed machine-gun was unbounded when he shot down an enemy two-seater.

'They say that his newer monoplane is even faster,' Leutnant Koch commented to Stein as they walked into the mess at Templeuve. 'So you were stationed here as an observer, eh? Are you glad to be back?'

'As a pilot, yes,' Stein replied. 'I can't wait to fly my first patrol.'

'There are only two of us, of course, flying the single-seaters. We have the whole sector to ourselves. Which gives us plenty of meat. I've already shot down two British reconnaissance machines. You've been taught the special manœuvre, of course?'

'Oh yes,' Stein said, resolving to equal Koch's score within a week. 'Surprise! That's the watchword, eh?'

'And secrecy. Under no circumstances do we fly over the front lines. We mustn't risk the mechanism falling into enemy hands.'


The wind had veered to the south and Corporal Jones was lending a hand to adjust the canvas landing-T when he spotted the tell-tale trail of smoke.

'Fire picket! Fire picket!'

At the sound of the urgent clanging on the swinging shell case, Triggers tore out of the Flight Office on to the field. The BE2, black smoke pouring from the engine, was just clearing the trees beyond Monsieur Flemmard's orchard. It was Gaylion's machine.

'I don't know what the hell happened,' Charles shouted through the billowing black clouds as he scrambled out of the cockpit. 'I heard a burst of machine-gun fire, but when I looked around I couldn't see — '

'Never mind that now,' Triggers cried, grabbing Charles's arm and hauling him away to a safe distance. The damned young fool seemed totally unconcerned. Had he no imagination at all? Had he never gazed into the flames of a fire and seen his flesh roasting there? 'You saw nothing at all?' he asked, when Charles had drunk the brandy and the horrors of what might have been had passed. Triggers had suspected that Charles's apparent calm and talk of an 'invisible enemy' were the manifestations of a frozen panic that the young man did not care to recognise. But Charles's bewilderment at the puzzling circumstances of the attack were genuine enough. He had heard a burst of machine-gun fire and turned immediately to starboard. When he had looked around, there was nothing to be seen. 'You were flying above cloud, you say?'

'Yes. So he must have dived into it.'

The obvious answer. But it still left both men puzzled as to the speed and surprise of the attack. For Charles to have seen nothing of the enemy machine either before or after the burst of machine-gun fire ...

'If I'd had an observer, he might have spotted whatever it was,' Charles grumbled. They had been awaiting the replacement observer for more than a week now. 'No idea when he'll be here, I suppose?'

'We've lost two machines in the last nine days,' Triggers murmured, looking thoughtfully into his brandy. 'And "A" Flight lost a machine on the long reconnaissance yesterday.'

During the following week, two more machines went missing in unreported circumstances, and on the Saturday morning, just before lunch, Triggers called his Flight together for one of his 'little chats'.

'In the last three or four weeks we've had rather more casualties than usual. Now I know that if you'd seen anything out of the ordinary you'd have included it in your Flight reports. However, it mightn't do any harm to have a little ponder on anything we might have omitted from our reports. Anything that might have seemed unimportant at the time. Well?'

There was a long silence. Everyone looked bewildered. Why was Triggers making such a mystery out of it? They all knew that their machines were to blame. The increase in casualties was not confined to Ste Marie; all Squadrons flying BE2s were suffering the same fate. The damned things were probably all falling apart.

'To be fair,' Triggers snapped, 'the BE2 is slow, clumsy and useless, but at least it is sturdy. Like a cart-horse. Sergeant Farmer? Any thoughts at all?'

'There are some new Archies that can reach about a thousand feet higher than the old ones, but I shouldn't think they'd account for the increase.'

'Mr Gaylion?'

'No, sir. I'm afraid I can't think of anything unusual. Except . . .'

'Yes?'

'I saw a Froggie I didn't expect, that's all. About fifteen minutes before that burst of machine-gun fire got me.'

Triggers looked annoyed. Why hadn't Charles mentioned it at the time? Was he sure it was a French machine? Had he seen the French roundels?

'No, it was too far away. Could have been French or one of ours. But it was quite definitely a Morane. I mean you can't mistake them, can you? A monoplane.'

That afternoon, Charles's new observer arrived. Corporal Jones was whistling his way back to the hangar after lunch when the dark-green Talbot sports swept through the entrance, the driver ignoring the saluting guard and honk-honking to attract the startled Jones's attention.

'You, Corporal,' the driver said, giving Jones an authoritative tap on the shoulder with his cane. 'Give my windscreen a wipe, will you? And later on, you can give her a wash down.'

Sergeant Mills leapt to his feet as the aristocratic

figure sauntered imperiously into the Flight Office, announcing himself as Lieutenant Conrad, and proceeding to hang his expensive-looking leather topcoat on the peg normally reserved for Captain Triggers' flying coat. He wore a brand new beautifully cut uniform, but what really took Sergeant Mills's eye was the row of medal ribbons, starting with the unmistakable purple of the Victoria Cross.

'Where is Captain Triggers?'

'He's flying this afternoon, sir.'

'But surely he was expecting me? Where is the mess?'

Mills opened the door and Conrad peered through to the lounge with the expression of a man being introduced for the very first time to a pigsty. 'Tell Captain Triggers he'll find me in my billet, would you?'

'You're sharing a room with Mr Bravington, sir.'

'That's quite impossible. I share my rooms with no one. In any case, I have already made my own arrangements.'

Triggers' engine failed soon after take-off and he sniffed at the back of the door as if Conrad's leather topcoat was to blame. 'Tell him I want to see him right away,' he barked at Mills, dropping Conrad's coat on the floor and hanging his own flying coat on the peg.

'You know how it is,' Conrad explained, when Triggers asked him why he'd decided to transfer to the RFC. 'One wants to fight. And this damned war, the cavalry just aren't getting a chance. So I pulled a few strings – my uncle is a full General – and I dropped quite a bit of rank, and here I am. The fact that I used to be a lieutenant-colonel, and – and this,' he swung his cane lazily, its point tapping his left breast, indicating the VC ribbon, 'I don't want *this* to make any difference.'

'It won't,' Triggers promised, with a thin smile.

'I was lucky, of course,' Conrad went on. 'I had the

chance to serve in a proper war. South Africa. But it seemed to me, things being what they are, the RFC was the next best thing to the cavalry. Oh. I've arranged my billet. The Château de Coutinard. Just down the road. The Marquis is a friend of the family.'

'Really!' Triggers took an extraordinary interest in some ridiculous memo concerning the laundering of mechanics' overalls and wondered about the reaction of the other members of 'C' Flight to this arrogant, over-bearing cavalry officer. But there it was, they were stuck with the man, and it was up to Triggers as Flight Commander to make Conrad fit in. And however much Triggers disliked the coldly disdainful smile, the imperious swagger, the conceited indifference in the shrug of the shoulders, there was one compensating quality in the man. Triggers had recognised it the moment he had walked into the office. And the purple ribbon, of course, confirmed it. Lieutenant Peter Conrad was absolutely fearless.

'I haven't time to send out messengers to the Château every time you're to fly. You'll be billeted here in the barn with the rest of "C" Flight. I've arranged for you to share a room with Mr Bravington. Is that your car just this side of the hedge?'

'Yes. I had it brought over.'

'Move it. If an aeroplane overshoots a bit, that's where they usually finish up.'

'Yes, of course. It wouldn't do the car much good, having an aeroplane land on it.'

'It's not the car I'm thinking about.'

Conrad's eyes were coldly piercing. 'Are you to be my pilot?'

'No. You're to fly with Mr Gaylion.' Then Triggers had a brainwave. 'That is, you *were* to fly with Mr Gaylion. But I've put Mr Bravington with him. Let's see now, who else have we got? As you've no experience . . .'

'No experience? I've had a damned sight more experience than any pilot you've got.'

'Military experience, may be. But horses don't count. For one thing, they don't catch fire.' Triggers wished he hadn't said that. It sounded so damned silly. But Conrad was getting his goat. 'You'll fly with Sergeant Farmer.'

Conrad looked as if the roof had fallen in. 'Fly with a sergeant?'

'Sergeant Farmer should be able to teach you what you need to know.' And by the same token, Triggers reflected, this lordly, ice-cold aristocrat would freeze Farmer into a more fitting awareness of the gulf between NCOs and commissioned officers. 'And before you go, Mr Conrad – don't forget your coat.'

Conrad picked it up from the floor. 'Captain Triggers,' he said, with dangerous politeness. He gave a knife-like salute and swept out of the office, leaving Triggers to curse himself for revealing his dislike for the man. It was a sign of weakness in a Flight Commander. From now on, Conrad would have no confidence in him. Damn the man! *And* his breeding! *And* his bloody VC!


'I thought you'd broken off with her,' Charles said, as Alan wiped the jam from the photograph of Lorna. The jar had broken and everything in the parcel was covered in jam, including the back number of *Flight*. 'So why has she sent you her photograph?'

'She hasn't. My mother sent it.'

'Ah! So your mother's on *her* side, is she?'

'It's not a matter of taking sides,' Alan said truculently. 'It's all off, and that's that. My mother doesn't understand, that's all. I thought I was – well – fond of Lorna. But I was wrong. It's as simple as that.'

'So she's a nurse now, eh?' Charles took the photograph and looked at it. 'Gosh! She looks more whole-some than ever in all that white.'

'It's a big house about five miles from the farm. Been turned into a hospital. She goes there three nights a week.' He changed the subject. Why was Charles there? What was all this mystery about the new chap, anyway?

'Oh, no mystery.' Charles shook his head and chuckled at Alan's bewilderment. 'Triggers has done me a jolly good turn, that's all.' He drew his finger along the little sticky sea of jam on the front page of *Flight* and sucked it approvingly. 'Here, did your mother make this? Jolly good. Ask her to send me a jar, will you? As for the new chap, Peter Conrad. You're flying with him tomorrow.'

Richard Bravington stamped around in the early-morn-ing mist looking for Corporal Jones, but he was told by a chirpy 2nd AM that the knocking sound had already been seen to. No, the engine spares still hadn't arrived but Corporal Jones had performed a minor miracle with a piece of old tin.

'Good God, my lucky day!' Bravington complained to Alan. 'Flying with Mr Gaylion and a cocoa tin.'

Alan had been due to take off fifteen minutes earlier, but there was still no sign of his new observer.

'Why the hell Triggers keeps on swapping us around is quite beyond me,' Bravington said, unaware of the imperious figure striding out of the mist. 'I pity you. Fly-ing with the new idiot.'

Alan gave him a warning look. But too late.

'Good morning,' Conrad said, with careful bonhomie. And as Bravington turned to him in wide-eyed surprise, he added: 'I'm the new idiot. Peter Conrad.'

'Oh, look here. I'm terribly sorry. I didn't mean . . .'

'I gather Charles Gaylion was originally detailed to fly with me. But Captain Triggers, for some obscure reason, changed his mind and decided that I should fly with a sergeant as my second-in-command.'

Bravington laughed. Alan knew better. Conrad was obviously quite serious.

'Second-in-command?' Bravington's laughter trailed away under Conrad's icy gaze. 'There's only two of us in a machine, you know. Anyway, whatever his rank, the pilot is considered to be the captain, as it were . . .' At that moment, something impelled him to look down at Conrad's feet. God, he couldn't believe it. Surely the morning mist was playing tricks with his eyesight? Conrad was wearing spurs. 'Oh. May I – er – introduce you to your pilot? Mr Conrad. Sergeant Farmer.'

'How d'you do, sir.'

Conrad made no reply. His eyes were fixed disapprovingly on Alan's scarf – the brightly coloured scarf that Lorna had knitted for him. 'There were two men back there,' he said. 'In the hangar, I believe you call it. They were not wearing their caps. I took their names. Lo and behold, I went along to the Flight Office to inform the sergeant, but was unable to find him.'

'It is rather early in the day,' Bravington said. 'Sergeant Mills doesn't need to be there until a bit later on.'

'If the flying personnel commence their duties at dawn, then in my opinion the Flight Office staff should do the same,' Conrad said sharply. And then, as if to point a finger at the root of the inefficiency: 'Captain Triggers was in the Royal Engineers, I believe.'

His tone was intentionally provoking, and Bravington responded. 'That's right. Where they judge a man by his expertise, not by the cut of his breeches.' And having got himself going, he went on to praise his Flight Commander in quite unaccustomed, and rather maudlin, sentiments. 'He's the best Flight Commander in the Corps. And we'd all willingly die for him.'

But it was all water off a duck's back. Conrad was glancing airily around as if he hadn't heard. 'Where is my mount?'

When Bravington had walked away in disgust, Alan led Conrad over to their machine. He was about to climb into the cockpit when Conrad tapped him reprovingly on the shoulder.

'Give me a leg up, sergeant.'

Alan gaped, and for the very first time Conrad looked him straight in the eye. 'You don't know how, eh? But of course, you weren't in the cavalry, were you? Cup your hands – like this – so that I can put my foot in.'

And that was just the beginning of Alan's humiliation. The moment their machine was airborne, Conrad stretched out his left arm, an imperious finger pointing towards the front lines. A few minutes later, he made a similar signal with his right arm and held up his hand like a traffic policeman when he wanted Alan to pull out of the turn. Crossing the front lines they ran into some Archie fire and when Alan began his evasive 'essing', Conrad glared sternly back at him, and bawled: 'Fly straight and level, damn you!'

'We could have been blown out of the sky,' Alan complained bitterly to Sergeant Mills as they walked to the mess for lunch. 'And he just sat there, cool as a cucumber.'

'The funny part of it is,' Sergeant Mills laughed, 'the purpose of the trip was for you to show him the sector.'

'The pilot is the captain of the machine,' Alan said, hotly. 'Everyone understands that.'

'Everyone except Mr Conrad, you mean. Here, that rifle he's got. It's a Mannlicher, you know. The finest hunting rifle in the world.'

'Trust him to be different to everyone else,' Alan grumbled. 'A Winchester is beneath him, I suppose?'

'And you'll have some competition,' Mills grinned. 'As the best shot on the Squadron, I mean. In the mess last night, Mr Conrad told them all he was the best shot in the whole of the cavalry.'

And two days later, Conrad appeared to prove it. On the way home from an artillery shoot, he pointed out something in the far distance. Alan could see nothing, but Conrad ordered him to turn and picked up his Mannlicher. For several minutes, Alan bewilderedly searched the skies in the direction in which Conrad was looking so intently. Once again, Conrad ordered him to turn, held up his hand in the now familiar 'stop turning' signal, and reached for his Mannlicher. He pushed up his goggles and took careful aim, his lips pursed in a soundless whistle. Alan spotted the machine just before Conrad fired. A second later it dived into the cloud.

'He reckons he almost got the pilot in the head,' Alan said, when Triggers, his curiosity aroused by Conrad's description of the 'enemy machine', called Alan into the Flight Officer for his version of the encounter. 'And I wouldn't argue with that, sir. He must have put the wind up the Hun because he immediately dived into the cloud for cover.'

'Mr Conrad says the machine was a monoplane.'

'Yes, sir.' Alan left it at that. Although he'd seen no more than a glimpse of it, he was sure the machine was a Morane, and that Conrad, with his limited experience, had mistaken it for an enemy machine.

'Mr Conrad says the machine turned, that he saw the crosses on the wings, and that's when he decided to fire.'

'Well, sir, I can only say that if there were German crosses and Mr Conrad saw them, then he's got very unusual eyesight.'

'Which of you spotted the machine first?'

'Mr Conrad, sir.'

'And when did you see it?'

'Several minutes later, sir. Just before Mr Conrad fired.'

'Then perhaps Mr Conrad *does* have unusually good eyesight?'

Alan couldn't resist the challenge. 'She was a Morane, sir.'

'You're sure of that?'

'Yes, sir. I mean, there's no other machine looks like a Morane, is there?'

An hour later, Charles and Richard Bravington supported Alan's opinion of the identity of the 'mystery machine'. They had been on photography reconnaissance and had seen 'the Morane' five or six miles from where Conrad and Alan had sighted it.

'A Morane right enough, and we can prove it,' Richard Bravington chirped as he took the heavy camera from its mounting on the side of the cockpit. 'The secret revealed for all eyes. What the butler saw – from six thousand feet.'

When the plate had been developed and Sergeant Mills was told it was on its way, Triggers sent once again for all concerned in the argument. Charles was quite adamant.

'I can't be sure it was the same Morane I saw on the day I was attacked and caught fire, of course. But it was definitely a Morane. Richard can vouch for it.'

'Oh yes, it was a Morane right enough,' Richard Bravington said. 'No doubt about that.'

'Did you see its markings?' Conrad asked. No, they hadn't. They weren't close enough. 'Well, *I* saw them. And quite distinctly. They were German crosses.'

Alan, Charles and Bravington exchanged sidelong glances. There was no point in continuing the argument. The plate would prove them right.

'Sergeant Mills has been making enquiries,' Triggers said. Despite his intense dislike of Conrad, Triggers was now reluctantly inclined to believe that the man's eyesight was quite as remarkable as his shooting. 'The French say they have no Moranes flying in this sector.'

This was a bit of a bombshell. Conrad gave a little smile of cold triumph. 'What did I tell you?'

'Then it must be one of *our* Moranes,' Charles said defensively. 'Because it *was* a Morane.'

'It could be a captured Morane that the Hun's put into service,' Triggers said, going to the window. Yes, it was the cyclist who had been sent to collect the developed plate. 'Then it would have crosses, of course. So you could *all* be right. Anyway, we'll know in a moment.'

Mills answered the tap on the door and came back into the room with the hasty importance of a head waiter bringing a very special dish. Triggers examined it first. Then Conrad, who 'humphed' and passed it to Charles. Alan and Bravington joined Charles as he held it up to the light. It *could* have been an aeroplane. It could just as easily have been a bird. Alan was sure it was a mark on the plate.

'Lord!' Charles snorted. 'So much for aerial photography.'

Talking 'shop' was taboo in the officers' mess, but nevertheless the argument continued until late that evening, when Conrad, incensed by accusations of his lack of knowledge of the various types of machines, ordered a nervous orderly to find the missing poster on pain of death.

'I knew I'd seen it somewhere,' Charles said, sliding the board from between two irate draughts-players. 'If you chaps will excuse me. Our game over there is more bitterly contested.'

The poster showed diagrams of Allied and German

machines for identification purposes. The Morane was there, and Conrad was convinced that it was not the machine he had fired upon. 'The tail thing's different. The nose is different. The whole damn thing's different.'

Several whiskies later, when the blurred diagrams had been returned to the draughts-players and the drowsy combatants had joined forces in condemning some idiotic French pilot who was obviously the cause of all the trouble, the orderly hurried up to the table to inform Triggers that Sergeant Farmer wished to speak to him. Tired and pleasurably drunk, Triggers waved the orderly away.

'Tell him I'll see him in the morning. Infinitely pref'r-able to seeing two of him this evening.'

'He says the matter is most urgent, sir.'

In the ante-room Alan was flushed with the excitement of his discovery. 'It's a copy of *Flight*, sir.'

'Yes, I can see that,' Triggers replied, irritably. 'This, I mean? All this sticky red stuff. Raspberry jam?' He handed it back to Alan. 'Thanks, but I've already eaten.'

'There's an article I'm sure you'll be interested to read, sir.'

'I'm not seeing awfully well.' He swallowed the remains of his whisky. 'You read it.'

Alan cleared his throat and read aloud to the swaying figure. 'Firing with a machine-gun between the blades of a propeller revolving at something like 1200 rpm strikes one as a very tricky, not to say risky pastime, but I have it on good authority that it is the latest exploit of Roland Garros, the famous French pilot, and resulted in bringing down two Taubes. According to — '

'Just a minute. What's the date of that magazine?'

'March the twenty-eighth. It was one I hadn't got. I asked my mother to order it for me and she sent it in the parcel.' He went on reading. 'According to a patent specification in a German paper, an inventive genius over there has a device enabling a machine-gun to be fired through the disc arc of the propeller by gearing the trigger of the quick firer to the engine, so that when a propeller blade is in line with the gun a lock prevents the shot being fired until the blade has passed out of the line of fire.'

Alan looked up from the magazine. Triggers had stopped swaying. In fact, Alan had never seen this extraordinarily restless man standing quite so still.

'So the Germans have invented a way of arming their aeroplanes that makes everything we're doing a waste of time.' Triggers went on looking at Alan for a time, then his eyes went down to the empty whisky glass in his hand. His fingers tightened around it. 'I tell my men to manœuvre their machines so that the Germans are kept flying directly towards them. Do that, and you're safe, I say. But what I'm really telling them is to use all their skills to get their aeroplanes into the one position where they are defenceless. The one position in which the Germans are lethal.' The glass in Triggers' hand suddenly shattered. He watched the blood trickling down his fingers. 'And how do I learn that every day I'm sending my men out to be murdered? From a document labelled "most urgent", sent to all Squadrons? No! From a copy of a magazine, bloody months old, and covered in jam.'

When Alan followed Lieutenant Conrad into the Flight Office, Triggers was loading his Webley revolver.

'I'm not ordering you,' Triggers said. 'But if you volunteer, you'll do exactly as I say. I believe the Germans are using a synchronised machine-gun in this sector.' He looked at Conrad. 'I believe you're right. It wasn't a Morane you saw. It was a German monoplane. Equipped with this gun. Anyway, I need proof, one way or the other. I'm going to fly over the airfield at Templeuve to see if I can provoke the enemy to attack me. I want you to keep your distance and watch. That's all. Your job is simply to fly back here and report on what you see.'

'I understand, sir.' Alan came to attention. 'I'd like to volunteer, sir.'

Triggers looked at Conrad, who appeared to be totally bored with the whole business. 'Naturally,' he said.

'Whatever happens, you will *not* intervene. I've a strong feeling the enemy will sheer off the moment he sees another Allied aeroplane. They're playing safe with this invention of theirs and won't risk being shot down and letting it fall into our hands. Mr Conrad, I'm asking you, not because of your VC, but despite it. I want you for your eyesight.' He looked at Alan. 'And I'm asking you, Farmer, because I can trust you to be sensible. We've already got enough heroes on that casualty list.'

Leutnant Stein had flown the dawn patrol and was eating a hasty breakfast when the 'possible enemy' was sighted. As he climbed into his Fokker E I, the enemy machine had turned away and was heading north. Stein took off and fired five rounds from his forward-firing Parabellum. He didn't want this early-morning 'gift' to slip through his fingers because of a jammed gun. Climbing west, he entered the layer of cloud, and turned to starboard. The enemy was now about two thousand yards ahead of him. Concealed in the cloud layer, Stein drew closer, noting the roundels. A British machine. He recognised the type. A reconnaissance machine, slow, and with a poor rate of climb. An easier prey than most. As it turned eastwards, circling the German airfield and making no attempt to conceal itself, Stein was curious about its purpose. Then he saw the empty cockpit. The two-seater had no observer. No defence against attack. The pilot must have lost his way. It was the only possible answer. No pilot in his right mind – no, not even a *British* pilot – would risk flying alone and unarmed so close to an enemy airfield. Stein was momentarily amused at the thought of the unsuspecting pilot approaching to land and suddenly finding himself in a hail of ground-fire. Then it crossed his mind that some lucky ground gunner might cheat him out of his 'kill', and the smile left his face. He pushed his Eindekker into a steep dive.

'There she goes!' Alan cried involuntarily as the monoplane swept down from the cloud. Conrad nodded. He had sighted the monoplane a full second before Alan had called out. They watched it pull out of the dive and fly on, straight and level, behind Triggers' BE2, and about five hundred feet below it.

In the light of the monoplane being able to fire forward, the German pilot's method of attack was all too plain, and Alan feared his Flight Commander would be taken completely by surprise. Triggers must have been aware that his plan had worked. He must have seen the monoplane taking off from Templeuve. But had he seen it diving into his 'blind spot'? Was he aware that the enemy was now preparing to swoop up and fire into the belly of his machine? There was nothing Alan could do to warn him. Hadn't Triggers ordered him not to interfere? He looked anxiously at Conrad, hoping for some sign, a gesture or a nod of the head, that would send him flying to their Flight Commander's aid. But Conrad made no such move. He just looked on, impassively. Alan knew that Conrad expected his own orders to be obeyed, precisely and without question, and he would *obey* his Flight Commander's orders in a like manner. He would sit there and watch Triggers being shot down, suffering no guilt, or even the slightest misgiving. Triggers had ordered him not to interfere. And that was that.

Triggers' eyes scanned the dark clouds above him, awaiting the appearance of the monoplane. He had seen it taking off from Templeuve and climbing into the cloud, and any moment now it would be diving into its 'surprise' attack. He would turn away, and as soon as he had shaken the enemy off, climb into the cover of the cloud and head for home. He wanted no more than a taste of what it was like to be on the wrong end of that forward-firing gun. Just enough for Conrad and Farmer to witness it in action. Not that it would help them to cope with it in the future; of that he was sure. But at least they'd have 'seen' what they were up against, and they'd have some idea, at least, of the monoplane's speed and method of attack.

Stein squinted along the fixed Parabellum towards the ring-sight over the engine cowling. He eased the stick back, and as the underside of the British machine flashed into view, he pressed the trigger.

The clatter of the burst took Triggers completely by surprise. Not knowing the direction of the unseen attacker, he was unprepared for the corresponding 'turn away'. He had been expecting the attack to come from above and in the second's delay before he pushed into the diving turn, he 'felt' the bullets ripping into the fabric behind him. As he pulled out of the dive, he saw the enemy above and behind, and turning after him. Blast! He had lost a lot more height in the dive so there was no hope now of climbing into the cloud and heading for home as he had planned. By the time his poor old BE2 made the climb this frisky-looking monoplane with its deadly gun would shoot him down ten times over.

Stein pushed into a dive, manœuvring his machine until the swaying nose pointed towards the BE2. As he fired, the BE2 turned steeply to port. Stein turned after him, and as the two machines levelled out, the Eindekker gaining on the BE2, Stein prepared to fire once again. From a much closer range this time, Stein decided; indeed, so close it would be impossible to miss. He manœuvred the nose of his machine with its fixed gun on to its target. His right hand reached to the butt of the Parabellum, the finger curling around the trigger and applying the steady preliminary pressure; the overture to the deadly squeeze that would surely end the life of the poor gallant Englishman already performing – or so it seemed – the dance of death before the jerking ringsight. Then a bullet whined between Stein's hand and head, nicking the rim of the cockpit.

'It was an absolutely splendid shot, sir,' Alan said to Conrad when they had landed. It had done the trick, Conrad replied, quite calmly. The Hun, obviously suspecting a trap, had gone haring for home. Alan wondered what Triggers' reaction would be as they watched him striding over. 'You were right enough, sir. A machine-gun firing through the propeller arc.'

'Mounted just to the right of centre,' Conrad added, tucking his Mannlicher under his arm.

'I told you not to interfere,' Triggers raged. 'Doesn't *anyone* in this Flight know how to obey an order?'

# 6

Harry had pumped the fire to a glowing red and Tom placed the cobnut on the front bar of the hearth. 'Right! Off you go! Say it!'

'I've said it once.' Lorna glanced uncertainly at the

two men. Were they pulling her leg, or what? 'It's made up, isn't it?'

'Not at all,' Tom said. 'It's truth! But you have to say it after the nut is placed. It doesn't work else.' Lorna laughed. It was just foolish country superstition. How could a cobnut know what was in Alan's mind? 'Go on, girl,' Tom urged. 'Say it!'

'If he loves me, pop and fly . . . if he doesn't, shrivel and die.'

They watched and waited. Lorna giggled. 'The looks on our faces. You'd think it was a matter of life and death with that old nut.'

There was a sharp crack. A piece of the flying nutshell stung Harry's cheek. 'A dangerous game, this,' he growled.

'You see, girl?' And there was a glow in Tom's old eyes that put the fire to shame. 'You've nothing at all to worry over.'

'They *all* pop and fly, don't they?'

'Not a bit of it. Most of 'em shrivel and die. We'll try another and you'll see.' He pulled aside his long leather apron to fish another nut from his trouser pocket. 'We'll try one for Harry. No doubt he's got a secret lady love tucked away somewhere.'

Lorna saw the fleeting concern on Harry's face before he turned away to pick up the urn. 'I've put a new handle on for you,' Harry said. 'I'll put it on the cart.'

'I can manage, thank you.'

Harry grimaced at the weight of the urn. 'Heavy enough without the milk in. How you manage the full ones is beyond me. Alan will have the strongest wife in Sussex, if not the prettiest.'

'He doesn't understand how it is,' Lorna said ruefully, when Harry had gone out. 'Why Alan broke it off, I mean.'

'Do you understand it then?' Tom asked, fitting a shoe-length of iron in the tongs.

'Yes. I do now. I thought he was afraid he might be killed. That I might be hurt. And somehow, by breaking it off, he'd save me from that. That's what I wanted to believe, I suppose. The truth is – as he said – we didn't have long enough to get to know each other before he joined up.'

'Not long enough? You've known each other since you were two foot high. Why, I remember Alan coming home from Lovell's Road School – and he'd not been there long, so he must have been a young 'un – his face covered in bruises. Ted Allsop was pulling Lorna's hair, he said, so I gave him what for.'

Lorna smiled at the memory. She had not learned about the incident until she was much older. Alan had never mentioned that he'd fought on her behalf.

'He's "over there", remember,' Tom said. 'And thinking differently about things. But the war has to end sometime. And he'll be thinking different again when he gets home.'

'He'll be changed though.'

'He may *think* he has for a while.' Tom gave her a reassuring smile. 'The Flying Corps. Mixing with the sons of gentry. He'll soon forget all that. Look at Harry. Eighteen years travelling about the world. Who'd have thought he would end up back in Becket's Hill? But here he is. And here he'll stay. Because he knows it's his rightful place.'

Lorna was curious. 'What you said about him having a secret lady love somewhere . . .'

Tom chuckled. 'Harry? No, not Harry. Joking I was, that's all. A man's better off on his own. Harry's always said that. Ever since he was a youngster. And he'll stick to it.'

Molly was looking her worst when Arthur Rudkin rapped on the door of the steam-filled washhouse. He was wearing his best suit and carrying a frail. 'I was in the garden yesterday evening,' he said. And with a diffident smile, he presented the lettuce. 'It's not a big one. I know there's only you in the house.'

Flustered, Molly took the lettuce, wiped back her bedraggled hair, and pushed the soaped pair of pink drawers down the washboard into the suds. She was sure he was going to ask her to go to the Electric Theatre and she'd already refused three times. She'd run out of excuses.

'There's carrots as well. And anything else you'd like. My mother and I can't eat it all. A shame it going to waste.'

'Thank you. Our garden's gone to pot since my Will died. Ashamed of it, really.'

'I wondered if you'd like to go — '

'I shall be ironing tonight, I'm sorry — '

'Oh, I didn't mean tonight. No, I meant Saturday. If the weather is kind enough, that is. A picnic.'

'Oh. A picnic?' What on earth could she say to that? She'd just wasted one excuse by being too quick off the mark. 'On Saturday afternoon, you say? What about the shop?'

'My mother will look after the shop.'

'Oh.' She heard Harry calling for her. Thank the Lord! 'Yes, what is it?'

Harry pushed the door wide open. 'Smithy coal is here. Shall I take the money from the tin?'

'Yes, please, Harry.'

He was staring at the lettuce, so she held it up, proudly, as if it might have been a bouquet. 'Mr Rudkin brought it from his garden.'

Concealed from Harry's view behind the opened door,

Arthur Rudkin now stepped toward the bubbling boiler; he didn't want Harry to think he was hiding deliberately. 'It's a nice day again,' he said. 'If you and Tom would like a lettuce, there's plenty there.'

'I told him our garden's gone to pot,' Molly said. She suddenly saw the answer to 'the problem'. 'What d'you think, Harry? Mr Rudkin wondered if we'd like to go for a picnic on Saturday.'

The clouds were as dark as slate by the time they reached the stile to Collins's field. Arthur Rudkin's mother, who had an eye for the weather, had assured them it would not rain. Harry had kept his mouth shut; though any fool could have seen it coming long before they had left the house.

'You're very quiet, Harry?' Molly said, as Arthur Rudkin helped her over the stile.

'Not a lot to talk about,' Harry mumbled, ignoring Rudkin's hand, *and* his offer to carry the basket. The damned man would keep drawing attention to his one arm, and carrying on like some bigwig from London with his brilliantined hair, his know-all chit-chat and the buttonhole from his garden. And Molly, the silly woman, tripping about like a schoolgirl and laughing like an actress. And in the hat Will had bought her a month before he was killed. Had she no sense of shame or propriety!

'Where should we sit then, Mr Rudkin?' Molly asked. She felt young and happy, and all the way down from the house she'd hardly heard a word Mr Rudkin had said. She'd been thinking of the picnic with Will, soon after they were married. If only she'd realised then how happy she'd been, instead of behaving like a spoilt child torn away from her prim little life in Lewes.

'In the middle of the field, I thought,' Arthur Rudkin

said, fanning a fly away from her neck with a gallant wave of his tweed cap. He had spent half the morning dithering between the cap and the boater, eventually deciding that the boater made him look quite handsome. 'Handsome, yes, and fickle,' his mother had declared. 'And as the poor woman has already lost one fickle husband in that flying machine contraption, she'll hardly be looking for another.' And so he had worn the cap. And oh, how he wished he had worn the boater. Molly was listening so intently to everything he said, and looking at him with such happy approval, the boater would surely have tipped the scales and swept her off her feet. 'It's very pleasant there in the middle of the field,' he said, waving an arm as if he owned half the county. 'And we'll have the sun when these clouds pass over.'

Walking at a distance behind them, Harry cast bleak prophetic glances up at the darkening clouds and down at the basket that he knew damned well would never be opened. They had hardly sat down when the storm broke.

'My God! A picnic?' Molly shrieked, as they ran, breathless and half-drowned, into the barn. 'A swim, more like.'

'Here, have my handkerchief to wipe your face,' Arthur Rudkin said. 'Well, well. It's coming down now.'

'Not going up, is it?' Harry said, inwardly cheering the downpour. It had put an end to the silly chit-chat anyway.

'Garden can do with it,' Rudkin said, watching Molly wipe her face and thinking he would treasure the handkerchief for evermore. 'Wet sandwich anyone?'

Molly looked horrified. 'Oh, they're not, are they?'

'No, no,' Rudkin laughed. 'A bit damp, that's all. Well. We can eat here, yes? I don't know about anyone else, but I'm ready for it.'

'Oh, look at my hat!' Molly cried concernedly. 'Will

gave me this. And my hair! What on earth do I look like?'

'You look fine,' Rudkin said quietly, as he loosened the straps of the basket.

Conscious of his unconcealed admiration, Molly, with a queenly air, throned herself on the bale of straw and demanded the basket be placed on her lap.

'Yes, madam,' Rudkin said.

Molly giggled. 'You sound as if you're in the shop.'

Embarrassed by the nonsense, Harry stared at the rain.

'I'm glad it rained now,' Molly said. There was cucumber and tomato, or chicken. Rudkin chose chicken. Harry chose cucumber and tomato. 'I haven't been down this way since Will died. Now what do *I* want, that's the thing? You know, I don't think I'm hungry.'

'Go on, you must eat,' Rudkin urged. 'The chicken's good.'

'Lorna brought it for me. She's ever so thoughtful, that girl. And sensible, too. A pity about her and Alan. Stubborn, he is. A bit of his father there. And they'd have made such a nice pair. So well suited.' She looked around the barn, as if the thought had just occurred to her. 'This is where they kept the aeroplane. Will and Conway Starke.'

'Yes, I brought my mother to see it one evening. Alan was sitting at the controls and wishing he was old enough to fly it.'

'Hours Alan spent down here when Will was tinkering with the engine. You're quiet again, Harry.'

'Listening to the rain,' Harry said, hoping it wouldn't stop. Rudkin was shivering a bit, and as he didn't look too strong, he might end up with pneumonia.

'He needs a good hot cup of tea,' Lorna said. She had seen them from the house and had run down with a piece of sacking over her head. 'I've got the big kettle

on for the men. I'll fetch some down in the billy-can.'
Molly insisted on giving her a hand. 'Right then! Under
you come!'

And they ran off into the rain, laughing like children
under the cover of the sacking.

'Chicken or tomato and cucumber?' Rudkin asked,
rummaging in the basket and wondering how to phrase
it. 'It must be hard for her. Her husband killed flying an
aeroplane. And now her son flying them over there. No
one could ever take his place, o' course. Your brother
Will's place, I mean. But I expect you've guessed that
I'm fond of her. When she first came to live in Becket's
Hill, all those years ago, I – well – even then I used to
think what a fine woman she was. I've got the shop. So
she'd be comfortable. I mean, when Alan comes home,
after it's all over, he'll want to live there with Lorna
Collins, won't he?'

'Not the way he's thinking at the moment. And he'd
hardly put his mother into the street, whatever.'

They ate for a time in uneasy silence.

'If I did get around to asking her to marry me,' Rudkin
said at last, 'I suppose you'd have no objection?'

Harry shrugged. What his sister-in-law did was no
business of his. Rudkin considered very carefully before
he went on. 'It's very strange. When a man becomes fond
of a woman, as I've become of Mrs Farmer – well – he
can tell when there's another man in the wind, as it
were.'

Harry turned away. 'It's slacking off,' he said.

'I am right, aren't I?'

Harry made no reply. Rudkin smiled and nodded.
'Was that why Harry had left Becket's Hill all those
years ago?'

'No, it was not,' Harry said, stiffly. 'Four men working
in the smithy, including my brother Will and myself.

Then Molly into the house as Will's wife. Five mouths to feed. Will and I went into the smithy to work with no breakfast in our stomachs many a day. Someone had to go. So. Off I went to the Army. Anyway. I wanted to see something of the world.'

'Strange, isn't it?' Rudkin said. 'As my mother says, she's no great beauty. Yet here we are. The two of us.'

He joined Harry at the door and they stood there watching the rain. 'The garden's in need of it, anyway.'

'You'll have some trouble digging with one arm, so I gave it a bit of thought.' Tom put down the hammer and plunged the spade into the bosh to cool it off. He had shortened the handle and inserted an iron crosspiece just above the head of the spade. 'You pushes your foot down in the normal way, then catches it under the crosspiece to lift the spade up to turn the earth.' He wiped the sweat from his brow in the towel hanging on the string over the forge hearth. 'And I'd sooner you than me. That garden hasn't been touched for years.'

On her way to the washing-line with the basket, Molly was surprised to find the heap of weeds. 'Well! I never knew you were a gardener, Harry.'

'Neither did I. But I thought it was time someone tidied it up for you.'

'Will used to have it looking nice. We hardly ever bought a vegetable.'

'That's what I thought. With money so tight, you should be growing your own.'

He hurried over to help her haul up the laden washing-line. Their hands touched as he handed her the rope to tie it off.

'You put this pulley up for me,' she said. 'All them years ago, and still working. D'you remember?'

'Just about.'

'Mr Rudkin won't like you growing vegetables. He'll have no excuse for calling here.'

Harry looked as if the thought had never entered his mind, and Molly took the empty basket into the house. A few minutes later, she came hurrying across the yard with a garden fork.

'I borrowed it from Tom. And it'll be a change from sitting in that kitchen knitting khaki gloves.'

When it had become too dark to carry on and Harry had cleaned the earth from the spade, he rapped on the open kitchen door to call 'goodnight'.

'Not quite,' she said. 'I've made a pot of tea. And there's something I want to ask you.'

Wondering what it could be, Harry sat on the step and unlaced his boots. Molly laughed. No need to take them off, earth on them or not. 'A different tale at one time,' Harry said. 'The place being scrubbed and polished till I hardly recognised it, and Will and I having firm instructions to take our boots off at the door, or else.'

'Yes, I must have been a devil to live with in those early days,' she said. 'How Will put up with me, I don't know, I'm sure. Now. What I wanted to ask you.' She had glanced at the empty left sleeve of his jacket. 'You've never told me how it happened.' She had never brought the subject up before this, sensing that Harry did not want to discuss it. However, something she had found on the previous day had made her curious.

'How did you know about that?' Harry asked, when she mentioned the medal.

'It was in the pocket of your best suit. I'm sorry, but I had to clear out the pockets to clean and press it.'

'Oh. So that was you. I thought it was Tom's Alice.'

'I couldn't help noticing in church. How shabby it was looking. So I asked Tom to fetch it over. Well? How did you win the medal then?'

'I didn't win it. Enough of my lot got killed, I suppose, so they gave me the DCM.' That was the end of that. But Molly wanted to know what happened. 'We were retreating. We did a lot of retreating in those early days. An artillery battery. We'd stopped to lend them a hand. In the artillery, the main thing is saving the guns. A shell had killed some of the horses. Some of the men. The gun was blown on its side. Sliding down into a ditch. We tried to hold it. I put my arm through one of the wheels. The gun slipped into the ditch.'

Molly was glad she hadn't lit the lamp. She could feel the memory of the pain in him; she had no wish to see it in his eyes. She poured the tea, and they drank it in silence, Harry glancing anxiously at the clock when at last the lamp was lit.

'I'd best be going,' he said. 'Tom's Alice locks up soon after ten o'clock.'

'You can knock, can't you?'

He shrugged and stood there, awkwardly, in the doorway. Then she realised what was concerning him.

'Wagging tongues, is that it—' She laughed. 'What nonsense! I mean to say – you *are* family, aren't you? Will's brother!' Indeed, he could have been Will himself, Molly considered, when Harry had gone; chalk and cheese when they were young, and yet, out there in the garden that evening, it might have been Will digging beside her. It was odd that she had never noticed before how like her late husband Harry had become.

The following evening, she was dusting the books in Alan's room when she heard Harry whistling his way across the yard. 'Gardening must suit you,' she called from the window. 'I've never heard you whistling before now.'

'You might close that window. I thought of burning those weeds.'

'Oh, a bonfire. That'll be nice. I'll make some tea and we can sit and watch the smoke.' Thinking she must have sounded like an excited nine-year-old, she added, in a more responsible tone: 'We'd best dowse it well before it's dark, or they'll put us behind bars for signalling to Zeppelins.'

And later, when the knock came at the door, she felt sure it was PC Royston.

'Oh, it's you, vicar' – she almost said 'thank God' – 'I thought we were going to be arrested. Won't you come in?'

'Thank you, Mrs Farmer.'

His expression was serious, his manner rather too formal, and when he mentioned Alan, Molly was gripped by a new and much more terrible fear.

'Alan? Have you heard news of him then? I mean, he's not hurt or anything?'

'No, he's not hurt. I've had a letter from his chaplain. We were at theological college together. I might have mentioned that to you ...'

'No, you didn't.' She was anxious, imploring, and he looked hesitant, wondering yet again if he was doing the right thing in telling her. All the way to the house, he had been in two minds. 'What's happened to Alan? Please tell me.'

'I'm afraid your son is facing a most serious charge.'

'You look white as a ghost,' Harry said, when Molly came to tell him she had made the tea but wouldn't bring it into the garden, after all. 'If you ask me, you need a drop of something stronger.'

'It's Alan. He's facing a court martial.'

'A court martial? What on earth for?' She told him, and he looked dazedly at her. 'Cowardice? Alan?'

'That's what I said to the vicar. Alan's not a coward.

And never could be. As soon as he was old enough he volunteered. Even when he was small, he was the one who'd stop any bullying in school. There must be some mistake.'

Harry's voice was hard. 'How does the vicar know about it?'

'He had a letter from Alan's chaplain.'

For Molly's sake, Harry strove to contain his anger. 'And the vicar came to tell you? The boy's mother? Why?'

Molly looked perplexed. 'He was in two minds, he said. But why *not* tell me? Why *shouldn't* I be told?'

Harry glanced away. Was it possible that the vicar did not know the penalty for a soldier found guilty of cowardice? The man was shot. But relatives, of course, were told that he had died gallantly in action. And rightly so! Why should the anguish of shame be added to the burden of grief? 'Let's have that tea,' Harry said, leading her firmly into the kitchen. 'No. You sit. I shall pour. What else did the vicar say?'

'It puts him in a difficult position next Sunday. He's adding a special part to the service, asking the congregation to pray for all the men in the village who are serving. He's reading out all their names. Now, he doesn't see how he can read out Alan's name.'

'And what did you say?'

'I said I didn't see why he couldn't read out — ' She shook her head, unable to go on. It was all too much for her. Harry handed the cup of tea. She shook her head again and started to cry. Harry felt utterly useless, not knowing what to say or do. He wanted to put an arm about her in comfort but he was afraid of revealing his feelings for the woman he loved.

'If they find him guilty of being a coward,' she said at last, 'what will they do to him?'

'I don't know,' Harry lied. 'I've no experience of such things.'

'But you were in the Army?'

'Yes, but I suppose it's different for fliers.'

Molly was silent. Since the vicar had left the house, a snatch of conversation she had heard in the village kept going over and over in her mind. Just four words from the babble of war-gossip wheezed by chesty old men who stood on the corner of Leadby Street, lighting up their spent-out lives with talk not only of the war in France but of all the wars ever fought, it seemed. They angered Molly with their endless lists of glorious victories, excuses for defeats, and their numbers upon numbers of maimed and dead, bandied and argued over as if they were scores on their precious cricket green. What, after all, did *they* know of wars on foreign fields when – God in Heaven! – most of them had never been a mile further than Caxton town. And what did they understand – or care – of the pain of the wives and mothers of their counted maimed and dead?

But try as she would she could not cast the four words from her mind, and on and on they went, long after Harry had gone. 'Shot for a coward . . . shot for a coward...' and when she drew back the curtain that night. and turned down the lamp, she stared into the darkness as if for all the world she could see beyond the far waters of the Channel as far as Ste Marie. But she was glad she could not truly see. The awful question might agonise her mind, but was not that easier than to be given an answer she could not possibly bear?

She wept through the darkness, and in the dawn light cried for shame at a mother's doubts in the courage and the innocence of her son.

The extraordinary circumstances that led to the arrest

of Sergeant Farmer began when Captain Triggers called his Flight together to warn them of the threat of the new monoplane with the forward-firing gun. He told them to forget everything they had learned about being safe when the enemy was coming straight at them. And they were not to go looking for trouble with this particular Hun. Their job was reconnaissance; they had enough problems without heroics, and in future, they would fly in pairs, for mutual protection. 'Sergeant Farmer? You and Mr Conrad will be artillery-spotting this morning. Mr Gaylion and Mr Bravington will escort you.'

Less than an hour after issuing those instructions, Triggers flew off on reconnaissance, *without* an escort, and did not return.

'A stickler for the rules,' Charles said, in the anger of shock, 'but he didn't damn well obey them himself.'

Sergeant Mills explained that the replacement pilot and observer had failed to arrive, having crashed in Kent, so Triggers had no option but to fly unescorted.

Alan, understandably perhaps, was mortified by the news. After all, Captain Triggers had given him his chance to train as a pilot. He owed part of his very existence to the man, and his angry refusal to bear the loss turned Triggers' flesh and blood into some godlike substance at the sight of which death paled away. The man who had raged against death on behalf of them all now became an indestructible hero. It was wholly impossible that he himself had succumbed.

When Charles stumbled, half-drunk, into Alan's tent, he thought he understood the reason for the tears. Had not Alan, as a boy, seen his father burn to death? Somehow, he identified *that* loss with *this* . . .

'Anger, that's all I feel!' Alan blazed at him. 'Anger that the rest of you behave as if he were dead.'

The next day, Charles, made Acting Flight Commander

F

until the arrival of Captain Triggers' replacement, briefed Alan and Peter Conrad to photograph an ammunition dump nine miles east of Templeuve. 'Remember to fly well south of the Hun airfield,' he warned. 'Though I hardly need to tell you that.'

'To hell with the Hun monoplane,' Conrad said to Alan as they walked to their machine. And in that now familiar tone of voice that brooked no argument, he added: 'We shall fly a straight course. There and back.'

Roughly five miles from the dump, Conrad suddenly reached for his Mannlicher and pointed urgently to starboard. The ominous-looking machine was two thousand feet below and snaking diagonally towards them. Alan's instinctive reaction was to climb and turn away, but Conrad's outstretched arm had already made his own intention plain enough; they were to attack the monoplane. Alan hesitated. Up until that moment he had never wilfully disobeyed a command from Peter Conrad. The chagrin, the humiliation he had felt on those first flights with his imperious observer had now settled into a certain wry amusement at the ridiculously commanding gestures. But *this* was a situation that was far from amusing. Whatever Conrad's confidence in his marksmanship, the Mannlicher was no match at all for the monoplane's devastating forward fire. As it was, they would be hard-pressed to make their escape. To tangle deliberately with the fast, manoeuvrable and reputedly deadly creature was sheer lunacy; the folly of a vain butterfly flopping down to challenge an angry darting wasp.

But there was really no dilemma here, Alan thought. He didn't have to make up his mind what to do. That had already been done for him. 'Hang on!' he called to Conrad, and turned steeply away to port.

'What the devil are you doing?' Conrad raved.

Obeying orders, Alan told himself. Hadn't Captain

Triggers told them not to go looking for trouble with this particular Hun?

'That way, I said!' Conrad stabbed a dictatorial finger in the direction of the enemy. 'That way!'

Alan looked right through the outraged features and absurd gesticulations, and headed for home. The damned man had to learn that a pilot, whatever his rank, was 'captain' of his machine.

Despite the cold anger with which Conrad made the accusation, Charles could hardly take the matter seriously. 'You look jolly cold, Peter. Here, have a nip!'

Conrad ignored the whisky-flask. 'I do not drink, as you know, this early in the day. I took it for granted you'd take Sergeant Farmer's part in this matter.'

What the 'matter' was, Charles was not at all sure, but Conrad's manner now began to disturb him. And as Acting Flight Commander, he had enough problems without the frozen-faced tantrums of this relic of the South African war. What the devil was he Acting Flight Commander of, anyway, an RFC Flight or a troop of poker-backed Dragoons? 'For God's sake, Peter, don't be so damned stuffy. It was simply a question of judgment. Sergeant Farmer thought it necessary to take evasive action.'

'He disobeyed an order from a superior officer.'

'Superior' was most certainly the word, Charles thought. 'The pilot *is* the captain of his machine, you know. Here, come on. Let's have lunch. Monsieur Flemmard has given us a pig in the vague hope of bribing us not to go on pestering his daughter. Smells absolutely delicious. The pig, I mean, of course.'

'I demand that Sergeant Farmer be court-martialled.'

Charles was stunned. He turned at the door, looking back at Conrad in utter astonishment. 'Court-martialled?

Oh, look here, Peter, you can't be serious?'

'I am, as you know, new to the Flying Corps. But I do happen to know the difference between judgment and cowardice. I also happen to know that cowardice in the face of the enemy is a court-martial offence.'

Damn the man! Spelling it out to him as if he were a child of seven. Charles closed the door and walked back to the desk. Triggers' desk! Where in Heaven's name was Triggers' replacement? Why wasn't he here to deal with this ridiculous situation? 'Look, Peter, let's try and be reasonable about this.' What was he to say now? Lord, his father had hopes of his becoming a General one day, and here he was, unable to cope with a storm in a teacup.

'Look at it from your point of view, Peter. I mean – well – you're not awfully popular in the Mess as it is. And if you do go on with this rather ridiculous . . .'

'I didn't join the Army to be popular.' Conrad's contempt for Charles was all too plain. He stabbed it home. 'Did you?'

The guard on the tent snapped smartly to attention. Charles ducked under the flap and tossed the packet of cigarettes on to Alan's bed. He'd put off telling Alan on his previous visit but this time he had to face him with it. 'Anything else you need?'

'Just a nice big patch of sky,' Alan said, the touch of a smile on his pale features. 'Penned up in here for two days, even a BE2 would be a pleasure to fly.'

'At least you're safe from the Hun,' Charles said, inwardly comparing the 'gallant enemy' with the 'insidious enemy within'. But who was *he* to carp at Peter Conrad? Had not he, Charles, made a mess of a situation that could so easily have been resolved – as Charles's father would have said – 'with a firm hand and a modicum of tact'?

'I've some news for you at last. They're going through with it.'

Alan was eating the dinner that had just been brought to him. He put down his knife and fork and flicked an earwig from the lid of the ammo box serving as a tray. 'That's what I thought,' he said quietly. 'But you said there was no chance.'

'It's a matter of procedure, that's all.' He didn't tell Alan that Conrad, blast the man, had written to his uncle, the General, and such a stink had been made they'd just had to go through with it. 'There'll be a President. And a couple of other officers acting as judges.'

'Who actually charges me?'

'Another officer. He'll be the prosecutor.' At first Charles had thought it would be Conrad himself. But he'd been mugging up; with an end in view. He had to do something for Alan, for God's sake. 'Then there are witnesses. Just one, in this case, of course. Mr Conrad.' Now his tone was deliberately offhand. 'Then, of course, there's the Prisoner's Friend.'

'Who's that?'

'He's whoever the prisoner asks to act as his – well – sort of lawyer, really. You can choose who you want.'

Alan looked at him appealingly. 'Would you do it, Charles?'

'My dear fellow, of course I'll do it.' He sat on the bed and explained to Alan that the prosecutor was a Lieutenant Walker, who used to be a solicitor. The man wasn't a flier and therefore might not be too sympathetic. 'So I've managed to change the President to a chap who *is* a flier. Major Cashman. He's grounded now. Landed a Gunbus upside-down or something and can't walk properly. But he won't have a lot of time for a prosecutor who doesn't know a damned thing about flying.'

Alan's look was half-accusing. 'I didn't realise it had all gone so far.'

'I've been putting off telling you,' Charles said bluntly. 'The reason is, I haven't handled it all that well.'

Alan smiled wanly and thumped a fist on Charles's arm. 'Well, I've got nothing to worry about now, have I? You defending me.' He glanced at the screwed-up sheet of paper on the bed. The letter to Kate. He had opened up his heart in a well of self-pity. Thank God he hadn't posted it; he'd never have been able to face her again, let alone ask her to marry him. 'I read somewhere that there's a sword on the table. If they point it towards you, they've found you guilty.'

'Not in your case. Only commissioned officers.'

Alan smiled inwardly. Then there *were* advantages, after all, in having lived by the sweat of one's brow. '*We* don't get shot then?'

Charles avoided his eyes. 'Aren't you going to finish your dinner?'

'No, thanks.' Charles gave Alan a cigarette and lit it for him.

'Waited on by officers,' Alan grinned. 'Living in the lap of luxury, aren't I?'


'My, where on earth have you been?' Molly enquired when she met Harry striding down the lane in his best suit.

'Looks a bit better now you've pressed it up,' Harry said evasively. Alice would have the evening meal waiting so he wouldn't stop.

'A secret, is it?' Molly laughed. 'Is she a Becket's Hill girl, then?'

'I've been to see the vicar,' Harry said, though he had fully intended not to tell Molly of the visit. She'd have found out for herself on Sunday, and conversation on the subject would only serve to magnify the terrible anxiety he knew she was feeling, despite the face she put on. He had not been at all confident in persuading the vicar to change his mind, but it had been easier than he had thought. The foolish, unthinking man had already realised that he had made a grave error in telling Molly of her son's court-martial, and when Harry had made his quiet 'demand', the vicar had readily acquiesced. Harry decided that in this particular parish, the Lord certainly *did* work in the most mysterious ways. 'Alan was mentioned,' he said, as if the subject had been a trifle arising out of something of importance, 'and in the special service on Sunday, the vicar will, after all, read out Alan Farmer's name along with the rest.'

The vicar's actual words had been 'the rest of the brave and gallant men serving their King and Country', and pronounced with the barely perceptible irony that can only be conveyed through the righteous art of a preacher.

'Thank you for telling me,' Molly said, her face betraying no more than a morsel of the gratitude she felt. Harry was deliberately belittling his act on her behalf. She understood why. Harry lived his own life, content in his aloneness: 'living like the wind', he had once told her, 'touching all and abiding nowhere'. He had seen fit to persuade the vicar to change his mind, and he had done so. He'd make no great song of it, and wanted no show of thanks for it, and Molly was more grateful for that than for the act itself. Such was the turmoil inside her at this time that any show of comfort would have caused her to make a fool of herself. And that would never do. For two nights now she had wept, her grief for her husband resurrected by her fears for her son, and in the early hours, smothering in the powder from the guns of the dream, she had run to the window, flinging it open to gasp in the cold dark air. Then she had howled into the night, cursing Will for not being there when she needed him most. She had sat in Alan's room until gone ten o'clock, and had not shown her face in the smithy all day in case they had heard her shameful cry. 'The suit is still up there in the wardrobe,' she said, with a glance at Harry's fraying cuff. 'Will hardly ever wore it, and it worries me every time I see it. A good suit, going to waste. I can't see for the life of me why you won't make use of it.'

When she arrived at the house, Lorna was standing in the yard. She was in her nurse's uniform, on her way to The Grange, the mansion near Hopford that had been converted into an emergency hospital. She was hesitant and self-reproving, apologising to Molly for not having called on her for so long. 'I see you in the mornings with the milk,' Molly said, curious to know why she was there. 'What is it then? You'll tear a hole in that apron if you fidget much more, girl.'

'It's Alan!'

Molly's heart leapt. How had the girl heard of it? Only Harry knew and he wouldn't have told her, surely?

'I've had a letter,' Lorna went on. 'It's all clear now. It's Charles's sister. Her name is Kate. He mentioned her once, you might remember. Anyway, after his last leave, when he left here – he called at her house in London.'

Molly tried her best to be sympathetic, but what did it matter who Alan loved or did not love when at this very moment he might be facing a firing squad?

# 7

The comfortable assortment of refugee armchairs 'rescued' by an enterprising adjutant had been cleared from the Mess lounge and replaced by upright wooden chairs more in keeping with the stark proceedings, and their creaking and scraping in the cold morning light reminded Charles of school examinations and the accompanying forebodings of failure. Lieutenant Walker, the prosecuting officer, was polishing his glasses as if he fully expected to polish off his business there with equal ease. He was in his late thirties, and his coldly intelligent features had regarded Charles's genial welcome that morning with aloof suspicion; he hoped Charles did not think there should be one law for the infantry and another for rather pampered pilots.

When Major Cashman limped to the President's chair at the centre of the table, Charles's hopes sank even further. The President had the expression of a man who lived in eternal pain and could not find an ounce of sympathy for himself, let alone a man accused of cowardice in the face of the enemy. Despite the reassuring sight of the 'wings' on the tunic breast, Charles knew the man was there to see justice done with a capital J, and from the irritable urgency of his manner, to see that it was done as quickly as possible. In the presence of two such men, humanity would not get a look in, of that Charles was certain. Not the slightest concession would be made to human frailty, and any glimmer of sympathetic understanding would be barked or glowered away in the harsh light of this bristling business. The tiresome episode was quite obviously a blessed nuisance to all concerned, and the prime object was to get it over and done. Dammit, there was a war waiting to be fought.

'The court is in session. Bring in the prisoner.'

'Prisoner and escort, 'shun! Left, right, left right, left right . . .' Pale and strained, Alan was marched into the courtroom between two armed guards. Charles's indignation rose at the sight. God, if there was one man in the whole of the Flying Corps who was entirely unworthy of this humiliation it was Sergeant Alan Farmer. 'Prisoner and escort, 'shun!' The guards booted to attention and Charles had an awful vision of the body as it fell to the ground under the murdering rifle fire. The Flight Sergeant saluted the President's table. 'Sergeant Farmer, sir!'

Alan, erect, his eyes unseeing, was facing Charles. He looked petrified, Charles thought; then, considering that Alan might be thinking the very same about him, he gave a bare smile and looked confidently down at his papers. Alan had such faith in him. God knows why! Oh that they were both flying this morning; *six* Huns on their tail would be a honeymoon compared with this bloody funeral parlour game.

Walker began for the prosecution by calling his only witness, Lieutenant Conrad. 'When you saw the enemy aeroplane, where was it?' he asked in his thin, dry voice.

'It was two thousand feet below and on the starboard side,' Conrad replied, in firm ringing tones.

'And what did you do, Mr Conrad?'

'Naturally, as we were in the perfect position to attack, I signalled to Sergeant Farmer to go down.'

'And what did Sergeant Farmer do?'

'He turned away and headed for home. The airfield at Ste Marie, that is.'

'And what did you do then?'

'At first, I couldn't believe what was happening. When I realised Sergeant Farmer really was running away, I ordered him once again to turn and attack the enemy. But he ignored the order. When we landed I reported the matter to — ' and he glanced at Charles, 'to Mr Gaylion, the Acting Flight Commander.'

Walker gave a curt, appreciative nod, allowed his eyes to rest on the purple ribbon of Conrad's VC, thanked him, and sat down. Now it was Charles's turn. Fighting down a growing sense of panic, he came to his feet.

'Mr Conrad. Nobody here would dream of criticising — '

'Would you speak up, please, Mr Gaylion?' the President said, in deep, hollow tones.

'Mr Conrad. Nobody here would dream of criticising your personal courage. But I would suggest that what we're talking about is nothing to do with courage.'

'Damn it, I gave Sergeant Farmer an order — '

'Mr Conrad.' The President rapped his knuckles on the desk like a schoolmaster reproving a boy for inattention 'I would remind you that you are now a Lieutenant in the Flying Corps, and no longer a Lieutenant-Colonel in the Dragoons.'

Good for 'Painface,' Charles thought. Conrad looked rattled now, and Charles went on with more confidence. 'What we're talking about here is not courage, but military common sense. Would you agree that this new German monoplane is a far better fighting aeroplane than the BE2 which you and the prisoner were flying?'

'No, I would not. How could I? It is a *new* monoplane, as you've just described it. We know so little about it, so how can anyone say that it's a far better fighting aeroplane than the BE2? In any case, we were in a position to attack, and the German monoplane was not. *We* had the advantage.'

Damn the man! He knew well enough, despite his being new to the Flying Corps, that the BE2 was distinctly inferior. 'On this particular flight, Mr Conrad – how were you armed?'

'With a Mannlicher.'

'A rifle?'

'It is my own personal gun. The finest hunting rifle in the world.'

'Nevertheless, it *is* a rifle.' Charles noted the interest of the two judging officers at the President's table. Neither were fliers, but they were sure to appreciate the point he was about to make. 'Whereas the enemy was armed with a machine-gun firing through the propeller arc at the rate of something like five hundred rounds a minute.'

One of the judges whispered to the President, who nodded, and said : 'Mr Conrad? What were your orders? What was the purpose of this particular flight?'

'To identify and photograph an ammunition dump.'

'And did you carry out those orders?'

'No. We were five miles or so from the dump when we sighted the enemy and Sergeant Farmer turned for home.'

A hammer blow against them, Charles reflected dismally. He had no further questions for Mr Conrad. 'You can't argue with that bit of purple ribbon on his chest,' he murmured to Alan, as Lieutenant Walker announced that Lieutenant Conrad was the only witness for the prosecution.

Mr Gaylion was now asked to present his defence, and Alan stood to face the court. 'Sergeant Farmer. How long have you been in France?'

'Since the end of May, sir.'

'Four months. I see. And in that time, how many hours have you spent flying?'

'About six or seven a day, sir.'

'And of your Flight, how many of the fliers who were

here when you arrived are still in action?'

'Just you and me, sir. And Mr Bravington.'

The President interrupted the questioning. 'I should remind the Prisoner's Friend that the fact that the Flying Corps has been suffering casualties is no defence to this charge.'

'I was just trying to indicate, sir, that Sergeant Farmer is a lot more experienced than Lieutenant Conrad, even though he is inferior in rank.'

'You may make that point either by examining a witness or in your final speech. You may not do it in the way you are doing.'

Charles apologised and asked Alan if he had ever turned back from a mission before the occasion in question. Yes, he had done; twice with engine failure and once when Archie had ripped up a wing. But he had never turned back when he saw an enemy machine? No, he had not done. 'Then why did you turn back on this occasion?'

'Because we were up against the new monoplane, sir.'

'Have you ever seen this monoplane in action before?'

'Once. When I was escorting Captain Triggers, my Flight Commander.'

'And when Captain Triggers encountered this monoplane, what did *he* do?'

'After he'd made sure it was armed with this forward-firing gun, he tried to break away and get home, sir.'

The President beckoned. He wanted to ask Alan a question. 'You mean, Sergeant, that having seen that Captain Triggers didn't want to engage the enemy, you personally didn't feel capable of fighting him either?'

The President's tone was surprisingly gentle. What was he up to? Inviting Alan to take the easy way out by admitting that he had followed a bad example? Or was he hoping to provoke Alan into revealing his 'cowardice' by attempting to bluster his way around the question? Charles's fears were allayed by the simple honesty of Alan's reply.

'None of us are capable of fighting this new enemy machine, sir. Not with the aeroplanes and weapons we have.'

At the back of the court, Conrad leapt to his feet. 'Nonsense! I almost shot the pilot of that monoplane.'

'Mr Conrad! You will not interrupt!'

Conrad ignored the warning. 'Another foot or so and I'd have got him.'

'If you interrupt again, I will order you from the court.'

'I am prepared to face the consequences, sir. I almost got that Hun in the neck.'

'You will leave the court!'

Conrad put on his cap, saluted, and marched stiffly out. Charles felt sick at heart. Conrad's outburst, however reprehensible, had served to exhibit to the court the rashly brave man he undoubtedly was, and Alan's nervous presence in the intimidating atmosphere of the court suffered by comparison.

In questioning Alan, Lieutenant Walker's manner was dramatically grave. The war was all but lost, it seemed, by Alan's failure to carry out his orders to photograph the ammunition dump and his refusal to attack the enemy machine. Then Walker set out to prove to the court that the new German monoplane, as Mr Conrad had suggested, was not the superior fighting machine that the defence had proposed. Indeed, the monoplane's armament was, in fact, inferior to the deadly accurate fire from marksman Conrad's rifle, which, after all, could be fired in all directions, whilst the monoplane's gun could only fire in one direction. Charles protested that there was no comparison between the two aeroplanes, or the armament, and that Lieutenant Walker was talking through his 'non-flier's hat'. He had neither the first-hand experience, nor the theoretical appreciation, of the vast superiority of the German machine. Totally unconcerned, Walker let his argument rest, but after lunch, in his final speech, he used Charles's protest to cunning advantage. Since when had a supposed inferiority in equipment been regarded as a reason for a British soldier refusing to engage the enemy? He asked them to consider Francis Drake, and added, with a little acid smile at Charles: 'Another non-flier, of course.' The prisoner had been ordered to attack, and he had disobeyed that order. Whether or not the Hun monoplane was a superior piece of machinery had no bearing whatsoever on the prisoner's innocence or guilt of the charges of wilfully disobeying an order and cowardice in the face of the enemy. The argument that the prisoner had fled because he was 'more experienced than his observer', the prosecution had found hard to follow. Perhaps their view of the matter was too simple, too factual, and the facts were that the prisoner had abandoned his mission and disobeyed an order to attack the enemy. The officer who had given that order was a Lieutenant who had dropped from the rank of Lieutenant-Colonel in order to serve his country the better; a man of unquestioned gallantry, a man who had seen more active service than anyone in the court, and who, of course, had been awarded the Victoria Cross.

'The prisoner is charged with disobeying a lawful order,' Walker said in conclusion. 'The second, and more serious charge, is that of cowardice. The facts are clear, and not disputed. Ordered to attack the enemy, he turned tail and fled. He is guilty, as charged, with cowardice in the face of the enemy. And he must pay the penalty.'

The President thanked him and looked to Charles.

'Mr Gaylion?'

Charles came to his feet. 'Sir. There is something bigger even than military law. There is justice.' God, he had never felt so awful. He was talking a lot of rubbish. But what else was he to say? He had not one fact, one shred of evidence with which to plead Alan's innocence. There must be *something*, of course, but he had neither the experience nor the wit to realise it. Whatever had gulled him into thinking he was capable of defending Alan? What monstrous blindness had God inflicted on him to allow him to enter so blithely and confidently into the grave and exacting business of defending a man on trial for his life?

'We're waiting, Mr Gaylion.'

'Oh. Yes. My apologies, sir. I was just collecting my thoughts. I – Sergeant Farmer has been serving his country in the field – and in the skies – since the end of May. Some of us here know what he has gone through. Some of us here know the freedom and the fear of flying. It is an exceptional man who can keep his head at all times, in the cold skies above the battlegrounds . . .'

He suddenly realised no one was listening. They were all looking towards the doorway, where a man had entered. He was in RFC uniform; dirty, dishevelled, his face telling of the terrible ordeal he had been through. He stood there looking at the court like a man resigned to death might regard his own grave. It couldn't possibly be the man himself, Charles thought, mesmerised by the wasted features and haunted eyes; it was some ghostly trick of the panic that had by this time totally engulfed him.

Alan, of course, had no such doubts of the flesh and blood of the man, half-starved or not. He had known all along he could not possibly be dead, and was overjoyed to see him.

Captain Triggers apologised for interrupting the proceedings, announced himself, and explained to the court that he had escaped from a German hospital, fallen into the hands of some French Zouaves who didn't speak French let alone English and had been taken for a German spy. Eventually he'd persuaded them to let him go, made his way to the nearest RFC Squadron and got through to Sergeant Mills. Hearing of the court-martial he had come with all haste to offer himself as a witness for the defence.

'Well, Mr Gaylion,' the President said. 'Would you care to question this witness?'

Charles didn't know where to begin. How long had Captain Triggers known the prisoner? Six months! Where had they met? Triggers had taught Sergeant Farmer to fly. Would he agree that the prisoner was a brave man? That was a leading question and would he kindly phrase it some other way.

'How would you describe the prisoner? As a man?' Charles asked, swallowing nervously. Triggers was looking at him with what Charles could only interpret as cold contempt. Lord, whose side was the Flight Commander on?

'He is a very ordinary man,' Triggers replied. Ordinary? Yes! Charles now glanced at Alan, who was looking quite as unhappy as Charles was feeling inadequate. 'Are you aware, Captain Triggers, that the prisoner is accused of cowardice in the face of the enemy?' Of course he was, Triggers replied, or he wouldn't be there. Did the accusation surprise him?

'Very little surprises me,' Triggers replied.

The President concealed a smile. 'I'm not sure you're helping Prisoner's Friend, Captain Triggers.'

'I can only answer the questions he asks me.'

The President nodded to Charles to continue, and

177

Charles asked Triggers if he had ordered his Flight not to engage the new German monoplane.

'No, I did not!'

Charles was shattered. 'In your opinion, was Sergeant Farmer right in trying to avoid an engagement with this monoplane?' Triggers had no idea; after all, he wasn't there. Would *he* have attacked this particular enemy? Here, the President intervened.

'Captain Triggers has already explained that as he wasn't there he cannot have an opinion on what he or anybody else might have done.'

'Yes, sir.' Charles was at the end of his tether now. 'Would you be willing to have the prisoner back under your command, sir?'

'Yes, I would.'

Dazedly, Charles thanked him and sat down. Walker now came to his feet. As far as he was concerned, the business was over and done with. Sergeant Farmer would certainly be found guilty on both charges. But he had noted a point that he now felt ought to be made. 'You said that you did not give the prisoner any order never to attack this monoplane?'

'That is correct.'

'So that when Sergeant Farmer turned tail, he was not only disobeying an order from Lieutenant Conrad, he was disobeying an order from you, too?'

Triggers considered for a moment before replying. 'No!'

'But surely, can we not assume that anybody in the armed forces of the Crown is implicitly ordered to engage the enemy, unless ordered otherwise?'

'I told my Flight, including Sergeant Farmer, that they were not to go looking for trouble with this particular machine. There *is* a difference.'

'I see. Would *you* attack this monoplane?'

'Not without a very good reason, no.'

Why not? Because the RFC had neither the machines nor the weapons to give them a fair chance, Triggers replied, whereupon Walker consulted his notes and read aloud what *Flight* magazine had said of the BE2c. 'As a flying machine it is one of which any designer may be proud.'

'I'm not talking of it as a flying machine,' Triggers said. 'I'm talking of it as a fighting machine.'

Was Captain Triggers telling the court, then, that this German monoplane was a superior fighting machine? Infinitely superior, yes! Despite the fact that it could not fire backwards, or sideways, or upwards, or downwards? Yes! Despite the fact that the pilot was alone in the machine, that he was also observer and gunner? Yes!

'I see,' Walker said superciliously. 'And you have evidence, of course, to support your arguments? You have proof?'

'Yes, I have,' Triggers said flatly. '*I* am the proof.'

'I don't quite understand?'

'It was one of those German monoplanes that shot me down twelve days ago. So *I* am the proof. So is Lieutenant Howes, my observer. He's buried, such bits of him as they could find. So is Lieutenant Carey-Jones, Lieutenant Robertson, Sergeant — '

'We don't want a catalogue,' Walker snapped.

'I think, in a way, Captain Triggers is answering your last question,' the President said, greatly impressed by Triggers, and now trying hard to look grimly impartial. 'But I would ask Captain Triggers to confine himself to just that – answering questions.'

Triggers sighed impatiently. 'The trouble is, no one will ask the *right* questions.'

Walker was ruffled now. 'Do you think it normal practice, Captain Triggers, for a witness not only to be able to choose his own answers, but his own questions as well?'

'Oh, I'm not blaming you.' Triggers glared across at Charles, who shifted uncomfortably in his seat. 'It was Prisoner's Friend who made a mess of it. He asked me what sort of a man Sergeant Farmer is. And I told him. An ordinary man! You'd have thought he'd have the sense to ask what sort of a pilot Sergeant Farmer is.'

'The witness must confine himself to answering the questions,' the President barked. 'I won't warn him again.'

Walker reflected before putting his next question. He said he was sure everyone present was anxious to secure justice, and Charles thought for a moment that the man looked almost human. 'Perhaps it would help if *I* ask that question,' Walker went on. 'What sort of a pilot is the prisoner?'

'He is an exceptional pilot.'

Walker smiled. But his tone was dangerously incisive. 'Surely you've noticed, Captain Triggers, that the prisoner is not on trial for ineptitude. If, as you say, he is an exceptional pilot, then he used his exceptional skills to disobey an order and to turn tail and flee from the enemy.'

Triggers looked contemptuously at Walker, then, with sudden and surprising vehemence, he said: 'Whether you take Sergeant Farmer outside and shoot him, or just return him to duty, it's unlikely to make much difference.'

'Thank you, Captain Triggers,' Walker said, his old cool self again, 'that's all!'

But Triggers had hardly begun. 'Sergeant Farmer has been in action, continuously, for four months. He is, therefore, overdue to die. In the circumstances, you could argue that what the prosecution calls cowardice is, in fact, a virtue.'

'I can't see your argument,' the President said when he'd found his tongue. Triggers asked permission to explain. 'Very well. If you're relevant. And brief!'

'At the moment we have neither the machines nor the weapons to fight the enemy,' Triggers began. 'The most useful thing that any good pilot like Sergeant Farmer can do is to stay alive. He's no coward because he doesn't fight when he hasn't a cat in hell's chance. There's nothing heroic in committing suicide. And, incidentally, killing your observer.'

'One moment,' the President said. 'The court cannot accept that the first duty of a member of His Majesty's forces is survival.'

'Not survival, sir! As fast as our new pilots get to France they're being killed. They're being killed because they don't know anything about air warfare. Nobody's taught them! And the only people qualified to teach them – experienced pilots like Sergeant Farmer – they're being shot out of the skies by these new German machines.'

'I see,' the President said, deciding that in the interests of 'morale' the court had heard quite enough. 'Thank you!'

But there was no stopping Triggers now. 'A few more months without better aeroplanes and more efficient weapons, and the Flying Corps will never recover.'

'That's all! Stand down!'

'And it's not helped by daft ideas like this court-martial.'

'I have ordered you to stand down!'

'Sir!'

Triggers clicked to attention, turned, and marched to the back of the room. Alan felt like cheering. Charles watched a fly buzzing about his papers and longed for its mindless insignificance.

'Does Prisoner's Friend wish to continue with his final

plea?' the President enquired. As Charles was about to reply, he suggested: 'Or would he be willing to forgo it?'

The last thing Charles wanted to do at that moment was to face his Flight Commander. Yet, with the instinct of an erring son who, when in doubt, still looks towards the hated scolding father, he met Triggers' warning gaze. He turned to the President. 'The defence rests,' he said, with the very last remnant of composure.

On the first charge of wilful disobedience of a lawful command by a superior officer, Alan was found guilty and was sentenced to nine days detention, starting from the day on which he was first put under arrest. On the second charge, that of cowardice in the face of the enemy, he was found 'not guilty'.

'You're back on duty tomorrow,' Triggers snapped, as they left the courtroom. 'The long reconnaissance. Escorting me!'

# 8

'Go on, missus,' old Tom urged. He had run all the way down the lane with the note from the vicar, who had given it to the postman to drop in as he passed; and now Molly was afraid to open it. 'It won't be bad news.'

'How do you know?'

Tom was stumped. He had been warned to say nothing of Harry's daily visits to the vicar to ask if there was news from Alan's chaplain; if the news was 'the worst' it had been arranged that Harry should break it to Molly. 'Here, give it to me.' Tom opened the envelope, unfolded the note and held it before her eyes.

'Thank God,' Molly murmured as she read what was written there. 'Thank God, he's safe.'

'All this worry for nothing,' Tom grumbled. 'You need have known nothing of it.'

'An awful thought. My son shot for cowardice and me never knowing.'

'Not so awful, missus. Been better for you to have believed he'd gone bravely.'

Molly shook her head. She would sooner know the truth, always, whatever it was.

'Aye. Well. None of us will know that, will we?' He shifted uncomfortably under her sharp gaze. 'Don't get me wrong, missus. He couldn't have been guilty or he wouldn't have been let off.' He was anxious to be going. 'I'll run over and tell Alice the good news.'

Molly was taken aback. 'How does Alice know?'

'I said nothing, missus. Honest. But – well – these things have a way of getting about, don't they?'

In Rudkin's shop, Mrs Bates, whose son was in the infantry and up to his neck in mud, fighting the 'real war', was ever so pleased that Alan had 'got himself off'. 'It must have been terrible for him, accused like that of something he wasn't guilty of. It makes you wonder how they thought he *was* guilty, doesn't it? A big relief to you, Mrs Farmer, I expect.'

'And a big disappointment to some, no doubt,' Arthur Rudkin said, meaningly, as he gave Mrs Bates her change.

'You mean those who think the flying boys have a grand old time of it compared with the poor devils in the trenches?'

'Some people,' Rudkin muttered, when Mrs Bates had gone. 'A lad does well for himself, and they can't wait to tear him down.'

'What if Alan *was* a coward?' Molly said in a quiet

impassioned voice. 'He's eighteen! What do they expect from boys? Yes, boys! Do the Generals think their mothers don't know they're still boys? They join up – willing to give their lives – everyone cheering and waving flags for them – then, because they see common sense for one minute and they're fearful, they're shot for being cowards.'

She had been so carried away she had almost forgotten she was standing there in the shop and she glanced furtively around in case someone had come in. Rudkin looked at her for a moment, then he closed the shop door, slid the bolt home, and turned the card to 'closed'. It was dinner time and his mother would have made a pot of tea.

'I've something important to ask you,' he said. 'And this seems as good a time as any.'

Tom stared at the bruise on Harry's cheek. Where did he get it? Harry thought he was referring to the bicycle wheel he had picked out of the junk at the back of Ted May's shed. Tom had almost finished the brakes, so all they needed now was a rear mudguard.

'That bruise on your cheek, I mean,' Tom said. 'Here, you haven't been fighting with Arthur Rudkin, have you?'

Harry gave him a black look. Why should he be fighting with Arthur Rudkin? Tom looked pained. 'I'm not that soft in the head, Harry,' he said. 'Diggin' up the garden for her, worryin' yourself to death over her worryin' over Alan, and now – well – this bicycle for her birthday.'

Harry thrust his fist into Tom's face. 'You want a bruise to match mine, old man?'

But Tom was determined to have his say. What was Harry so frightened of? The missus'd be a lot better off with him than with Arthur Rudkin, going little grocer's shop or not. She wouldn't marry Rudkin, Harry said, sullen-faced.

'Will she not? Round here every five minutes. Free quarters o' tea with her order. Extra weight on the butter. Cups o' tea with his mother. Oh aye, potty little things, I know. But she's hanging in the balance, I'll tell you that now. And it don't take much to tip a scales one way or the other.' Then he delivered the bombshell. 'Anyway, he's already asked her. The missus told me so.'

They had finished fitting the left-hand brake before Harry found the courage to ask. 'Has she given him an answer then?'

'Not as I know of. She said she's thinking it over. And it's a wicked shame. 'Cos you're right for her. Even more right than Will was, I reckon. There! I've told you to your face.'

The damned old fool, Harry thought, spinning the back wheel to test its trueness. Did he know nothing of the law? How *could* he ask her to marry him?

Lorna had grave doubts as she helped Tom to cram the bicycle into its hiding place in the jam-packed paint shed. Harry would never persuade Molly into the saddle of the danger to man and beast. 'She can't abide anything on wheels, you know that. And if Harry doesn't, then you should tell him.'

'I'm saying nothing,' Tom spat. 'Every time I open my mouth I say the wrong thing, it seems. And I've spent three hours cleaning the rust from the creature. Harry's made it for her birthday, and she'll damned well be grateful and learn to ride it.'

Lorna knew about Harry's bruise; she'd heard that he'd got it from Ted Allsop, who had jeered something about Alan being a coward.

'Fancy picking on a man with one arm,' Tom complained.

'It was Harry who did the picking, I gather.'

'I hear you're walking out with an officer now,' Tom said, accusingly. Not just one, Lorna replied, but a half a dozen or more. In wheelchairs most of them. 'But one of them has been going down to your place to tea, hasn't he?' No, just to play the piano in their front room. There wasn't a piano available at the hospital, and Robert was very fond of music. So was Lorna. They played duets sometimes. 'Oh, aye. And what's Alan going to play when he comes home?'

'It's no business of Alan's,' Lorna said tartly. 'He broke it off between us. Not me!'

The matter was very important and Conrad asked to speak to Triggers in private. He had a request to make. In the circumstances, he would not have thought it necessary, but as Triggers had neglected the obvious . . .

'I'm hard-pressed this morning,' Triggers snapped. 'So come to the point, please, Mr Conrad.'

'I wish to fly with another pilot.'

'Why?'

Surely the reason was plain enough? Sergeant Farmer had been court-martialled for cowardice and it was Conrad who had accused him, so their flying together could prove to be an embarrassment. If Conrad thought so, Triggers replied, then he had better look into his motives for accusing Sergeant Farmer. Conrad said he had no other motive than his duty, and it was not his own embarrassment he was considering, but Sergeant Farmer's.

'That's most generous of you, Mr Conrad.'

'Generosity does not enter into it.'

'Speak your mind, man!'

Conrad reminded Triggers that Sergeant Farmer had been found guilty of disobeying an order, Conrad's order, and the same thing could happen again. Triggers looked threatening. 'I hope *you* won't be disobeying any orders, Mr Conrad, because in this Flight, *I* give them. You will not go looking for trouble with that Hun monoplane.'

When Conrad had left the office, Triggers had second thoughts. He hated giving in to the man but there was no point at all in risking a repetition of the tiresome business of Farmer's court-martial.

On his way to the hangar to find a rigger to check his flying wires, Alan had seen Conrad flinging out of the Flight Office, so when Triggers sent for him he had an inkling of what was coming.

'You and Mr Bravington got on rather well together, didn't you? So I'm going to put you back with him.' Triggers smiled and looked down at the papers on his desk. The interview was at an end. But Alan made no move to go. 'That's all, sergeant.'

'I'd sooner stay with Mr Conrad, sir.' And when Triggers looked up at him, he said: 'Unless you've a particular reason for changing us round, sir?'

Triggers was stymied. And he didn't like it. 'I ask the questions here, sergeant, not you. And if we're looking for reasons, then what's your reason for wishing to continue to fly with Mr Conrad?'

'He's a very good observer, sir.'

Triggers pushed back his chair and came to his feet. 'Don't be the clever Dick with me, sergeant. I don't need my NCO's opinions on the merits of commissioned officers. Now! Why do you want to stay with Mr Conrad?'

Calm and forthright, the shade of defiance barely discernible, Alan said that Mr Conrad was an excellent shot, and in times like these that was a comfort to any pilot, wasn't it? Whilst admiring the common sense of Alan's reply, Triggers knew that he was lying, of course. Intrigued, he took his whisky flask from the drawer and poured himself a drink. It was an old trick that rarely failed; it relaxed the atmosphere and lulled the man on the other side of the desk into talking more freely. 'Look, Farmer, what are you trying to prove?' Alan, apparently, did not know what he meant. 'That court-martial is over and done with. Forgotten!'

Alan said that he had already forgotten it, implying that it was Triggers who was resurrecting it. 'And I'd sooner carry on just as we were before the court-martial, sir. Otherwise, well, we're drawing more attention to it, aren't we?'

Triggers thumped his flask on the desk. 'Why are you so damned keen on flying with Mr Conrad?'

'I respect him, sir!'

Indeed! What sort of a fool did Farmer take him for? But Alan was adamant. In accusing him of cowardice, Mr Conrad had done what he considered to be his duty, regardless of what anyone else may have thought of him. Triggers, whilst impressed by Farmer's generous attitude towards the man who had caused him so much anguish, knew damned well that there was some ulterior motive for Farmer wanting to continue to fly with Conrad. 'Very well,' he said, at last. 'But if you will go diving into hot water, don't expect me to haul you out a second time.'

Charles was totally bewildered. Sergeant Mills, who had 'inadvertently' overheard a snatch of the conversation between Conrad and Triggers that morning, had given Charles advance warning of the switch of observers. Now, it seemed, they had been switched back again. 'I was told you were to fly with Dick Bravington from now on.'

Alan was putting on his flying gear and whistling unconcernedly. 'I asked to stay with Mr Conrad.'

Charles was dumbfounded. 'Lord, you really are a funny chap, Alan.'

'No,' Alan said, picking up his goggles. 'Just an ordinary chap.'

Charles remembered how Triggers had described Alan at the court-martial. Quite obviously, Alan had been offended. Why, Charles wasn't at all sure. After all, the pride of the working-class and all that. 'What's wrong with being an ordinary chap, then?'

Poor Charles, Alan reflected as he walked to the hangar. Charles didn't understand what it was like to have ambitions; he had no need of them, of course. Neither did Mr Conrad, whose batman was helping him into his flying coat when Alan walked up. 'Good afternoon, sir. I believe you wanted to speak to me before we take off.'

Conrad said nothing until his batman had gone, then he told Alan that he had made a request for another pilot but Captain Triggers had chosen to ignore it. He wished to make it perfectly clear to Alan that on the ground and in the air, he was Alan's superior officer. 'I've no need to remind you, I hope, that you *were* found guilty of disobeying my orders.'

'It won't happen again, sir.'

Conrad was somewhat taken aback by the willingness of the remark, and, for a moment, he looked steadily into Alan's eyes as if seeking some dark motive. 'Something else before we go. This monoplane and its damned forward-firing gun. It's ludicrous that one Hun machine should be allowed to plague a whole Squadron.'

'I would agree with that, sir.'

Conrad looked vaguely suspicious, as if he was wondering why this damned know-all sergeant had suddenly turned into an angel of obedience. 'Captain Triggers says we are not to go looking for trouble with that particular Hun. And I shall obey that order, of course.'

Alan nodded understandingly. As a commissioned officer, Conrad knew that to be able to give orders one had to be able to obey orders. And, to be accounted brave – in Conrad's eyes, at least – one had to seek out death and stare it in the face; it was not enough to wait for it to come to you. Very well then; that's just what Alan would do. He would do anything Conrad would have him do. How else was he to wipe clean the black mark that Conrad had put against his name? How else was he to be deemed worthy of a commission, and consequently of Kate Gaylion, the marvellous girl that he had made up his mind to marry?

'We are not to go looking for trouble with the Hun,' Conrad repeated, tying his expensive scarf in its careful knot, as was his custom. 'But I intend making sure that trouble comes looking for us.' Alan smiled in appreciation of the remark and Conrad's eyes narrowed. 'Is there something you wish to say, sergeant?'

'Nothing at all, sir.'

'Right, then. This is what I have in mind. On our way home, we shall fly a little off course. My – er – bad navigation, you understand.' Alan smiled again, thinking the man was becoming almost human. 'We shall fly close to the Hun airfield at Templeuve,' Conrad went on, inspecting his Mannlicher rifle, 'and this time we shall shoot down that damned Hun monoplane.' He started to walk out of the hangar, stopped, and looked steadily back at Alan. 'One other thing you should know,' he said. 'I am not a man to bend to the opinion of the majority. Or to be swayed by the verdicts of courts. I still think you should have been shot.'

When he took off that afternoon, Leutnant Stein had a

raging toothache and the bite in the air at seven thousand feet was an agonising prospect. On top of that, his wounded pride was still smarting. The surprise visit of the General had rocked the unit from the commanding officer down to the lowest-ranked mechanic and had culminated, explosively and quite unjustly, in Stein becoming the scapegoat for what the General regarded as the unit's dismal failure to sweep the enemy from the skies. The General had taken several leisurely years to change his mind about the military importance of the Zeppelin, but he had been shelled into submission over the value of the aeroplane in just a few short weeks. And he didn't like it one bit. However, he had been assured by an enthusiastic advocate of the Air Service that the genius of Anthony Fokker would surely put a stop to the Allied artillery-spotting machines. But in the sector covered by the unit at Templeuve, at least, the General's ground forces were still being accurately shelled with the help of British aeroplanes. The General refused to listen to the excuses of groundlings; he required first-hand knowledge from 'a driver' of one of these supposedly war-winning new machines. Stein was sent for. He explained that his Eindekker was the only one in operation at the moment; the other machine had crash-landed two weeks earlier and had been sent back to the Fokker factory for extensive repairs. The General was unimpressed. 'So you've only one of these miracle-working machines instead of two,' he raved. 'Then I am entitled to expect, at least, half a miracle.' And when Stein went on to speak of the difficulties of war in three dimensions as opposed to the relative simplicity of war on the ground, the General looked totally bewildered and interpreted Stein's words as a slanderous attack upon the courage of his soldiers, the men who were being slaughtered every day because of Stein's incompetence. Why, when they possessed this new flying weapon to which the enemy had no answer, were the British pilots continuing to wreak their havoc?

At three thousand feet, Stein turned south and went on climbing, wishing the fat old ground-bound fool could only comprehend the area Stein was expected to 'sweep clean'. The wooden-headed diehard had demanded figures; but how could one quote, in military measurement, boundless space? Oh, Stein might have told him eight miles long – the length of their sector – and, perhaps, two miles high; but how many miles 'across'? There was no way at all of measuring that. These foolhardy British pilots still went on flying deep into German-held territory despite the awesome reputation of Stein's new monoplane. Ah, well, if he was lucky, Stein decided, he might get a 'kill' today; and as the General was not leaving until late that evening, at least Stein would be able to hold up his head during dinner. Although he wouldn't be eating much. Not with his damned aching tooth.

As soon as he saw the orange flash, Alan swung the stick over to begin the customary evasive 'essing'. Conrad, in the process of signalling to the battery, glared back at him. Alan had performed the action instinctively, but his observer did not approve of *any* manœuvre – even those avoiding death, it seemed – without his prior command. Alan turned her back on course, and Conrad, oblivious of the deafening explosions, the terrifying flashes, and the mourning drifts of the distinctive black smoke of Hun Archie fire, went on making his signal. Alan had once made the mistake of telling Conrad that while they were flying straight and level Archie gunners could correct their range and so increase their chances of blowing their frail targets out of the sky. With his own inimitable brand of derision, Conrad had replied that in fearfully sidestepping death one was all the more likely to be caught by it. In his time he had been on the hot end of more artillery fire than anyone on the Squadron, and he insisted that 'essing' or not, if a shell had your name on it, that would be that. However, when he had finished making the signal, Conrad blinked at a flash that came alarmingly close, winced at the explosion, and with a lofty outstretched hand made a snaking motion. Alan, surprised that the man had condescended to agree with him for once, went gratefully into his evasive 'essing'.

When the Archie fire had stopped – temporarily, he supposed – Alan found his bearings and turned towards the target, an enemy supply dump. He turned quite steeply so they'd get a good view of the result of Conrad's correction to the battery's fire. A minute or so later, they saw three explosions. The first was a little north of the target, the second south-east of it. The third was a direct hit. The job had been done. Conrad held up a triumphant thumb and Alan could have sworn that he actually grinned. Then, with a significant look, Conrad pointed northwards. True to his word, he was going to 'lose his way' on the flight home. They were to fly via Templeuve in the hope of engaging the enemy monoplane.

Naturally, Conrad was the first to sight it. It was approaching directly ahead. It began to climb and Conrad motioned to Alan to follow suit. They did not want to give the Hun too much height advantage. But with its faster rate of climb, the monoplane soon loomed above them. As its nose dipped, Conrad signalled the turn and reached for his Mannlicher.

As the monoplane came hurtling towards their starboard side, Conrad pushed up his goggles and took careful aim. What cool nerve the man had, Alan thought, fighting his instinct to turn away from the threat of the forward-firing gun that would open up at any second.

But the seconds passed. Long, long seconds. What was Conrad waiting for? Why didn't he fire?

The machine-gun chattered and Conrad jolted back in his cockpit. Alan swung the stick over and kicked the rudder bar, sending the BE2 into a steep diving turn away from the killing fire. The monoplane flashed above him, pulling out of its shallow dive and hurtling ahead. Alan pulled his shuddering machine out of the tilting dive and centred his controls. Conrad was slumped in the cockpit. His head had lolled to one side so that Alan could not see his face. But the man was dead. Alan was convinced of that. He noted the two bullet-holes in the side of Conrad's cockpit; and God knows how many other bullets had entered his body.

Filled with sudden rage at the death of such a brave man, and furiously blaming himself for taking heed of Conrad's orders and not turning away sooner from the monoplane's murderous onslaught, Alan looked around for the enemy machine. It had turned some distance ahead of him and was circling on Alan's port side, preparing to make a second attack. Alan watched it fly on, passing him; the attack would come from above and behind. Not that it mattered much where it came from. Armed only with a revolver, he was virtually defence-less. And hardly a cloud in the sky, so there was nowhere to hide. He cursed the idiotic coolness of the man who had got him into this mess, and eased the stick back. He had to maintain his height; allowing the Hun a height advantage was just asking for trouble. The opportunity of diving added yet more speed to the fast monoplane and gave the pilot even more advantage with his for-ward-firing gun.

Seeing the monoplane turning on to his tail, Alan stub-bornly went on climbing, and as soon as he heard the burst of fire he pushed into a steep diving turn. When the monoplane had passed overhead, he pulled out and began climbing again. The monoplane turned, flying across the path of Alan's climb, turned again, and dived towards him. Alan shoved his stick forward until the BE2 was plunging almost vertically. The machine-gun chattered and the monoplane swept across Alan's tail.

Alan eased back the stick, coaxing her out of the wing-tearing dive. The monoplane was climbing away from him, gaining height for its next attack. Alan had lost a good deal of height and was now in a most vulnerable position. Once again, he pulled her into a climb; as he did so, the body in the front cockpit lurched towards him. It was as if the dead Conrad had suddenly come to life. The barrel of the Mannlicher, the butt still gripped by the dead right hand swung to and fro like a topsy-turvy pendulum. The monoplane was turning high above him, and Alan glanced down at his petrol gauge to see how much longer he could afford to go on playing death's ducks and drakes with this fiendish enemy. His heart sank. He had little more than enough petrol to get him back to Ste Marie. Looking up from the gauge, a second shock awaited him. Conrad's eyes were open, staring, unseeingly, into his own. Then the eyes blinked. The hands clawed at the cockpit rim and Conrad drew himself up, raising an arm like a man calling a halt to his own funeral cortège. Then his face contorting with the sudden realisation of the terrible pain, he sank back into the cockpit.

Alan's mind was now fully made up. The petrol situation had partly convinced him that the only thing left to do was to make a run for home. Now Conrad's plight made it imperative. But with the Hun on his tail, his only chance was to fly at low level, risking Archie and any other fire from the ground and hoping to hell the Hun wouldn't fancy doing the same.

As Alan pushed the stick forward, Conrad caught sight of the pursuing monoplane. He looked dazedly over the cockpit side, staring at the uprushing earth. What the hell was going on, he seemed to be saying as he looked questioningly at Alan. Then, in a pathetic parody of the old imperious gesture, he held up a hand. Alan simply ignored it. *He* was in charge now. The pilot! The captain of the machine! All the vows he had made about obeying Conrad's every order were forgotten. He had to get the man to hospital. He was dying. Didn't the fool realise that?

Alan glanced around. The monoplane was still in pursuit. He pushed the stick forward to steepen the dive and increase his speed, his eyes looking past Conrad, ignoring the man's accusing stare. The Mannlicher was lying in the cockpit. Conrad picked it up and swung it around. He was going to take a potshot at the Hun, Alan thought. Some hope! The man looked only half-conscious.

Alan, however, had misconstrued Conrad's intention. When the rifle was lowered it was aimed at Alan's head; the muzzle just three or four inches in front of his eyes. Had the man gone crazy or what? 'What are you doing, for God's sake?' Alan cried. Conrad made no reply. He appeared too weak even to speak. Then, in his mind, Alan heard the words Conrad had spoken in the hangar just before they had taken off: 'I still think you should have been shot.'

The rifle was in Conrad's right hand, the finger on the trigger. Now, with his left hand, Conrad motioned to Alan to pull out of the dive. Alan made no move to obey the order. His eyes looked over the muzzle of the Mannlicher into the growing ferocity in Conrad's face. He knew damned well that the man might press the trigger at any moment. Conrad truly believed that Alan should have been shot as a coward. And by his present action, Alan was proving that belief beyond all doubt; for here he was, once again, disobeying orders and fleeing from the enemy. Why then, in the knowledge that his own life was fast ebbing away, should Conrad *not* take justice into his own hands and pull the trigger?

Alan pulled his eyes away and glanced back at the pursuing Hun. He had rapidly closed the distance and was now within certain killing range. As if to confirm Alan's thought, an orange spark appeared just above the monoplane's nose and bullets ripped into the port upper wing of the BE2. The barrel of the Mannlicher lifted above Alan's head. Conrad squinted and fired. Then he twisted convulsively as a bullet entered his brain.

In the Eindekker cockpit, Stein's raging toothache had suddenly stopped. The monoplane's nose dipped in response to the pressure of the dead hand on the stick, and the pride of the German Air Service plunged to its doom.

Alan was taking the Mannlicher from the cockpit when Charles ran up. He had just heard the good news. 'You got the beggar then?'

'Not me, Mr Conrad.'

Charles looked suitably solemn. Yes, he had heard Conrad was dead. 'I'm sorry.'

'Are you?'

Charles was taken aback by Alan's hard stare. 'Well, I know I never thought much of the chap . . .'

'But now he's a hero, and a dead one, he wasn't such a bad chap after all, is that it?'

Charles bit back an angry retort. He partly understood how Alan must have been feeling. 'I heard you had a pretty bad time of it.'

'Mr Conrad insisted that I should have been shot as a coward. And I reckon he was right.'

'Oh, for Heaven's sake, Alan — '

'He was right,' Alan said adamantly. 'We're all cowards compared with a man like him.'

When Triggers read Alan's flight report he sent for him immediately. He was still looking sourly at the report when Alan came into the office. 'What's all this about you disobeying orders again and Mr Conrad threatening to shoot you?'

'It's an accurate account, sir.'

'It is also meant to be a reconnaissance report. I suggest you make another, much shorter report, and that you confine it to reporting on the task you were given, and which you successfully accomplished.'

Alan knew by Triggers' tone that his Flight Commander was on his side in the matter and was advising him for his own good. Yet he remained stubbornly silent. 'Look, sergeant,' Triggers remonstrated. 'You got that Hun monoplane. That's to your credit. Very much so.'

'Mr Conrad got the monoplane, sir. Not me!'

'Don't quibble! You deserve your share of the credit.' He tapped the flight report. 'This can bring you nothing but discredit.'

Alan, however, insisted that the report was a full and truthful account of what had happened and he did not want to change it.

'I see. You want to make a martyr of yourself, do you, Farmer? I suppose you know that following a certain period of service in the field, an NCO can be recommended for a commission?' Yes, Alan did understand that. 'Well, then,' Triggers went on, 'you've already been found guilty of disobeying an order from Mr Conrad — ' and he stopped, a thought occurring to him. 'Tell me, sergeant, is that why you wanted to continue flying with Mr Conrad?'

Alan knew it was no use beating about the bush. He explained to Triggers that he somehow hoped to wipe out the black mark against him. 'You're a contrary beggar, aren't you?' Triggers said. 'Now you want to give yourself another black mark, as you call it, by admitting that you disobeyed him yet again.'

'I vowed not to disobey him again, sir. But I did. And if I'd not done – well – if I *had* obeyed Mr Conrad, he might still be alive.'

Triggers gave an impatient sigh. 'Look, sergeant. This report would spoil any chance you might have of getting a commission in the future. So we'd better forget it, hadn't we?'

'I'd rather not accept any favours, sir.'

Triggers looked as if he might erupt. 'What makes you think I want to do you favours, sergeant?'

'I'm sorry, sir,' Alan said tightly.

'The fact is, the General Staff's opinion of us is low enough as it is, without reading your little personal trials.' He picked up the flight report and tore it in half. 'Write another one,' he snapped. 'And this time, make it brief. And relevant.'

Alan was just finishing the letter to Kate when Charles came into the tent with the splendid news that the Squadron Commander was at last granting leave. They had to take it in turns, of course, so Triggers had drawn the names from a hat. 'And guess whose name came out first? Aren't you the lucky blighter?'

'Thanks for coming over to tell me.'

'I expected whoops of delight.'

'Whoop, whoop!'

Puzzled by Alan's lukewarm reaction, Charles said Alan's 'mum' would be sure to be pleased; *and* the farmer's daughter, of course. Alan reminded him, churlishly, that it was all off between them. Charles gave a little smirk and indicated the pages of the letter scattered on the bed. 'Eight pages to a dear old aunt, I suppose?'

'Nine pages,' Alan said, gathering them up. 'To Kate!' Charles's expression hardened. But he'd been drinking in the Mess, and was tired, and certainly not in the mood for another of their fights over his sister. Nine pages, indeed? What on earth did Alan find to write about? His ambitions for after the war, Alan told him, and Charles shook his head bewilderedly. 'You're a strange chap, Alan.'

'An ordinary chap, you mean, don't you?'

Lord, he was off on that tack again, was he? 'After the war, you say? Good God, you're the first chap I've heard to even mention it. The rest of us have the feeling we'll never see the happy day, and the most we can hope for is the absence of some heavenly Captain Triggers when we fly through the Pearly Gates – bawling us out for getting our harps the wrong way round.'

Alan smiled faintly. Then he said: 'We ordinary chaps *have* to think of the future. We have to earn everything we get, you see.'

'Like your commission, you mean?'

'May be,' Alan said, truculently. Charles nodded wearily and wished he'd not troubled to leave the cosy warmth of the Mess to bring Alan the good tidings. 'And you may as well know,' Alan went on, 'I intend to earn your sister.'

'You're likely to earn no more than a kick in the teeth,' Charles replied. And as Alan made to retort, he added: 'No, not from me! From Kate!'

'I don't know whether or not she wants to see me again,' Alan said, with an accusing stare. 'She was going to tell me that in the note you burned. But I've made up my mind to see her. And now I've got this leave – well –

I shall be spending most of it in London.'

Charles shook his head and left. A moment later he shoved his head through the tent flap. 'He wasn't a bad chap – that ordinary man. A shame he's become an extraordinary bore.'

# 9

The news of Alan's leave came at the end of a day of surprises for Molly. The first was the bicycle; Molly had just taken the men's morning tea into the smithy when Harry proudly wheeled in the well-kept secret. 'Happy birthday,' he said, doffing his cap and standing stiffly with one hand on the handlebar. 'I thought it would be handy for you. You can ride it in to Caxton of a Thursday. It's a lot cheaper than the bus. And when the weather's fine – well – it's very pleasant just riding round and about.'

Molly stared at the bicycle as if it might have been a dragon. Tom, deeply conscious of Lorna's remark about Molly's aversion to anything on wheels, was anxious to suppress any negative comment. 'It's not new, o' course. New ones cost. Harry's put it together from bits and parts picked up here and there. Harry's gone to a lot of trouble with it.' And to allay any fears before they could be voiced, he added: 'The brakes is hand-made by yours truly, so you'll be safe enough. The frame had a lot of rust on it. We spent three days scraping — ' At this point he caught sight of Harry's reproving look. 'As Harry says – it's very pleasant riding around the countryside.'

Molly smiled, fixedly, and felt obliged to smooth the

saddle. 'It's very nice. Very nice, indeed. Thank you.'

'He thought you needed cheering up a bit,' Tom said. 'After all the business of Alan's court-martial.'

'There's something else,' Harry said. He had been intercepting the postman for the past week, and sure enough, two days earlier, a package had arrived from France. 'I hope you didn't mind. But I thought you'd sooner have it on the proper day.'

'It's from Alan!' Molly cried, taking the small, oblong package. 'I wonder what it is?'

Tom had already opened his penknife to cut the string. 'My word, a Regent Street jeweller,' he murmured, seeing the gold lettering on the lid of the dark blue box. 'Only the best for you, eh, missus?'

It was a military badge brooch, in fifteen-carat gold; a pilot's wings with the 'RFC' at the centre. Molly's eyes glistened. 'A pin on the back. Shan't try it now. Wear it with my best.'

Tom winked at Harry. 'Not till she's learned to ride this bicycle, eh, Harry?'

Molly looked wonderingly from one to the other. Harry grinned. 'Tom's right,' he said. 'Like Alan – you'll have to earn your wings.'

Soon after eleven o'clock, Arthur Rudkin called with a huge bunch of flowers. Molly took him into the garden. 'To show him how well you're getting on with it,' Tom said to Harry as they poured the buckets of water on the red-hot iron tyre to shrink it onto the cartwheel. 'So she says. But I reckon she's ready to give him his answer.'

'She'll not marry him,' Harry growled.

'You keep saying that. But you don't do anything about it, do you?'

'How can I, you damned old fool?' Harry said in sudden anger. 'The law won't allow it.'

They had reached the bottom of the garden and Arthur Rudkin had remarked three times what a good job Harry was making of it before Molly found her tongue. 'I've been thinking over what you asked me, Mr Rudkin. Thinking it over very carefully, in fact.'

'There's no need, Mrs Farmer,' Rudkin said. And he gave a little self-deprecating smile. 'I know the answer.'

'I'm sorry,' Molly said, thinking what a nice man he was and wondering why she was refusing him. 'There's no reason I can give. No reason at all. And I expect you think I'm a foolish woman.'

They wandered back along the path to the house. Harry was in the yard, filling a pail from the tub. 'Morning, Arthur,' he said, immersing the pail in the tub and hiding his anxiety behind a fixed smile. 'The garden is not quite up to yours yet, eh?'

'Not quite,' Rudkin said. 'But I don't know what will happen to mine now, I'm sure.'

Harry looked questioningly at Molly. She laughed. 'I'm as wise as you are,' she said.

'I went into Caxton yesterday afternoon,' Rudkin explained. 'For some of that ointment for my mother's back. And there they were, next door, all queuing up. It's funny, really. It's not like me at all. Always been cautious. Take a month o' Sundays over any big decision. Yet, before I knew it, there I was in the queue. My mother will manage the shop. Though she'll have to get some help, o' course.'

'What have you joined?' Harry asked.

'Nothing fancy. The infantry.'

Harry felt like patting him on the back. He might even go to the station to cheer him off. Molly did not speak until Harry had gone back into the smithy. The uniform would suit him, she said. Rudkin grinned. 'Aye. A pack and a rifle can give a hero's swagger even to a grocer, they say. So! When I come home on leave – well – maybe you'll see a new man altogether.'

'He asked me to marry him,' Molly said, as they walked to the end of the quiet lane beyond Lovell's Hill, Harry pushing the bicycle. 'D'you think I did right to say no?'

Harry ignored the question. 'No, not that foot. Why don't you listen, woman? The right foot. You push off with your right foot and then you lift your — ' He hesitated. She giggled and he looked sternly reproving. 'You'll never learn to ride if you don't listen.'

'I'm sorry,' Molly said, assuming an intensely interested air. 'Now, what was it I have to lift?'

'Your seat. Once you've pushed off, you lift your seat up on to the saddle.'

Molly looked perplexed. If her foot was going down, how was her seat to go 'up'? Harry gave an impatient sigh. 'Like this!' He held her by the waist and lifted her into the saddle.

'I see! Well, that seems easy enough.' She looked at him, awaiting his next instruction. Harry, conscious of her nearness, took his hands away. 'I'm falling off!' she cried.

'Nonsense!' Harry said tetchily, gripping the handlebar and the underside of the saddle. 'You just put your foot down and you can't fall over.'

'I feel safer with you holding me,' she said.

She would never learn that way, Harry said, looking coldly into the distance. He would give her a push and off she'd go.

'Right then! Push down!'

And off she went, wobbling and wavering, laughing and screaming, and finishing up in the hedge. 'They must have heard you all over Becket's Hill, I should think,' Harry said, irritated.

'Why, is it a secret then?'

He pulled the bramble from her sleeve and wondered if he'd been wise to spend three weeks of his spare time in putting the thing together. 'I think that'll do for the first day.'

'Not a bit of it,' Molly said, determinedly. 'I'm getting a taste for bicycle riding. Now, this time, until I'm well started – hold on to me, not the bicycle.'

She put her foot on the pedal, lifted into the saddle, and Harry held her, once again, at the waist. This time she was conscious of his holding her, he thought. 'Are you ready then?' Yes, she was! Impulsively, Harry pressed his lips to her cheek. Molly stiffened, but said nothing. She did not even look at him. 'I'm sorry,' Harry murmured. She seemed not to have heard. She looked down at her foot on the pedal as if she had been totally unaware of the kiss; or as if it had been of such unimportance she had already dismissed it from her mind.

On the walk back to the house, Harry's boots felt like lead. If only she had slapped his face or reproved him in some way. But to ignore him like that . . . he felt such an utter fool.

As they turned into Haverton Lane, Tom came running to meet them with the letter. 'He's coming home on leave,' Molly cried when she had read it. 'I shall bicycle to the station to meet him. Won't he be surprised?' And she looked undecided about something. 'No. I shan't ask Lorna. But you must both come to tea. He'll be down there to see her before a day has passed, I'm sure.'

And just wait until he found out about 'Robert', Tom told himself; that would make him sit up.

'And we'll just forget that court-martial trouble,' Molly said, with a warning look at Tom. 'It's all over and done with. So it's best he thinks we know nothing of it.'

'Registration Sunday, they called it,' Tom said, tucking his napkin into his collar. 'Every man and woman between the ages of fifteen and sixty-five had to fill up the form.'

'That let you out, Tom,' Harry grinned, passing the bread and butter to Alan. 'The first step to conscription, they say.'

Alan looked thoughtful. 'Kate won't be very pleased about that.'

'Kate?'

'Charles Gaylion's sister. She's against men being ordered to fight for their country.'

'A sensible girl,' Molly said, with a significant glance at the empty chair. She had placed it next to Alan in the hope of reminding him of Lorna's absence. 'Lorna said you'd called at Charles's home at the end of your last leave.'

Alan caught the reproving glance from Harry, whose manner had been vaguely hostile since the moment Alan had shaken hands with him in the smithy. 'Yes, I decided to call on Charles's mother. I knew Charles wouldn't be getting leave for some time and I thought she'd like to know how he was getting on.'

'Very thoughtful of you,' Molly said. 'And you saw Kate, then?'

'Yes, I did,' Alan replied, unable to resist the note of defiance. They were all looking down at their plates as if he had committed some terrible crime. God, just because he'd chosen to spend one day of his leave in London. Wait until he told them he was to spend six days of his present leave up there. 'The garden looks nice.'

'Harry, that is,' Tom said. 'And he's painted the front windows, too.' And he went on to tell Alan all the other jobs Harry had been doing for Molly, adding, with a little satisfied smile, that Arthur Rudkin had joined up.

'How are things in the smithy?'

They were managing, Molly said reticently. In Tom's opinion, things could have been a whole lot worse. They had Harry to thank for keeping their heads above water. Molly agreed. 'We'd never have managed without your Uncle Harry.'

In all this praise for Harry, Alan felt they were blaming him for joining the Flying Corps and not giving a second thought to the running of the smithy. They thought him a shirker instead of a man who was willing to give his life for his King and Country. 'It's very strange,' he said, with a little tight smile. 'That walk from the station. Nothing changed. You wouldn't know there was a war on. Except, may be, for that Union Jack hanging from Mrs Edwards's bedroom window.'

'Some say it'll be over by the end of the year,' Molly said.

She couldn't wait to get him back home again, Alan thought, so she could run his life for him. 'Oh yes, Kate has a mind of her own,' he said, and they all stared, waiting for him to go on, so he'd tell them now and get it over and done with. 'I shan't be staying at home for the whole of my leave.'

Molly was stunned. 'Not staying at home? Where are you going then?'

'Up to London. The day after tomorrow.'

Harry had stopped stirring his tea and was staring darkly into the cup as if he had found some alien substance floating there. 'Your mother's been looking forward to you coming home. But you'll know that without us telling you, I'm sure.'

Alan made no reply and they went on eating in uneasy silence.

'Aye, we're running the place fine together, Harry and me,' Tom said at last. 'Nothing for you to do when you come home after it's over. You can stroll round the village like a toff, eh? Swinging your cane. Your medals on your best coat.' He was busily concerned with the blob of jam on the best tablecloth and so did not see Harry's warning look. 'They'll be making you an officer before long then?'

Alan looked sharply at his mother. 'That's news to me,' he said. Molly shifted uncomfortably in her chair. Alan looked at Tom. 'Where did you get that idea from?'

'He got it from you,' Harry said in a low voice. 'One of your letters to your mother.'

'A long time ago,' Molly said, sensing the conversation was turning towards the subject she desperately wanted to avoid. 'You could be made an officer in the field, that's how you put it.' And she went on quickly to say: 'You'll be staying here at home until Friday then?'

'I might have been lucky enough to be made an officer,' Alan said tersely. 'But there's no chance of that now.'

Molly looked anxiously at Tom. But she was too late. 'No chance?' Tom enquired. 'Why not?'

'Oh, what does it matter?' Molly said quickly. 'An officer's uniform! What difference would it make? He'd still be the same boy.'

'Yes, that's very true,' Alan said. 'I have to tell you. I was court-martialled for cowardice.'

His words were greeted with such heavy silence that he understood at once that they already knew. Harry explained that Alan's chaplain had written to the vicar.

'I see.' Alan looked accusingly at his mother. 'Why didn't you say before?'

'It didn't come up before, did it?' Harry was looking steadily at Alan. 'Anyway, it's all over and done with, isn't it?'

'Oh, yes,' Alan said bitterly. 'So my Flight Commander told me.'

'Oh, we knew you wasn't guilty,' Tom said, cutting a slice of cake. 'You don't mind me helping myself, do you, missus? No, we knew all right. As Harry said – the fellow that accused you, it was him who should have been shot.'

'He *was* shot! He's dead!'

'Oh. Well, then – that's proper justice, eh?'

Alan pushed his plate away. 'Mr Conrad. *He* was an officer. The bravest man I've ever met. And if I hadn't disobeyed his order, he might still be alive.'

No one felt like eating any more. Not even Tom. Molly insisted on pouring Alan another cup of tea and he murmured an apology for spoiling the 'splendid' homecoming tea his mother had prepared for him. Molly laughed it off, but Harry knew she was close to tears.

'I'm glad you're managing the smithy so well,' Alan said, when Tom had gone, and he and Harry had settled into the armchairs in front of the kitchen range. 'Flying. That's my life now. They'll be wanting fliers when the war's over. More and more people will be travelling by aeroplane, bound to be. So they'll be needing pilots.'

Molly had just come in from the yard and she stood aghast at Alan's words. 'You mean you won't be coming back to Becket's Hill?'

'Of course he will,' Harry said. 'They'll be in need of pilots, yes. But by the time this lot is over, they'll have more than enough to choose from.'

'They'll choose the best. And I'll be one of them.'

'Modest, isn't he?' Harry said, a bite behind the smile. And he reminded Alan that the Farmer smithy had been in the family for four generations. 'Who's going to carry on here?'

'From all accounts, you're making a good job of it,' Alan said. 'And you'll be staying on here, won't you?'

Harry glanced at Molly before he answered. She was

folding the washing; he felt sure she was thinking of the kiss he had given her on the day of the bicycle riding lesson. 'I don't know about that,' he said. 'It was agreed that I give a hand here while you were away. And in any case, I won't have a son, will I, to carry on after me?'

'It's my life,' Alan said stubbornly. 'I'll give it for my country. Or live it as I choose.'

Harry rose angrily from his chair. 'Why wait till Friday to go off to London? It strikes me you'd have done better going straight there, and not bothered with us at all.'

'Now, now, Harry,' Molly murmured, smiling foolishly in an attempt to heal the situation.

'Harry's right!' Alan went to the yard door. 'I'm sorry I've upset things here.'

'Alan!' Molly cried. 'Where are you going?'

'Arthur Rudkin said I could use his telephone.'

'You shouldn't have upset him like that,' Molly said when Alan had gone. 'We all know what he's been through.'

'He's just like his father,' Harry raged. 'Too big for his bloody boots.'

'That's wicked,' Molly said, her face crumpling. 'Wicked!'

She ran upstairs and Harry glowered at the photograph in the mahogany frame. Damn his brother Will, and his foolish notion of learning to fly. His death was to blame for it all.

The shop was empty when Alan arrived, and Arthur Rudkin discreetly closed the door to the kitchen, leaving Alan alone at the telephone. But by the time he had got the number, and Levin had enquired who was calling and had gone upstairs to fetch Miss Kate, four customers were talking excitedly about the latest Zeppelin raid,

Arthur Rudkin was cutting sheets of greaseproof paper, and his mother was dragging a chair to reach the top shelf.

'I said it's me – Alan!'

'Excuse me, Alan dear,' Mrs Rudkin said. 'If you could just move that way a bit. Thank you, dear.'

'Hello, Kate! It's me – Alan!'

Yes, Levin had told her that. Why was he calling? It wasn't Charles? Nothing had happened to Charles? Oh, thank God! Why was he shouting? Yes, she'd got his letter. It was awfully long, wasn't it? Yes, she remembered his saying he was coming home on leave. His *second* leave. Wasn't he lucky? When was poor Charles going to get some?

'I'm coming up to London on Friday. I shall be staying there for six days. I said so in my letter, if you remember?'

Oh dear, London was so very crowded these days and the traffic was simply awful. She had only become so terribly conscious of it since she had been riding her motor cycle.

'Motor cycle? You riding a motor — ' Alan winced as a tin clattered from the top shelf to the floor. Mrs Rudkin tut-tutted and reproved her son for keeping them so high up. 'What Corps did you say?'

The Driving Corps was doing such a terribly important job and the uniform so suited her, especially the hat. Wasn't life odd? She'd turned her back on all that No-Conscription Fellowship nonsense, gone all patriotic, doing her bit, but her mother was terrified at the way she went whizzing around Regent's Park.

'If you remember – in my letter – I said I wanted to see you again.'

What was that?

'I'm sorry! It's the noise in here!' Alan shouted, and

found himself glaring into four, dumb, curious faces. He mumbled an apology and turned his back on them. 'I shall be catching the ten-to-nine train on Friday.'

What was that? Why was he whispering? Friday? Oh no, she couldn't see him Friday, and Saturday she'd be on her motor cycle all day and hoped to God it wouldn't be raining again, and Sunday she was off into the country with her mother, and how was his leg? The wounded leg, silly?

'Oh, it's fine now. Fine. Perhaps I could see you on Monday then?'

No, not Monday, she was going out with Roland, and how was Becket's Down – or Hill? – or wherever it was?

'Oh, it's – it's just the same. Who – who is Roland?'

Roland was a Lieutenant who'd come to the house with her father one afternoon last week and was terribly sweet and if the truth was known that was why she had suddenly gone all patriotic.

'Well, when – when do you think I might see you then?'

What was that? Levin was calling her again and she simply had to fly. She hoped Alan would enjoy his leave and please, please, would he ask Charles to write to mother just a little more often, and it was goodbye then, and thanks once again for the awfully, awfully long letter.

Stunned and humiliated, Alan hurried out of the shop and walked at a furious pace until he was halfway down Lovell's Hill. Here, he left the road and ran through the coppice into Collins's big field. He ran the length of the field and with bursting lungs flung himself down in the long yellowing grass beneath the elms, lying on his back and gazing up at the branches, now swaying gently in the evening breeze. This was the haven of the grief-stricken boy in the weeks that followed his father's death. He remembered the weight of the great stone inside him, the burning of the tears that dissolved it, and the shame he felt in the presence of his mother, who had borne the loss so bravely. And he remembered, above the swaying tree-tops, hovering like a huge butterfly, 'The Flyer', as he had seen it on that Saturday afternoon: hovering, then falling. He heard the rending of the fabric, the agonised creak of the twisting booms, and the snapping of twigs as the delicate creature fell aslant in the branches. And then he heard Tom's voice, harshly protective, as he pulled the boy aside so that he should not see the horror of his father's burning body.

Damn Kate Gaylion! Damn his mother, too! He was no longer a boy! Despite his eighteen years, he was a man. God in Heaven, had he not seen more of life and death in his few months in France than old men like Tom who had never put a foot beyond these cloistering fields?

Turning the bend at the bottom of the hill, he was surprised to see Harry standing on the bridge. He was lighting his pipe, and he puffed and nodded thoughtfully when Alan apologised for his rude behaviour back at the house. 'Aye. Well. I lost my temper, too. And I should have known better.' And he smiled faintly at the memory of the turmoil he had felt on his return from France in the January of that year. Alan thought he understood what was going through Harry's mind. He glanced at the empty left sleeve and murmured that it must have been harder for Harry, of course. 'May be,' Harry said, looking down into the slowly moving waters of the stream. 'Eighteen years I'd been away. Travelling all over. And thinking myself to be all different kinds of men, no doubt.' He smiled and shook his head and gazed for a time at the hazy evening scene. 'Then I came back and looked at all this. And I knew I hadn't changed one whit from the young fool I was when I left here.' And his smile broadened. 'Whoever or whatever I thought myself

213

to be, I still had the Becket's Hill earth on my boots.'

'Well, well! If it isn't Alan Farmer.'

The cheery-faced young bull of a man was coming through the gap in the hedge that bordered Richards' farm. Ted Allsop had been in Alan's class at school and in his work as a farm labourer he had never outgrown the rough and tumble joys of the play-yard. He was followed by two bodgers from Hopford, who walked to Becket's Hill on Friday evenings to admire Ted Allsop's provoking wit. Ignoring Alan's friendly greeting, Ted made a comment on Alan's 'wings' that sent the Hopford lads hooting and stamping, then he spat into the stream. 'We heard you had some trouble,' he said.

'And he's looking for more,' Harry murmured, giving Alan's sleeve a meaning tug. Molly would be wondering where Alan had got to.

'What about you, Ted?' Alan enquired. 'Still hiding behind a haystack? You'll have to come out soon, you know. There's talk of conscription.'

Ted shrugged the word away as if he knew what it meant and grinned at his companions. Their boots and knuckles were itching to go. 'They join the Flying Corps to dodge the fighting, they reckon.'

'Come on, Alan,' Harry said, firmly. He had already had one dust-up with Ted Allsop, of course. 'He was a bit more than I could manage, I'm afraid.'

'Just like him,' Alan said vehemently. 'Picking on a man with one arm.'

'Not a bit of it. It was me who did the picking.'

'Over something he said about me?'

Harry told him to forget it. He gripped Alan's arm and led him away. Ted jeered after them. 'So you can understand him turning his back on the enemy, can't you? And he talks different now, d'you notice? Mixing with the sons of gentry, that is. Like his father.

But he came down to earth in the end, didn't he? With a bloody big bump, too.'

Alan brushed away Harry's restraining hand. Harry sighed. 'Three arms against six,' he said. 'What d'you reckon?'

Alan's mind was made up. 'My father used to say a blacksmith's arm is worth two of any other man's.'

'Just look at the state of your uniform,' Molly cried, as if the cuts and bruises ran a poor second place. 'I shall be hours cleaning it up.'

Harry winked at Alan. 'Ted Allsop's mother is lucky, eh? And the other two with him.' He spread his cut lips in a proud bloodied grin. 'They're cleaned up already – to finish matters off, we pitched them in the stream.'

Molly glared the grin from Harry's face and wrung the flannel as if it were Alan's neck. 'Fighting, fighting! Can men think of nothing else? And at your age, Harry Farmer, you should damned well know better. Encouraging the boy to go behaving like a hooligan.'

'I am not a boy,' Alan muttered.

'What are you then?' Molly asked, dabbing dirt from the cut on his cheek. 'An officer, by God! You're not fit to be a sergeant yet.'

Alan's mouth was closed by Harry's warning look. 'Listen to your mother, Alan.'

'Did you talk to Charles's sister?'

How had she known what he had in mind? God in Heaven! Mothers! 'Yes, I did.' And he left it at that. But when she had finished her dabbing and scolding he told her he was not going up to London, after all.

'Indeed? I'm supposed to wave a flag in delight about that, am I? Did Kate decide – or you?'

'Kate.'

'I see.'

Alan gave a little 'humph'. 'The hero's return, eh?'

'Not *me* that wanted a hero, remember. I never wanted you to join up, even.' And while she was top dog she decided to make the most of it. 'As for that poor girl down there at the farm – you've broken her heart. You know that, I suppose?'

'Yes,' Alan said, stiffly. 'I realise that.'

'Well, then? What are you going to do about it?'

Mrs Collins was feeding the pigs when Alan walked up. 'I thought sure you were Robert coming up the track. But I should have noticed the uniform, shouldn't I? Robert is an officer.' And she sniffed over the pail of pig food as if it was good enough for NCOs, too.

'I wondered if I might talk to Lorna,' Alan said.

'She's on duty at the Grange,' Mrs Collins told the piglets. And she picked up the empty pail and squelched through the mud between the stye and the house.

Alan spent the rest of the afternoon mooning about the wilderness that overlooked the farm. As far as he knew, Lorna nursed up at the Grange in the evenings only. Not that he thought Mrs Collins would deliberately lie to him; no, he had an uneasy feeling that Lorna had asked her mother to make some excuse to him. And the reason was plain enough. Who the hell *was* Robert, anyway?

Lorna's father was hedging on the bottom field. Alan ran the half a mile or so at full pelt and sauntered by the hedge as if he was going nowhere in particular. 'Smoking a pipe now, I see,' Mr Collins called. 'No wonder you're looking so pale. Yes, she's up at the Grange this afternoon. Call down this evening. She'll very likely be there.'

'Very likely,' Alan muttered as Molly placed the steaming bowl of stew on the table. 'At one time you could count on her always being at home. And why didn't you tell me about Robert?'

'Robert? Who's Robert?'

'An officer, I gather.'

'You've got officers on the brain.'

'So has Lorna, by the seem of it.'

'Are you calling there this evening as Mr Collins suggested?'

'I might do,' Alan said, with a vision of another court-martial for punching a much too handsome Second Lieutenant through a parlour window and then hurling him into a pigsty. 'They call it "leave",' he said, burning his mouth on the spoonful of stew. 'A soldier's respite from the strife. Good God, France is a blessed Beulah Land compared to Becket's Hill.'

At the foot of the cart-track he changed his mind and went the long way round. Passing the barn, he saw the door and could not resist a quick look inside. It was much smaller than he remembered and he wondered how on earth it had housed 'The Flyer'. He stood there filling his pipe, lost in memories of summer evenings, recalling the boy's hands and feet working the controls from the precarious seat of the wood and wire wonder, eagerly practising for the faraway day when he would actually be allowed to take her into the air.

'You should know better than that, Alan Farmer.'

Startled, he turned to see her between the stacked bales of hay, her face grimed and perspiring, her black-ened hands gripping the cord of the heavy bale. She nodded at the pipe. 'Don't want to start a fire in here, do you?'

'Oh. No. I – er – I wasn't going to light it.' He was so taken aback by her sudden appearance he didn't know what to say. 'It's smaller than I remember it.'

'Everything looks different when you're older, they say. And the place is full now. That makes a difference, I suppose.'

'Yes. Of course.' And recovering from the shock of finding her there, he was pleased that she was looking far from her best. It made the hurdle of their first meeting easier somehow; and seeing her like this revived the old protective feelings, his indignation at her father for making her work so hard. Oh, he wasn't quite the winged knight come home to rescue her from her drudgery, but his armour, if not shining as bright as he'd hoped, was creditably dented.

'Is that why you got leave?'

He realised she was referring to his cuts and bruises. 'Oh. My face, you mean?'

She shook her head, heaved aside the bale, and looked thoughtfully at her skirt as she brushed away the leavings of hay. 'Those poor men at the Grange,' she said. 'We had a new lot in this afternoon. It was terrible to see them.'

He felt her indignation at the well-intentioned lunacy of men who incited other men to inflict such horrors on one another, and feeling somehow shamed, he passed a hand over the cut on his cheek. 'It wasn't a crash or anything like that,' he murmured. 'I had a bit of an argument.'

She was so engrossed in her own thoughts, she seemed not to have heard him. 'Up at the Grange they're mostly soldiers.' She said it as if 'airmen' did not really count, and quite unwittingly turned the knife in the wound when she added: 'We only get officers up there, of course.'

When she had asked after Charles and Alan had waited for the conversation to lead on to Charles's sister, she went on to ask how much leave he had. She seemed to have forgotten the very existence of her 'rival'.

'Seven more days,' she repeated, as if it were a life-time. 'What on earth will you do with yourself? And in a place like Becket's Hill?'

It was as if she was reproving him for the 'fine old time' he had been having 'over there' where real soldiers were being killed and maimed.

'You've changed,' he said, quietly.

She gave a short laugh. 'The last time you were home on leave, it was *you* who had changed.'

'That's right,' he said, smiling rather foolishly.

'The new lot we had in this afternoon. One of them had lost both his legs. Another with half his face gone. When you see what the war has done to others – well – it's silly, isn't it? Selfish, I mean! To even stop to consider the petty ways in which we think *we've* changed.'

Alan just looked at her, not knowing what to say or do.

'Here, I have to be going,' she said. 'We've got someone coming this evening. Enjoy your leave, won't you?'

She was half-way to the house when he caught her up. 'Just a minute. Someone coming this evening. I just wondered – would that be – I mean — ' God, she must think a shell had blown his wits away. 'Your mother mentioned someone called Robert.'

'Yes, that's right. I used to wheel him out on Thursday afternoons, but he's walking quite well now. He may be up at the house already. I never know what time he's coming, you see. If he took the omnibus – it stops outside the Grange now, you know – then he won't be there yet. But if Mr Starke's driven him down, then he will be. Mr Starke! D'you remember how he used to cherish that motor car of his? A speck of dust and he'd worry. Now, there he is, every day, a free taxi service for them. Crutches banging about! Plastered limbs! To hell with the bodywork, he says, *their* bodies are much more important.'

'So Robert comes to the house?'

'Yes. There's no piano up at the Grange, you see, and Robert needs the practice. He wants to be a professional after the war. Mother was ashamed of the piano, of course. You know what she's like. Wanted to get it tuned. But Robert wouldn't hear of it. He's ever so nice. Mother treats him like the King, of course.'

Yes, she would, Alan thought, but how did Lorna treat him?

'He's marvellous fun. We play duets together.'

Alan's heart sank. 'I was just thinking – wondering, really – if you might have liked to come up to the house tomorrow for tea.'

'I'm sorry. But I'm on duty at six. I have to catch the half-past five omnibus from Lovell's Bridge.'

'We could have tea earlier. Say – four o'clock?'

She looked as if she wanted to please him but it was going to be such an awful nuisance.

'Look, there's no need to make up your mind right now. I shall be walking down to the stile tomorrow, anyway. I'll wait there at – say, quarter to four?'

She was awfully sorry but she really had to fly. They were the very words Kate had used, Alan thought, as he watched her hurrying up the path; and, astonishing as it was, Lorna now seemed just as unattainable.

At quarter-to-ten that night, Harry called to ask how Alan had 'got on'. He was fast asleep, Molly told him, and Lorna would come to tea the next day if she could find the time. 'Don't rush away. I've made a pot of tea.'

Harry glanced at the clock. Ten minutes or so and Alice would be bolting up. He sat at the table, took out his pipe and tobacco, and watched Molly fetching the china from the dresser. 'That cup and saucer. One of the set you bought when you first married Will.'

'You've got a good memory.'

'For some things, aye. Like the fire I used to light when I lay up there in bed at nights.'

'Fire? In bed? What are you talking about?'

'A great log fire. And I'd sit you on top of it.'

Molly laughed. 'What, did you think I was a witch, then?'

'Seventeen, remember. And never known my mother. So. Took some getting used to, taking orders from a sister-in-law. And a woman from the town at that. A clever tongue, and sharp, too. Boots off at the door and having to scrape the smithy dirt from my nails before sitting here at the table.'

Molly smiled at the memory of it all and went to the larder for the milk.

'The flames of that fire,' Harry went on, quietly. 'They been burning away inside me ever since. But I reckon you know that.'

She came back to the table with the milk. 'No, I didn't. At least, not before that bicycle riding lesson.' She poured the tea and Harry lit his pipe, and nothing more was said until it was time for Harry to go. 'Alan asked you a question today,' Molly said. 'And you didn't answer. He asked if you were staying on here.'

'I don't think he put it quite like that, did he?' He saw from her look that it was she who wanted the answer. 'I've no other plans. Not yet, anyway. I'm quite content where I am.'

She turned away from him, looking into the fire. 'You're a good man, Harry. And I don't know how I would have managed here without you.'

He stood there for a moment, then, as he opened the door, she ran up and kissed him lightly on the cheek. There were tears, but she was smiling happily. 'There,' she said. 'Now we're evens.'

Nothing could come of it, of course, Harry mused, when she had closed the door behind him. But she wanted him there. She depended on him. And at least he had told her how he felt. He tapped out his pipe and whistled all the way back to his lodging.

Alan arrived at the stile at half-past three and tapped his foot on the bottom bar for the next twenty-five minutes, looking expectantly at the gap in the hedge on the far side of the field. At four o'clock he took a short walk down the lane in the vague hope that she might appear when he wasn't looking, and at ten-past four he resigned himself to the fact that she was not going to come. It was all over between them and he had only himself to blame. His intention had been fine and noble enough when he had told her he no longer felt the same about her; he had wanted to save her hurt in the event of his death. But that fine and noble sentiment had flown out of the window when he had become infatuated with Kate Gaylion. Then, he had thought he just had to snap his fingers and Lorna would fall at his feet again. He had been so busy congratulating himself on becoming a man that it had never occurred to him that Lorna had been just as busy becoming a woman. As a nurse she had seen as much of life and death up at the Grange as he had done in France. Much more, no doubt! Had she not made the point herself? 'Up at the Grange they're mostly soldiers.' Soldiers! Airmen were not involved in the horrors of the war that she knew; they were above the terrible mutilations that she witnessed each day.

As he turned away from the stile, he caught sight of the arm waving above the hedge. Was it really Lorna? Surely not? But of course, the navy blue uniform! It was the first time he had seen her wearing it. As she came through the gap in the hedge, he vaulted the stile and ran to meet her.

'Sorry I'm late,' she said, 'but we couldn't miss seeing him off. We shan't see him again, you see. He's been discharged and sent home to Berkshire. Robert!'

'Oh, Robert? Well. Fancy that.'

'And I'm sorry about yesterday. If I seemed a bit odd, I mean.'

'Oh – no – no, not at all.'

'Whenever we get a new lot of those poor wounded men come in – well – one feels so angry and helpless.'

She straightened the brim of her uniform hat, and Alan thought she looked so capable, so womanly, and so very, very beautiful; he wanted to take her in his arms and tell her that he loved her, that he had always loved her, that he had been a damned fool and was ready to fall at her feet as he had expected her to do. But this was hardly the time, and anyway, there were seven more days yet.

'It's very strange,' she said. 'Do you remember, just before you joined up, the first time you asked me to your house for tea?'

'Do I remember?' Alan smiled. 'My mother does. She spent weeks prodding the courage into me to ask you.'

'You'll laugh, I expect,' she said. 'But leaving the house just now, I felt just as nervous as I did that first time.'

'Well,' Alan said. 'Fancy that.'

He helped her over the stile, and as they walked in silence down the lane, he reached out and took her hand in his.